THE MYSTERY OF
THE FOLDED PAPER
AN AMOS LEE MAPPIN MYSTERY

THE MYSTERY OF THE FOLDED PAPER

AN AMOS LEE MAPPIN MYSTERY

HULBERT FOOTNER

COACHWHIP PUBLICATIONS

Greenville, Ohio

ISBN 1-61646-255-8
ISBN-13 978-1-61646-255-0

Cover: Paper © Stephen Rees; Knife © Oleksiy Fedorov; Hulbert Footner
   (George H. Doran Co., 1921)

CoachwhipBooks.com

CONTENTS

CHAPTER ONE

FINLAY CORVETH HUSTLED in the direction of the Lackawanna terminal. When it was a question of getting the low-down on anything
in Hoboken, he immediately thought of Henny Friend, big boss
and proprietor of the Boloney Bar. Fin was not more hard-hearted
than the run of young men; he was genuinely sorry for his friend
lying dazed and half sick amid the wreck of his poor belongings
but . . . Gosh! what a situation was opening up! What a chance for
a free-lance writer! Ought to make his ever-lasting reputation if
he handled it right. He thrilled with the possibilities of mystery
and danger. "Dearer to me than life!" Nick Peters had muttered.
Naturally, a woman was suggested.

Fin took Hudson Street because it was less crowded than Washington. He had not gone a hundred paces before he discovered that
he was being followed. It was the first time in his life, so far as he
knew, that anybody had ever considered it worthwhile to follow
him. It gave you a feeling like no other. Not exactly fear. Fin did
not consider there was much danger of being shot down in the open
street. Just wants to see what I'm after, he told himself.

And if there was a sensation of fear mixed with his excitement,
he wasn't going to let anything on. He coolly stopped in front of a
small haberdasher's and made believe to admire the satin ties in
the window. His trailer could not stop, because the pavement was
empty at the moment and there was no other convenient store window. Slowing down, the man passed behind Fin. Whereupon Fin
went on and passing him, got a good look. A weird foreign-looking

cuss, tall and excessively lean; dressed in black broad cloth like
the deacon of some outlandish church. Fin was reminded of the
portraits of Robespierre with his greenish complexion and lank
black hair.

He wondered if this was the man who had struck down Nick
Peters, and anger made his throat tight. However, this one had
not the look of a hired spy such as Nick had described; there was
too much crazy fire in his sunken eyes. Perhaps this was the principal, then, the chief of Nick's enemies. Why go to Henny for
information if the man himself was in his grasp? But if I grabbed
him without evidence I'd only make a fool of myself, thought Fin.
I've got to beat him at his own game—lead him on.

The Boloney Bar is on River Street near the Lackawanna ferries. There it functions exactly as in the old days, with its long
mahogany bar to pound the seidels on, brass foot-rail, sawdust-
covered floor, and free-lunch counter displaying every variety of
the delicacy which gave it its name. Behind the bar is a long range
of mirrors covered with a film of soap as a protection from fly
specks. In the soap Ed Hafker, the chief bartender, is fond of trac-
ing toasts with a flowing forefinger, such as: Prosit! Here's How!
Drink Hearty! Never Say Die!

Fin's trailer did not follow him inside, but remained watching
from across the street. The Boloney Bar is always crowded, for men
will make a long pilgrimage nowadays to plant their elbows on the
veritable mahogany. Fin was well known there, and his friends the
bartenders greeted him jovially as he passed down the line: "'Lo,
Fin! . . . Howsa Boy? . . . What's the good word, Fin? . . . What'll
you have?"

To which Fin replied: "See you later, fellas. I'm lookin' for
Henny."

"Well you know where to find him."

Henny Friend's sanctum was in the corner room upstairs. Like
other magnates, his days were spent in "conferences." A diverse
collection of humanity passed unobtrusively in and out every
twenty-four hours. The door was always locked. Fin knocked, and
Henny's thick voice was heard from within.

"Who is it?"

"Fin Corveth."

"Half a mo', Fin."

When he was ready, Henny pressed a button and the latch clicked. As Fin entered, somebody left by another door. Henny never allowed his callers to meet unless he had an object in it. A huge, toadlike hulk of flesh planted in an oversize chair behind a desk, with an over-size cigar elevated from one corner of his mouth. Notwithstanding his name, he was certainly Italian; swarthy, smooth, and expressionless. "Henny Friend" had been adopted for professional purposes in a German community. His brown eyes were as bright and hard as agate.

"Well, Kid, how's tricks?"

Fin wasted no time in beating around the bush. With his tough friends he sported a tough accent. "I run into a damn queer story up the street just now," he said. "I only got the half of it and I thought maybe you could piece it out."

"Well, shoot!" said Henny, leaning back in his swing chair.

On the way down Fin had naturally figured out what line he would take; tell Henny the whole truth, but omit any reference to the missing brass ball from Nick's bed.

"In my business I got all kinds of friends . . ." Fin began.

"Just like me," said Henny, with a fat chuckle.

"Sure! Well, up on Fourth Street, near Washington Square, there's a guy named Nick Peters has a little store where he repairs watches and jewelry. It's a real poor little place, that's what attracted me inside in the first place, I thought there would be a story in it. He hasn't even got a safe, but he says when anybody brings him a valuable piece to fix he tells them to come back for it the same night. The rest of the stuff he puts under his pillow.

"He's a foreigner, but of what kind I don't know. Never would talk about himself. Lives all alone in a room back of his store. He's a damn good workman; I've watched him often; too good for the cheap jobs he gets. When I asked him why he didn't go to work for one of the big houses he said he made more on his own. I reckon it's a fact, because he seems to have all he can do. Works day and night. He's a good head, Henny; me and him has had many a talk together. He's what you call a philosopher."

"Yeah?" said Henny, good-humoredly. He cocked the cigar at a steeper angle.

"Well today, after I left the Three-Hours-for-Lunch Club," Fin went on, "I fluffed up there to have a talk with Nick, and I found the store closed and the blinds pulled down. The kids in the street said he'd been closed all day. I didn't know what to make of it, because that guy was always working. I went through the hall of the tenement house to try to get into his room at the back. The door opened in my hand, and, Gosh! Henny, when I looked inside, the place was completely wrecked!"

Henny shrugged cynically, and flicked the ashes off his cigar.

"It was like a madman had been let loose in there," Fin continued. "The table was turned over, the shelves swept bare, and all Nick's stuff lying on the floor and trodden on. I couldn't see Nick first off, but I smelled a sweetish smell on the air. Chloroform. The store in front was just the same. The fellow had even torn the paper from the walls and knocked holes in the plaster. Some of the boards of the floor had been pulled up. Certainly looked like a crazy man's work, because the watches and bits of jewelry Nick had been repairing was scattered on the floor with the rest.

"I heard a groan from the back room and run in there again. I found Nick lying on the floor between the bed and the wall. He was just coming to, and I laid him on the bed. He looked bad, all bruised and bloody about the head. Made me hot, I can tell you; such a good little guy, never harmed nobody. Well, I gave him water to drink and washed his head. I found he wasn't hurt bad, but only knocked silly.

"When he was able to talk, either he couldn't or he wouldn't tell me what the fellow was after. He said he must have come in by the window and chloroformed him while he slept. The window opened on an air-shaft. Easy enough to climb up that way. Nick said when he came to in the morning the fellow was still there, looking. He snatched a brass ball offen the foot of the bed and cracked Nick over the head with it. That was all he knew. The fellow must have let himself out into the hall then. As I told you, the door was unlocked when I came. That's the story."

"Yeah?" said Henny, coolly. "I'm sorry for the guy if he's a friend of yours; but what's remarkable about it? It happens ev'y day."

"There's two things funny about it," said Fin. "The fellow that beat him up didn't take anything. The watches and jewelry and all was still lying around the place. And, secondly, Nick's going to keep his mouth shut about it. Made me promise to keep away from the police."

"What do you make out of that?" said Henny.

"This fellow was after something special," said Fin. "Nick let on as much, but he wouldn't tell me what. The fellow didn't get it because, as Nick said, he had it safely put away somewheres outside."

"What do you come to me for?" asked Henny, with a hard look. "Do you think I beat up this bozo?"

Fin affected to laugh heartily. Like many a lad with an open and honest face, he made it work for him when he had need of it. "Quit your kidding!" he said. "I came to you because you know everything that happens this side of the river, or you can find out if you want."

Henny was silent for a moment or two, twisting the big cigar between his lips. "You better keep out of this, kid," he said at last. "'Sall right for me to tell you stories of what's past and gone. That don't hurt nobody. But you can't use this story. It's too new. The police would get on to it."

"How could they?" persisted Fin. "They don't know nothing and they won't know. Nick Peters won't say a word, and I'll change it round like I always do. You know me, Henny. I treat it as fiction. . . . Aw, there's a swell story in this," he went on, cajolingly, "and I need it for my Sunday article in the *Recorder*. Don't be a crab, Henny."

"Did this guy give you a description of the guy what hit him?" asked Henny.

Fin shook his head. "He couldn't see him good."

"Well, I'll ask around," said Henny, cautiously. "Go down and have a drink and come back in fifteen minutes."

From the bar Fin could see Robespierre (as he termed him to himself) still loitering in front of the bank across the street. That's all right, old fella, he thought; this joint has a door on the alley!

When Fin was admitted to Henny's room for the second time, the big man was not alone. Beside his desk sat a comely, well-dressed lad, like Henny, of Italian extraction, and, like Henny, with a smooth blank face and wary eyes. Quick work! thought Fin. However, he dissembled his excitement.

"This is my friend Tony Casino," said Henny. "Meet Fin Corveth, Tony."

Fin shook hands. The Italian lad got up and sat down with a bit of a swagger.

"Well, spill your stuff, Fin," said Henny.

Fin felt embarrassed in having to speak of burglary and assault in such company. However, he plunged ahead. "Fellow I know, a watchmaker, was beaten up today," he said. "I just wanted to get the rights of it."

Tony cocked an inquiring eye in Henny's direction.

"'S all right," said the latter, with a comfortable grin. "Fin ain't lookin' for revenge. He only wants the story. He's one of these, now, fiction-writers. He'll change the names and all."

Tony, assured there was no danger in it, swelled a little at the idea of seeing his exploit in print. "Yeah," he said, with a great air of unconcern, "that was my job, all right. I didn't aim to hurt the old Slovak, but it took longer than I figured to search the place, and he come out of the gauze before I was troo. So I hadda bump his bean. I didn't hurt him much." Tony spoke in an oddly husky voice for one so young, and dropped the words out of the corner of his mouth like a ventriloquist.

Fin held in his anger. It was no time to indulge private feelings. "Sure," he said, propitiatingly, "he wasn't hurt much. Who hired you to do the job?"

"I don't know the guy's name," said Tony, coolly, "and I wouldn't tell it if I did. I seen him hanging around town once or twice. He was a guy you wouldn't forget easy, and one night he come into the bar downstairs. I seen him lookin' at me, and I seen him askin' Ed who I was. So I let him buy me a drink. After we had three or four we got friendly, and after he stalled around awhile he put it up to me—would I take on a little job for a hundred smackers paid down and a grand to follow."

Fin perceived that he need have no delicacy in discussing these matters with Tony.

"I says sure I would," Tony went on. "Give me the dope. And he told me a story how years ago a Slovak jeweler stole an emerald off him that belonged to his family, and disappeared. The guy finally traced him here to Hoboken, and found him keeping a little repair shop. He couldn't have the Slovak arrested, he said, because he didn't have no proof he stole the emerald, but he'd give me a hundred smackers to search his place, and if I found the emerald and brought it to him, it would be worth a grand to me.

"Maybe it was all hooey. What did I care? I saw a hundred in it, anyhow, and I took it on. I prospected around the joint and I found the Slovak hadn't no safe, so it looked like a cinch. I found I could get in easy through the cellar, and up the air-shaft to the window of his back room. He always left it open nights.

"I fixed on last night to pull it off. The Slovak worked late in his store ev'y night. I watched until he put his light out, then I waited an hour for him to go by-by and went in. I give him a whiff of chloroform to keep him quiet. Then I searched the place. Cheese! I near pulled it down, bookin', because the New York guy told me if he had it he would hide it good. Well, I didn't find no emerald at that. The rest of the stuff wasn't worth lifting. I'm no small change artist. . . . Well, you know the rest," Tony concluded; "the Slovak come to while I was there, and I had to put him to sleep again."

"What did you hit him with?" asked Fin, casually.

"Didn't have nothing with me," said Tony, "so I unscrewed a brass knob offen the bed, dropped it in my handkerchief, and soaked him with that."

"That was a neat one!" said Fin, with a grin that concealed more than it expressed.

"Well, that's all," said Tony, with his conceited swagger. "I told you there was nothing to it."

"Oh, I don't know," said Fin. "That was a good touch about the emerald. What like emerald was it, did he say?"

"It was in the shape of a heart, the guy said," answered Tony, "about so big." He measured an inch with thumb and forefinger. "It was in two halves joined together with a gold band," he said, and there was a little ring in the top to hang it by. Been in his family hundreds of years, he said. All hooey, I guess. Said I was to bring it to him just as I found it if I wanted the grand."

"What like guy was this New York guy?" asked Fin.

Tony shook his head. "I won't furnish no description," he said. "It ain't professional." Henny nodded in agreement.

"Have you seen him since last night?" asked Fin.

"Sure. I met him on the ferry-boat *Bergen* this aft., as agreed. He was sore as hell too, not to get the emerald, but what did I care? I already had the hundred off him."

"Will you see him again?"

"Nah! Why should I?"

"It's a good story, all right," said Fin. "I'll have to fake up what we don't know about it. What did you do with the brass knob after?" he asked, very carelessly.

"Cheese! I dropped it in me pocket and forgot all about it," said Tony. "I found it there later, and I was for pitching it in the river first off, but it made an elegant dropper without being incriminating—get me?—so I kept it. Just about that time I met Kid River, a pal of mine. He had a job over in Manhattan tonight and he was looking for a nice dropper, so I give it to him."

Fin quietly absorbed this piece of information. There was nothing more he could say without showing his hand. He threw out a little smoke screen of flattery. "Cheese! Tony, you sure are one nervy kid! It's a treat to hear you! You must tell me some more stories!" And so on.

Tony could take any amount of this. "Sure; anytime you like," he said, condescendingly.

The meeting broke up.

Fin made his way down to the bar alone. He accepted a beer from Ed Hafker, and they fell into idle talk across the mahogany.

"Do you know a guy called Kid River?" asked Fin.

"Sure. He comes in here."

"I'd like to know him. I hear he's got a good story."

"I'll tell him when I see him."

"Know where he lives?"

"In the old tenement at Second and River. One block up."

"What's his right name?"

"You can search me. Everybody calls him Kid River."

Fin was in no haste to be gone. Ed must have one with him first.

Robespierre was still loitering across the street. Fin naturally supposed that this was the man who had hired Tony Casino. He silently addressed him over his beer glass: What wouldn't you give to know that the emerald heart was inside the brass ball, old fella? Your man lifted it without knowing that he lifted it!

CHAPTER TWO

THE OLD TENEMENT HOUSE had a row of broken letter-boxes in the vestibule but nobody troubled to put names in them. The people who lived in this house gave little work to the letter-carrier. Fin as before, applied to the sidewalk children for information.

"What floor does Kid River live on?"

Several voices answered at once, "Top floor front, left-hand door."

Another said, "He ain't home."

"Is there anybody there?" asked Fin.

"Sure. His girl is home."

Still another voice volunteered: "They had a fight this afternoon. I heard her hollerin'."

Fin made his way up four flights of dark and smelly stairs, and, knocked at the designated door. It presently opened a crack, revealing part of a pale, pretty face not over-clean and unmistakably tear-stained.

"What you want?" she demanded, sullenly.

"Is Kid River home?" Fin asked, pleasantly.

"Nah!" she said, and made to close the door; but Fin had inserted a toe in the crack.

"Aw, don't be a crab, sister," he said, with his most insinuating grin. "I ain't no bill-collector."

The girl took another look at Fin's mirthful blue eyes and white teeth, and opened the door wider. She bridled slightly, and put a hand to her hair. "What do youse want with Kid River?" she asked, with a sniff.

"I just want to get a story out of him."

"A newspaper guy?" she asked, suspiciously.

"Not exactly," said Fin. "I write fiction for the Sunday papers and the magazines."

"Cheese! the Kid is popular this afternoon," she said, with a sneer. "Youse are the second stranger that's been after him."

Fin pricked up his ears. "Who was the first?" he asked, carelessly.

"An old guy," she said, indifferently. "Real swell dressed."

This was certainly not Robespierre. A new factor in the case. "Swell dressed?" he said. "Real swell or Hoboken swell?"

"New York swell," she answered. "Cheese! you want to know a lot!"

"Always on the lookout for a story," said Fin, grinning. "Whadda ya mean, New York swell?"

"Great big guy," she said; "pop-eyed. Had a white edge on his vest, and a spiky mustache, and carried a cane."

"A cane!" said Fin, scornfully. "Go on!"

"That's what I said. And he had one of them single eyeglasses too, but he didn't put it up, or I'd a give him the razz."

Thus Fin obtained a pretty good description of the man, whoever he might be. "What did you tell him?" he asked.

"Nottin'!" she said, quickly. "He was too fresh with his my girl this, and my girl that, and pinching my arm and all. I hate an old freshie! I shut the door in his face and left him standing!"

This sounded as if it might be true, and Fin breathed more freely. Still he was anxious. It appeared there was to be a race for the brass ball. He must make no mistakes!

"Thanks for the hint," he said, facetiously. "I see I gotta watch my step around here."

She gave him a sidelong look as much as to say that what was "fresh" in an old gallant might be something else from a young one. "You can come in if you want," she said, leaving the door. "It's a hell of a dump," she added, with youthful bravado. "I've been accustomed to better."

She did not belie the room. A sordid setting for love's young dream. To be sure, there was the view over the river, but it is doubtful if they ever looked at it. The girl in her soiled and sleazy silk dress was of a piece with the room. Yet Fin had seen worse looking girls installed in splendor on Park Avenue. There was something touching in the way her half-grown brown hair curled at her neck. This one simply had not had any luck, he thought.

"You're worth better," he said.

She gave him an extraordinary look, half sullen, half wistful. To her Fin was like a creature from another world. She was wondering, without hope, if this might prove to be her Prince Charming.

It made Fin uncomfortable. "Where is the Kid?" he asked, to create a diversion.

"Search me," she said, sullenly. "If I knew I wouldn't tell you."

"Why not?"

"I don't know who you are. I'm not going to get him into trouble."

"He don't seem to have treated you any too well," suggested Fin.

"That's all right. Wouldn't do me no good to have him sent up."

"Come on," said Fin, grinning. "On the level, do I look like a cop?"

She shook her head.

"When will he be back?"

"I don't care if he never comes back!" she said, with a painful sneer.

"Has he left you flat?" asked Fin.

She made no answer, but her eyes filled with tears; however, they were tears of anger, not grief, Fin noted. He saw her thin hands clench.

"It's a dirty shame!" he said. "A good-looking girl like you!"

With a grievance on one side and plenty of sympathy on the other, it does not take two long to reach an understanding. The girl said, eagerly:

"I'd tell you where you could find him if you'd promise to hand him a stiff one for me."

"I'll do that," said Fin, quickly. He salved his conscience with the assurance that most men would lie to a woman for no reason, whereas this was a matter of life and death.

"All right," she said. "He's on a job tonight; I don't know where it is; but when he comes off a job he always goes to Sheeny Moe's speakeasy. Sheeny takes the stuff off him and gives him a hide-out if he wants it. Sheeny's place is the last house on Essex Street by the tracks. An old shanty standing by itself. It's a bad neighborhood. Have you got the nerve to go there?"

"I reckon," said Fin, grinning.

"Some time near morning he'll come there. . . . Knock him down, will you?" she said, passionately. "Knock him down and say, 'That's for Milly, you skunk!' Will you? Will you?"

"Sure!" said Fin, grinning. "What's the guy look like?"

"He's your height," she said, "but slimmer. Walks with a kind of lope like a kangaroo. Here, I'll show you his picture."

From a drawer in the dresser she took a little photograph of the sort you get in a slot machine. It depicted two smiling, comely young faces pressed cheek to cheek, taken evidently before the rift appeared in the lute. Somehow the cheap photograph gave Fin a wrench. It would have been hard to explain. Well, he knew what it was to be young.

Handing it back he said, "Well, I must be pulling my freight."

"There's no rush," said the girl, wistfully. "You won't find the Kid until near morning."

"I got other work to do, sister. So long."

"Will you come to see me tomorrow?" she murmured, lowering her eyes.

Fin lied blithely, "Surest thing you know!"

It was evident from her pale, downcast face that she was not deceived. The young man was attacked by sudden compunctions. She was so pale, so listless in her movements.

"Have you got anything in the house?" he asked, diffidently.

She slowly shook her head.

"Oh, gee!" murmured Fin, compassionately. He was always broke, but he could spare a dollar to one who was hungry. He folded the bill up small and tucked it under the pillow on the bed. It seemed more delicate to dispose of it that way. "So long, kid!" he

cried. "Keep your dander up!" He scuttled downstairs, whistling
to drive away painful thoughts. . . . The poor kid! The poor kid!
Didn't look a day over seventeen. How she would bloom out if somebody was good to her!

FIN HUSTLED UP WASHINGTON STREET, seething with excitement. He
was on his way back to see how Nick Peters was getting along. His
spirits were alternately up and down. Well, he was still hot on the
trail of the brass ball; he hadn't done so badly for a novice sleuth.
But, gosh! there were a thousand things that might happen before
he got it safe in his hands. The trouble was, the damn thing was of
so little apparent value. Kid River was going to use it for a blackjack tonight. After he had cracked his man on the bean, ten to one
he'd throw it away. It was maddening.

It suddenly occurred to Fin it was dinnertime and he was hungry as a hunter. Nick would need to be fed, too. He stopped and
looked up and down the street for the nearest delicatessen store.
When he stopped a man behind him stopped, and by that he learned
he was being followed again. This was a man he had not seen before—a cagy individual with two sharp eyes in a face as blank as a
death mask. Private detective was written all over him.

Where does he come in? thought Fin. Gosh! what's the use of
asking? There's an army of them! Is he after me or is he trying to
find Kid River through me? If it's Kid River, I'm a lap ahead because I know where to look.

Fin foresaw hot work during the coming night, and a mouse
with cold feet scampered up and down his spine. It would provide
the test of his nerve that every young man dreads a little while he
welcomes it. He thought desirously of a gun he had hidden in the
bottom of his trunk in New York, but he would not turn in his tracks
to fetch it, because it seemed important not to let his trailer know
he had been spotted. So he kept on his way. Entering a delicatessen store, he bought the makings of a supper for two, and carried
it on to Nick Peters' without another glance behind him.

The store contained literally nothing but Nick's workbench and
stool, and a kitchen chair for waiting customers. During Fin's

absence Nick had cleaned up as well as he was able, and one could never have guessed from his calm face that anything had happened. He was working under pressure to make up for the time he had lost. He was wearing a black skull cap to hide the abrasions on his bald poll. A gaunt little man with deep-sunken eyes, when he screwed in the watchmaker's glass he had the look of a kindly gnome.

As Fin entered, Nick dropped the glass from his eye and glanced with strained intensity in the young man's face. Seeing instantly that Fin had not brought back what he desired, he put back the glass and resumed work with a bitter half smile. He had expected nothing better.

Fin, reading that look, said, "Just the same, I've got a clue."

"What's that?" asked Nick, eagerly. He spoke excellent English, but with an accent Fin had never been able to identify.

"Lock up for half an hour and let's have some supper," said Fin. "You'll be needing it. I'll tell you everything while we eat."

Before they sat down in the rear room Fin took care to see that the door on the hall was locked, and the window on the airshaft. He pulled down the blind to discourage spies. Nick looked on at these precautions with his bitter smile.

"What matter if they come again?" he said, "The prize is gone."

"Sure," said Fin, "but we've still got our skins to save."

Nick shrugged apathetically. "You have," he said. "You are young. You got your life before you." His deep-sunken eyes dwelt on the young man with wistful kindliness. "You're a good fellow," he went on. "Keep out of this. Stay away from here."

"A fat chance!" said Fin, more moved than he cared to show.

As they sat down to *Leberwurst*, salad, and rye bread, Fin said, with a touch of resentment, "You wouldn't tell me anything, but I found out a few things for myself." He described the lantern-jawed individual who had followed him away from Nick's place earlier.

"I know him," murmured Nick.

"If you know him, why don't you have him arrested?" said Fin.

"It's not so simple," said Nick.

"At first I thought he was back of it all," said Fin, "but later I got on the track of one who seemed to have more sense. This one suspects there may be something in the brass ball." Fin described the fat man. "I reckon he's the main guy."

Nick slowly shook his head.

"Then who is?"

"A great personage," murmured Nick.

Fin stared at him. "But you know this fat man?"

"I think I see sometime in this street, watching," said Nick. "A new man. There are so many! I notice this one because he is American. So I call him to myself, 'the American.'"

"Good God!" cried Fin, amazed. "So many of them! And all pitted against you!" He looked around the bare little room as if seeking the answer. "What does it mean, Nick?"

The little watchmaker shrugged wearily. "What's the connection between the fat man and Robespierre?" demanded Fin.

"No connection. There are two parties."

"Two parties!" echoed Fin.

"One look for the brass ball to save it," said Nick, coolly; "one to destroy it!"

"You're talking in riddles!" cried Fin. "Why should anybody destroy a valuable emerald?"

"There is more in it than an emerald," said Nick, with his quiet, bitter smile.

"Good Lord! why do you tantalize me with hints!" cried the exasperated Fin. "Why not tell me the rights of it?"

"I say no more," said Nick, pressing his lips together.

"How does a poor man like you come to be mixed up with a great personage?" demanded Fin. "If you had this valuable emerald, why do you live so poor?"

"It is not mine," said Nick. "I keep for somebody."

"Then you ought to let me go to the police. You need protection here."

From the first, Nick had become agitated at any mention of the police. "No! No!" he said. "If you go to police you get in the newspapers. I got to keep secret. For sixteen years I keep secret."

"Can't you tell me?" said Fin. "I'm your friend. Don't you trust me?"

"I trust you," said Nick with a quick warm glance. "You are a good fellow. . . . But it is too dangerous. If the brass ball is lost, there is no use. All better be forgotten."

"Maybe I'll get it back!"

Nick shook his head gloomily. "You not get it back. What is a brass ball? It will be thrown away."

"You might as well tell me," persisted Fin. "I'm in it up to the ears already. They've spotted me. There's a man laying for me outside now. Why not give me the satisfaction of knowing what I'm up against?"

"I will not tell you," said Nick, firmly. "If the emerald is lost there is no use."

"But if I bring it back to you?" said Fin, eagerly.

Nick considered. "Yes," he said, "if you bring it back I tell you the whole story—if you wish to risk your life."

"Risk!" cried Fin. "That's all that makes life worth living! . . . All right, that's a go! You can depend upon it, I'll do my damnedest!"

For a while they ate in silence. "Nick," said Fin, persuasively, "just answer me one question. Which party was it that engineered the attack on you last night? The fat blackguard or the lean?"

"Truly, I do not know," said Nick.

"I think it was the fat one," said Fin, thoughtfully, "because he suspected there was something in the brass ball."

"Maybe so," said Nick.

As soon as they finished eating, Nick returned to his bench. Some of the watches had been damaged in being flung on the floor and he had extra work to do. Fin sat in the other chair, smoking, and they left the blinds up and the door open to suggest to anyone who might be watching that they had nothing to fear and nothing to conceal. While they talked a workman came in with his watch to be fixed, and another called for his.

Nick would answer no more questions. Instead, he resumed a conversation he had had with Fin before all this happened. It dealt with his favorite theme—the future of man in the universe. Nick, who was no pessimist philosopher (though he had good reason to be, Fin thought) was obliged to concede that man's present situation in a partly mechanized world was bad; but he had faith in the spirit of man. "When man perfect the machine," he said, "he master it."

Fin marveled at such detachment; such sang-froid. Truly, courage chooses strange vehicles. The wizened little man with the watchmaker's glass screwed into his eye, giving his conscious mind to philosophy and his unconscious to the watch he was repairing, was a first-class hero, he considered. Fin himself, thinking of actual men prowling in the street, was unable to concentrate on man in the abstract.

As it drew on towards midnight Fin got up. "I've got to run over to New York," he said. "I hate to leaveo you here alone, Nick."

"I have a gun," said Nick, quietly. "I lock the window tonight. They not catch me so easy again."

Nick arose, and their hands involuntarily shot out. Nick gave Fin's hand a little shake. The watchmaker's deep-sunken eyes dwelt on the young man with infinite feeling. Fin was never to forget that look.

"There is much I have not say to you," Nick said, quietly. "Words so poor to express! just say this: I am lucky I have you for friend."

Fin, deeply moved, turned away his head. "Don't, Nick, don't!" he mumbled. "You make me feel rotten. . . . I want to say you've given me something . . . something big! . . . I mean . . . something to measure up to. . . . Hell! I can't say it right!"

Nick patted his shoulder, and then, when Fin thought all had been said, he suddenly came out with a piece of vital information: "Listen, my friend. In Miss Folsom's School at Pompton Lakes there is a young girl who look to me for everything. She is called Mariula Peters. She not know her own name, her history. Unless I produce her heritage she must never know. The wolves are waiting to tear her! . . . I tell you because . . . well if my skull was not so thick tonight she have no friend in the world. So I am scared for her. I ask you to befriend her. She has noble nature."

"Gosh, Nick!" faltered Fin, pressing his hand. "I'll do my very damnedest! . . . Why do you stay here alone?" he added, with a kind of anger. "Go to a hotel; go any place where there are people; you would be safe among people."

Nick shrugged indifferently. "I safe enough here," he said. "They know the prize not here now. It is you who will be in danger to-night."

CHAPTER THREE

MIDNIGHT. Fin supposed the private detective to be at his heels, but made it a point not to look behind him. He crossed Washington Street and headed south, looking for a taxi bound in the right direction. The busy main street was quiet now, and the cats were coming out. A cab came along and Fin jumped on the running board, hoping there might be no other for his tracker.

"Hudson Tunnels," he said to the driver, "and step on it!"

However, when he drove up to the entrance of the tunnels there was another cab close behind him. Its occupant did not immediately get out, but Fin had a glimpse of a masklike face through the front window. Fin descended to the upper level of the tunnel station and hung about, gaping at the magazines on the newsstand, until he heard a warning cry from below announcing the departure of a train. Dropping his money in the box, he ran downstairs. However, he was not so quick but the detective boarded the rear car as he made the front one.

Leaving the train at Christopher Street, Manhattan, Fin found a single taxi waiting at the station, and congratulated himself. Here's where I shake him! he thought. He got in, giving the address of his own hang-out in MacDougal Street. But the detective was having the devil's own luck tonight. He found a taxi somewhere. As Fin unloaded at his own door, his pursuer turned the corner. Fin shrugged. Oh well, the night is young!

In his room Fin changed to an old suit badly in need of the pressing iron, and a battered felt hat that he could pull down well over his eyes. He loaded the gun and dropped it in his pocket. He possessed no license to carry a gun, but under the present circumstances a man could not stick at that. He was mighty thankful he had a gun.

As he reviewed in his mind all the curious facets of this case, none of which seemed to match, Fin's thoughts turned desirously toward his friend Amos Lee Mappin, the famous writer on crime. There would be the man to consult in such an emergency. And how he would enjoy getting his teeth into it! But I shan't go to him, Fin thought, hastily. His reputation would blanket me entirely. I must work this out on my own.

On the way back Fin employed every stratagem he could think of to throw off his tracker, but it was all in vain. The detective landed in Hoboken at the same moment he did. His persistence was uncanny. Fin began to be a little worried.

Always looking for a chance to shake him, Fin visited the resorts that were still open. In Meyers' he sat down in a corner of the bar, since he still had time to spare. He could not see his detective, but he had no doubt that the man could see him.

Presently Fin got a shock. Looking through the archway into the restaurant, he could see the end of a table where a noisy party was supping. The host, an old rounder extraordinarily big and fat, was directly in line with Fin's vision. At first the young man scarcely noticed him, but presently certain significant details stole on him: red cheeks, protuberant blue eyes, waxed mustache, dangling monocle.

"Gosh! it's the American!" thought Fin. "What's his game here?"

Immediately afterwards he got another shock. Within the bar, alongside the archway, there was a small table occupied by a single figure—a queer, lean, writhen figure—peeping around the arch at the supper party in the adjoining room. In short, Fin's Robespierre! His back was turned towards Fin, but a noise behind him made him jerk his head around nervously, and Fin had a glimpse of his green face distorted with anger and hatred. He did not spot Fin.

Fin instantly left the building. I don't know what it all means, he said to himself, but my job tonight is to find the brass ball, and I can't afford to get mixed up in any fresh complications.

The detective was waiting for him outside, and Fin soon received fresh evidence of his skill in tracking. He was able to take advantage of every bit of cover afforded by the deserted streets, and it was but rarely that Fin got a glimpse of him. Fin led him half the length of the town, turning many a corner, and frequently doubling in his tracks. But the detective appeared to have an uncanny faculty of forecasting what a hunted man would do, and he was never caught napping. At last Fin could waste no more time. When he finally turned into Essex Street, it is true, he had not seen the man in half an hour, but he assumed that he was still on the scent.

Essex Street begins back of Castle Hill, and runs downhill both actually and figuratively until it loses itself among the rusty tin cans and rubbish heaps of a former, dumping-ground under the Heights. The dumping-ground is bounded by a pool of stagnant water, and beyond run the tracks of the belt railway. It is as foul and ugly a spot as that waste where Childe Roland found the Dark Tower. Nothing will grow there except, oddly enough, clumps of gigantic sunflowers.

The last house stands out in the middle of the hummocky dumping-ground. It appeared to have been constructed out of what odds and ends might be found in such a place. New rooms had been tacked on at random as additional materials were collected. The whole straggling mass had a kind of sinister picturesqueness under the night sky. It was surrounded by a crazy fence built of discarded sheets of tin roofing, with a wooden gate in front. No sound was to be heard from within and no crack of light appeared anywhere.

It was a clear, starry night, and after having been out for an hour Fin could see pretty well. He looked about for the best point of vantage. All he knew was that Kid River was coming to this house sometime toward morning. The most direct approach was down Essex Street, but the thief might have reasons for avoiding a direct approach. An examination convinced Fin that his man could not climb the tin fence anywhere without making an ungodly racket, so he determined to watch the gate.

There was no lack of cover among the hummocks of ashes and the cast-off articles bestrewn over the dump. Fin hated to lie down in such a place; his nose wrinkled up at the sour smell that hung over it; however, he could not afford to be squeamish now. Looking for a hiding-place near the gate, he was greatly astonished to stumble over a soft body. A man started up, cursing him in a whine.

"Sorry, 'bo," said Fin. "I didn't see you lying there."

"What the hell are you looking for?" asked the man.

"The same as yourself, I reckon," said Fin, quickly, "a place to lie down in."

"Well, it's free to all comers," said the man, mollified. "You ain't got a cigarette on you, have you?" he asked, eagerly.

"Sure," said Fin producing a packet. "But hide the light. We don't want to bring anybody down on us."

"Hell! I wasn't born yesterday," said the other.

With the expertness born of long practice he lit a match inside his coat and stuck his head down to it. When he got the cigarette going he cupped it within his hand so that not a spark showed. "Cheese! that's good!" he murmured. "That's a life-saver!"

Presently they saw a dim figure where the street ended in the dump. Flattening themselves behind a hummock of ashes, they watched it. In another moment Fin recognized the squat figure of the detective. He came down to the gate of the shanty, stood watching and listening for a while, as if in uncertainty, and then went back out of sight in the dark. But Fin did not suppose he had lost him.

"It's a bull!" muttered the man beside him, savagely. "Damn their dirty hides!"

"Yeah," said Fin, sympathetically. "It's a nice thing if they won't let a man sleep on the dump! If they chase us off the dump, where the hell else is left for a man to go?"

"You said it, fellow. Them people has got no bowels. Them lousy millionaires has got the whole earth fenced off for theirselves; they won't even leave the dumps to the workers!"

Fin had the impulse to ask when he had worked last, but restrained it. Full sympathy was his line. "Yeah," he said, "what we got to do is to join together and take what we want. Throw a scare into them pot-bellied millionaires!"

"That's what I say," returned the other, truculently. "Some day we'll show them where they get off at. We'll let them millionaires sweat down their fat on the road gangs while we ride round in their Rolls-Royces and spit out of the window!"

Thus they conversed in great amity while the stranger smoked Fin's cigarettes. "Cheese! you're a good fellow!" he said, warmly. "You're a man after my own heart! . . . You ain't got a drink on you, have you?"

"Wish to God I had," said Fin. The lower you go in the scale, he reflected, the easier it is to make friends.

After a while the man lay down and slept again, while Fin continued his vigil. What queer sights the stars look down on! he thought. Nobody came out or went in at the gate he was watching.

Dawn was heralded by a loud crowing of cocks within the ramshackle tin fence. Fin grinned to himself. This cheerful sound that everybody associates with the clean countryside had a weird effect on the dump. Well, it's all one to a rooster, thought Fin. Daylight revealed the full hideousness of the place with its piles of ancient rubbish. It was chilly, and an unwholesome steam was rising from the stagnant water near by.

The sleeping man beside him, with his bristly face and ragged, dirty clothes, was of a piece with the other cast-off articles. He was a small man in garments much too big for him; in age he might have been anything between thirty-five and fifty-five. Fin noted with surprise his small hands and feet and delicate features. Just a little different turn of fortune's wheel, he thought, and he would have been twirling a cane on Park Avenue. Fin perceived other derelicts lying here and there. So much the better, he thought; if it's a regular hang-out for tramps, I won't be conspicuous.

One by one these deplorable figures arose and shuffled away with shamefaced glances from side to side. No man can feel at his ease rising from a dump pile. The little fellow beside Fin opened his eyes and looked at his partner of the night with strong curiosity. At the sight of Fin's shaven chin and fairly good clothes his cameraderie dried up. Feeling that he had been taken in, he arose, muttering:

"Aah, what the hell . . . !"

It did not suit Fin to be left alone on the dump, and he said, quickly: "Wait a minute. That's a speak-easy yonder."

"Sure, I know it is," returned the other.

"Fellow I know said he'd buy me a drink if I waited till he come in the morning," said Fin. "Stick around awhile and I'll get you in on it."

"Oh, all right," said the little man, wiping his mouth with the back of his hand in anticipation. He sat down again.

They had a long wait. Conversation did not prosper by daylight because Fin did not look the part that he was trying to play, and the little man was ill at ease. No sign of life showed outside the rambling shanty, but smoke started to issue from one of the leaning tin chimneys. Fin could not see the detective anywhere.

It was after eight before Kid River appeared. He came from the north, circling around the fence to reach the gate. Fin knew him first by the loping walk Milly had described; a moment later he recognized the weak, comely face of the photograph, with deep lines etched between nostrils and lips. Fin ran to intercept him before he should reach the gate. There was no time to parley with the man, who might have a dozen friends in the shanty; he must strike and strike quickly.

The instant Kid River saw Fin's eyes he knew what was coming to him. With a scared face he turned to run back the way he had come. Fin overtook him and, still running, struck him a blow under the ear that toppled him forward on hands and knees. Fin fell on his back, bearing him flat to the ground. Kid River struggled weakly—he was a weedy lad—but made no loud outcry.

"What's the matter with you? What's the matter with you?" he kept gasping, as well he might.

The thought flitted through Fin's mind: Anyhow, I'm keeping my promise to Milly. Kneeling in the small of Kid River's back and keeping a hand on his neck, he frisked his pockets with the other. He pulled out a little canvas bag which from the feel of it contained rings and brooches. This was no good to him and he put it back. Kid River must have been astonished. A hasty patting of the Kid's bony frame all over satisfied Fin that the brass ball was not upon him. A sickening disappointment.

"The brass ball," he said. "The ball Tony Casino gave you yesterday. That's what I want. Where is it?"

"What the hell! . . . What the hell. . .!" stammered Kid River in witless amazement.

"You heard what I said!" cried Fin. "Where is it?"

"I gave it to some kids in the street," gasped the Kid.

"You lie!" cried Fin, tightening the grasp on his neck.

"Honest! Honest!" stuttered Kid River. "I didn't know there was anything special about it. I come over on the Fourteenth Street Ferry. I walked down Bloomfield. On the corner of Eleventh there was a bunch of kids playing duck on a rock in a lot there. I handed them the brass ball to pitch with because I didn't want it found on me."

This had the ring of truth and Fin arose from the prostrate figure. "All right," he said. "If you're lying, I'll come back and smash you. I know where to find you."

Kid River, getting to his feet, cringed and gaped at him.

As Fin turned to go he saw the little scarecrow tramp sitting in the ashes, and likewise gaping at him with ridiculous hanging jaw. But his astonishment was not sufficient to make him forget what he was waiting for.

"Hey! Where's the drink I was going to get?" he cried.

Fin pitched him a quarter. "There's the price of it," he said. "And keep your mouth shut!"

Fin ran up Essex Street. At the corner of the first north-and-south street he came upon the detective lounging against some railings. Fin's hand instinctively went to his gun. The man gave him a hard look as he passed. However, there were a number of people about, and he could not attack Fin, supposing that to be his intention. But perhaps he knew that Fin had not secured the prize.

Bloomfield was another of the north-and-south streets that ran the whole length of the town. Eleventh Street crossed it several blocks to the north. By this time of day all Hoboken was abroad and the sidewalks were thronged. Fin had no doubt but that the detective was jogging along behind him. He refused to give the man the satisfaction of seeing him turn his head.

At the corner of Bloomfield and Eleventh Streets there was in fact a vacant lot, and Fin saw the stones still in place that had been used in the game of duck on the rock. The only children in view at the moment were three wizened boys of eleven or twelve sitting on a piece of heavy timber, blowing clouds of cigarette smoke through their nostrils. Fin approached them.

"How long have you been here?" he asked.

"What is it to you?" answered one, impudently. "You don't own this lot."

"I don't aim to chase you," said Fin, mildly. "Was there a fellow come by here a while ago and gave you a brass ball?"

"I think you're coocoo," answered the boy.

"He stole it off me grandmother's bed," said Fin. "It's worth a half a dollar to me to get it back."

The boys looked at one another in chagrin. "Cheese!" said one, "and we sold it for a dime!"

"Sold it!" said Fin, with a sinking heart. "Who to?"

"The rag, bone, and bottle man."

Fin silently cursed his luck. "Would you know him again?"

"Sure. He comes through here regular."

"Do you know where his hang-out is?"

"I know," said one boy. "What is it worth to you if we show you?"

"Dime apiece," said Fin. His heart rose again.

"Come on."

They set off up the street, the small boys surrounding Fin and scampering to keep up with his long strides. It was like Gulliver led by the Lilliputians. The boys' street-sharpened instincts suggested to them that there was a mystery about the brass ball, and they kept glancing inquisitively into Fin's face, trying to read the secret.

"How did you know the guy give it to us?" one asked.

"I collared him," said Fin, "and forced him to tell."

"Cheese! It's funny the guy would swipe it off you only to give it to us!"

"Yeah," said Fin, smoothly, "he's bughouse. What they call, now, a kleptomaniac."

"Cheese!"

At Thirteenth Street two blocks farther north, the boys turned to the left and led Fin to a point where the street ended against a high board fence bounding the freight yards. There on the right was the junkyard heaped with its hopeless-looking impedimenta. Tucked into the corner where the two fences joined was a tumbledown store and dwelling displaying a few so-called antiques in the dusty window.

"This here's the place," said Fin's conductor, "and there's the guy himself inside."

Fin distributed dimes all around, and entered the store. He ordered the boys to wait outside. The junkman and his wife were a browbeaten pair who had obviously outfitted themselves from their own stock. They cringed at the entrance of a well-dressed customer. Fin wasted no time.

"Those boys told me they sold you a brass ball awhile ago," he said.

At the suggestion that something in their possession might be valuable, a cunning look appeared in the faces of the man and woman. They sought to mask it under expressions of abysmal stupidity.

"I don't recollect it," said the man, dully.

"Well, let me see the stuff you just brought in on your cart and I'll look for myself," said Fin.

There was a side door from the store into the yard, and the junkman's handcart with its row of cow-bells stretched between two upright sticks, was visible just outside it. While Fin watched, the man went through the door and thrust his hand under a pile of bags in the cart. When he returned to the store he had the gleaming brass ball in his hand.

Fin's heart gave a great leap of joy. If it had been a ball of pure gold it would not have meant so much to him. He had seen the other three balls on Nick Peters' bed; he knew what he was looking for, and this was it. So furious was the coursing of his blood that it dizzied him for a moment. Masking his excitement, he said, casually:

"Yes, that's it."

"You can have it back for five dollars," said the junkman.

Fin believed that this ball was worth a thousand times five dollars, yes and a thousand times that again, but a man hates to have an advantage taken of him. "Five dollars nothing, you swindler!" he said, indignantly. "I'll give you a dollar, and that's four times what it's worth to you. If that don't satisfy you, I'll fetch a cop and take it for nothing. It was stolen!"

The junk dealer surrendered with a shrug. "All right, you can have it for a dollar," he said.

Glancing over his shoulder, Fin saw the three small boys staring in through the open door at the transaction—and behind the boys the hard, wary face of the hired detective. The man's eyes were fixed on the brass ball in the junk-dealer's hand. The sight administered a check to Fin's rising tide of joy. He said, quickly:

"Come into the back room. I don't want them to see me paying you for it."

The back room served as living-quarters for the couple. Junk doubtlessly has a demoralizing effect on those who deal in it; the place presented a hideously squalid aspect. Here the dollar and the brass ball changed hands. Fin had the blessed object in his possession at last. He dropped it in his pants pocket with a thrill of satisfaction.

This room had a door looking toward the back of the yard. The railway fence ran alongside. Once he had his prize safe, Fin said:

"That fellow outside is laying for me. Can I get out this way?"

"It's nothing to me," said the junkman, surlily. He felt that he ought to have had more than a dollar out of this curious situation, whatever the rights of it might be. "The railway detectives will run you in if they see you," he added.

"I'll chance them," said Fin, grinning.

He jumped for the top of the fence, hauled himself up, and dropped down on the other side. There was no one in sight in the yard. Suspecting that the junk-dealer would promptly sell him out to the detective, he ran with all his speed to the nearest gate. This gave on Fourteenth Street, one of Hoboken's principal thorough-fares. By good luck he picked up a taxi, and two minutes later he was aboard a ferry pulling out of its slip, with his prize in his pocket, and free of espionage at last.

Fin experienced a fine moment of exultation. He snatched off his hat to let the river breeze cool his throbbing forehead. Unable to keep still, he walked up and down the deck, singing an inward paan: "I've done it! I've done it! I've done it!" He pictured how beautifully Nick Peters' worn, grave face would light up when he saw the prize. Fin felt like a king.

In thus dashing for the ferry he had yielded to a blind instinct to shake off the dog that was sniffing at his trail. As he cooled down he began to perceive he had made an error in tactics. What good was it to shake him off? As soon as it was reported to his master (whoever he might be) that Fin had recovered the brass ball, what would he do? Simply lie in wait for Fin outside Nick Peters' store. The young man's ebullient spirits subsided. He saw now that what he ought to have done was to head straight for Nick's place in an effort to get there first.

Well, it was no use wasting his time in regrets. What he had to do now was to study how to reach Nick in spite of them. He re-membered that Nick's store was in the first of a row of tall tene-ment houses, the last one of which abutted on Hudson Street. These houses all belonged to the same estate. Suppose he entered the end house and made his way to Nick's place either through the cellars or over the roofs?

At Twenty-third Street, Manhattan, Fin merely changed to one of the Lackawanna ferries, and returned to the other end of Hoboken. At the ferry terminal he took a taxi and had himself set down near the house on Hudson Street that he intended to enter. Discovering that there was no communication through the cellars, he climbed to the roof. Here it was clear going over the parapets to the house where Nick lived. In each house there was a door giving on the top of the stairs.

As he was about to descend through the last house, Fin was stopped by a thought. Suppose the enemy to have three or four men on the job by this time, would they not be stationed in the halls of the house? In that case Fin would be running directly into a trap. He recollected that the airshaft on which Nick Peters' window opened also served the house next door, and he determined to go down through that house and endeavor to gain Nick's window through the shaft. The decision undoubtedly saved his life.

Through a cellar window he reached the bottom of the air shaft. Over his head he saw that Nick's window, was open. A heavy iron waste-pipe with joints at three-foot intervals enabled him to reach the sill. So Tony Casino had gone two nights before. Fin threw his legs over the sill and ducked his head under the raised sash.

The airshaft was a narrow, one, and it ran up four more stories before opening to the sky. Consequently, it admitted but little light to Nick Peters' room, and for a moment Fin could make out nothing. An ominous silence hung over the place. "Nick! Nick!" he called softly. There was no reply. The bed faced him from across the room, and with growing horror he perceived that there was a motionless body upon it.

Springing across, he discovered his friend lying in a twisted position, his face horribly contorted, the eyeballs starting from his head. A twisted cord was cutting deeply into his neck. The body was still warm; the deed must have been committed within five minutes. Fin was afflicted with an agony of self-blame. If I had only come straight here perhaps I could have saved him!

Whipping out his pocket-knife he cut the cord. Straightening the limbs of the body he climbed upon the bed and endeavored to promote artificial respiration. But his efforts were in vain. Nick's heart had stopped beating. His body was growing cold under Fin's hands, Too late! Too late! he thought, despairingly.

He heard furtive sounds out in the stair hall of the house, and sprang to the door. The key was in it. As Fin laid a hand on it he found it was unlocked. He no more than got the key turned when the handle was softly tried from the other side.

The young man paused in the center of the room, distraught with grief and irresolution. What shall I do? What shall I do? His

friend was dead beyond recall, and the instinct of self-preservation moved strongly within him. If they know I'm in here, they'll
soon cut off my escape by the airshaft. Like a flash he was out of
the window again. Gaining the cellar of the next house, he ran up
to the roof three steps at a time.

CHAPTER FOUR

WHEN FIN, flying blindly from the scene of the murder, found that he had reached the ferry terminal without being followed, he paused to try to take stock of the situation. But his brain was spinning like a teetotum; it was impossible for him to think clearly. He was shocked, upon looking into the mirror of a slot-machine, to catch a glimpse of his own face. Pale, haggard, and wild-eyed; no wonder people in the street had stared.

Under the circumstances an honest man's first impulse is to communicate with the police. But Nick Peters, when the first attack was made on him, had been so desperately averse to seeking the aid of the police, he must have had a good reason for it. Fin felt that he owed it to his dead friend to find out what his reason was, before going counter to his wishes. On the other hand, if he delayed notifying the police it would leave him open to grave censure if not to the suspicion of having murdered the man himself. He could decide nothing.

In addition to the confusion of his thoughts, his heart was heavy with grief for the loss of his friend, and the self-accusation still rang in his ears—If I had acted with better judgment I might have saved him!

In his helplessness the young man remembered Amos Lee Mappin. At such a moment the thought of that humane, cool-minded man was like a ray of light in impenetrable gloom. Of all men living, Mappin, the expert in crime, the high-minded gentleman, was the best qualified to advise in such a crisis. Fin made up his mind to consult him before taking any other step. How thankful he was he had such a friend.

He took the tube to Manhattan and a taxi to Mappin's apartment. Taxis during the last twenty hours had taken all his money, but he reflected that he could certainly borrow from his well-to-do friend in such an emergency.

Mappin lived in one of the big apartment houses overhanging the cliffs bordering the East River. In addition to the luxuries common to such houses, this one provided its tenants with a yacht-landing in the basement. You approached the building through a slum, but the windows of Mr. Mappin's vast living-room on the twentieth floor commanded a panorama embracing the whole river between the Queensboro' and the Williamsburg bridge.

Fin found his friend serenely breakfasting out on his lofty balcony in a flowered dressing-gown. Mr. Mappin was a small man, always beautifully turned out in a style that held a true line between the conspicuous and the common. He had a neat round belly, a round bald head, and he wore round spectacles with thin gold rims. It was his passion, to treat himself—and his friends—to the best in life, and he had the means to satisfy it; good pictures, fine bindings, incomparable wines and cigars. A dilettante in the fine old sense. He wrote for the love of writing. His infrequent books did not sell by the hundreds of thousands, but they were instinct with a grace and wisdom that made them prized by the discriminating the world over. Mr. Mappin was a bachelor.

He exclaimed in dismay at the sight of his young friend's white face and staring eyes. "Good God! Finlay, what's the matter? You look as if you hadn't slept for a week."

"Matter enough," muttered Fin.

"Have you breakfasted?"

Fin shook his head. "Can't stop to eat now."

"You must eat," said Mr. Mappin, firmly.

"Let me tell you . . ."

"Not a word until I have ordered your breakfast."

Mr. Mappin pressed a button that summoned Jermyn. Jermyn naturally, was the *ne plus ultra* among gentlemen's gentlemen, and he was a good deal more beside; he was counted a friend by his master's friends. He greeted Fin cheerfully.

"A quick breakfast for Mr. Corveth, Jermyn, please," said his master. "Fruit, bacon and eggs, fresh coffee."

When Jermyn had retired Mr. Mappin said: "Bring a chair, out Finlay, and fire away. You will excuse me if I go on eating. Food chills so quickly in the open air."

Fin sat down, and pressed his aching head between his hands in an effort to bring some order into his thoughts. He desired to tell a plain and concise tale. He began to talk.

Now Mr. Mappin prided himself upon never being taken aback by life, but on this occasion his *savoir faire* deserted him. Fin had not uttered half a dozen sentences before the older man laid down his knife and fork and stared.

"Good God!" he muttered. "Amazing! . . . Amazing!"

It was an immense relief to Fin to get it all off his chest. Mr. Mappin was a wonderful listener. He grasped a situation with half a word. Upon finishing his tale Fin could have wept with gratitude and weariness and sheer heartbreak, but breakfast appeared in the nick of time to give him fresh courage.

Mr. Mappin had Jermyn spread the meal inside, so that while Fin ate he could walk up and down and question him. He said he required leg action to induce his wits to work properly. Maybe that was why he had provided himself with a living-room fifty feet long. His questions went unerringly to the heart of the matter.

"First of all," he said, briskly, "you must get rid of this notion that you are to blame for Nick Peters' death. That is merely weakminded. Suppose you had gone directly to his store, what would have happened? They would expect you to go there direct. They were certainly laying for you. They would have got you and Peters both, and would have recovered the brass ball into the bargain."

Fin began to feel better. "Why did they kill Nick before he got the brass ball back?" he asked helplessly.

"To prevent him from telling you its secret," Mr. Mappin answered, instantly. "Have you got it?"

Fin handed it over. The little man weighed it and studied it—just a common brass ball that had ornamented a cheap bedstead, but it made their hearts beat fast. It had a hole in the bottom where it had been screwed to the bed. Mr. Mappin thrust the point of an orange stick into the hole and delicately probed it.

"Three-eighths of an inch thick," he murmured. "One can feel the hard object inside. It has been wrapped in something to protect it." He pointed out a line showing where the ball had once been sawed in two, then brazed together again and buffed to hide the joining. "An expert worker in metals did it," he remarked. "Probably Peters himself. . . . I'll open it while you eat."

Fin, however, leaped from the table. They adjourned to the small room that Mr. Mappin called his "shop." He built ship models in his hours of ease. His present work, a quaint galleon of the sixteenth century, complete down to the last tiny detail, rested upon chocks, waiting to receive her rigging. All the tools that they required were on hand here. Mr. Mappin screwed the brass ball between the jaws of a vise and started to saw along the faint line that marked the previous joining, stopping often to turn the ball that the saw might not damage its contents. Fin looked on with a fast-beating heart.

The two halves finally separated, and they saw a little cotton bag lying within. When Mr. Mappin ripped the stitches, the great emerald slipped out on his palm, and a sigh of satisfaction escaped them both. So far so good. It was not a single emerald, but two matched halves set in gold and put together to form a locket. There was a gold ring in the top to hang it by. Upon being held to the light it was seen to be opaque. A marvelous jewel! Magical green fire gleamed from its depths.

"This in itself would provide the girl with a handsome dowry!" said Mr. Mappin holding it up by the ring to flash in the sunlight.

"Never mind the emerald!" said Fin, breathlessly. "See what's inside!"

Mr. Mappin found the hidden spring, and the locket opened on his hand. Within it lay a square of white paper folded up small. Mr. Mappin himself forgot the emerald then. It clattered to the bench unheeded while he opened up the paper with trembling fingers. Fin looked over his shoulder, his eyes fairly starting from his head.

A groan of disappointment broke from them both. The paper was blank. Mr. Mappin turned it over and back again. Blank on both sides!

"O God! what a sell!" cried Fin.

Mr. Mappin said nothing.

"They have over-reached us!" cried Fin.

"That's impossible!" said Mr. Mappin, sharply. "We are the first to see it."

"Well, we're sold, somehow."

"Perhaps not," said Mr. Mappin, thoughtfully; "it may not be so blank as it seems!"

"What!"

"We can't stop to make tests now. Murder will not wait."

He locked the emerald and the paper in his safe.

CHAPTER FIVE

WHILE FIN RESUMED HIS BREAKFAST, Mr. Mappin paced back and forth, smoking a cigar. "Did Peters give you no clue to his nationality?" he asked.

Fin shook his head.

"I suspect that the whole head and front of our problem lies in that," murmured the older man, thoughtfully. "It is clear from his reference to 'the American' that this is a foreign intrigue which has been imported to our shores. Tony Casino referred to Peters as 'the Slovak.' There may be a hint there."

"What is a Slovak?" asked Fin.

"Strictly speaking, it's a Hungarian Slav. But as the word is used in the streets it might refer to a member of any of the Balkan peoples. Peters is no doubt the Americanization for business purposes of some unpronounceable foreign patronymic. His real name may have been Petrovich, Petrovsky, or Pitescu."

He asked Fin a score of questions tending to clarify the story and divest it of non-essentials. "Then the matter stands thus," he said at last; "the emerald heart contains the heritage of the girl who goes to school in Pompton. According to Peters it is a very great heritage, but the girl does not know anything about it, and now Peters is dead. If we can't solve the riddle ourselves, we will have to look for the answer either from the man known as 'the American' or the one you term 'Robespierre.'"

"What shall we do first?" asked Fin.

"Do!" cried Mr. Mappin in exasperation. "We will have to notify the police! . . . Was ever a good citizen put in such a position before? Nick Peters foresaw that it would be fatal to divulge the facts of this case prematurely. . . . But there's no help for it. One cannot compound with murder. We must go to the police. It's heartbreaking!"

"Couldn't we send them an anonymous notification?" suggested Fin.

"Too dangerous! They might bring the crime home to you then. . . . Besides, I must visit the scene. All the evidence is there. I must look it over before the police mess it up."

"It's not safe for you to go there," said Fin. "The murderer is still hanging about."

"Why me any more than you?"

"Oh, I'm of no importance to the world," said Fin.

"I confess I don't like it," said Mr. Mappin, a little waspishly. "I'm not of the stuff that heroes are made of. But there's no help for it."

"You must arm yourself," said Fin.

"Bless you, I don't own a gun," said Mr. Mappin, with a rueful smile, "and if I did I wouldn't know what to do with it."

"Well, I have one on me," said Fin.

Mr. Mappin continued to pace the room, thoughtfully rolling the cigar between his lips. "I have it!" he cried at last. "We will notify the police, but we'll say nothing about the brass ball or the emerald. You went to call on your friend yesterday. You found his place had been broken into and he had been beaten. He forbade you to notify the police. Today, when you went back to see how he was, you found him foully murdered. He never took you into his confidence and you have no idea what lies behind it all. This is almost the truth, and it is what you must tell the police."

Fin nodded.

"You see," Mr. Mappin went on briskly; "it all hangs together; it exactly coincides with the story you told Henny Friend yesterday afternoon. Your interest in the case is merely that of the free-lance writer looking for copy. If we say nothing about the emerald we may be sure that the murderers will not. Neither will Henny Friend, nor Tony Casino, nor Kid River give us away, for good reasons of their own. It is possible that the boys in Hoboken or the junk-dealer may break into the newspapers with their story, but there will be no support for it; we'll simply laugh it down."

"I get you," said Fin.

"I hope under the circumstances we may be said to be justified in keeping a part of the truth from the lawful guardians of the peace," said Mr. Mappin, with a sly twinkle in his eye. "However, justified or not, I mean to take the responsibility."

"The police will never solve the murder by their own efforts," suggested Fin.

"So much the better," said Mr. Mappin, dryly. "If it turns out that we have to seek the solution of the mystery through the American or Robespierre we want them to have full liberty of action. We couldn't get anything out of them if they were locked up. . . . But as a matter of fact," he went on, "we have to lay bare the motives for the crime before we can hang it on anybody."

"It is hard to have to let them go," said Fin, somberly.

"We are only giving the murderers rope enough to hang themselves with," said Mr. Mappin. "Understand, since I am deliberately hampering the police in their investigation, it is up to me to see that justice is done in the end. I pledge myself to that."

"I'm not worrying," said Fin. "I know justice will stand a darn sight better chance with you than with the police."

"Swallow another cup of coffee," said Mr. Mappin, briskly making for the door. "I'll get into my clothes."

In a remarkably short space of time he returned wearing a double-breasted gray suit of French flannel, a tie like nobody else's tie, and a distinguished Panama hat. Fin, whose style as yet was somewhat sprawling and immature, always sighed over the effect that Mr. Mappin was able to create; it was neither too youthful nor too aged; it was right.

"Let's go," he said. "I've been thinking about the best manner of notifying the police. I suggest we let Jermyn telephone them after we have gone."

Jermyn entered the room to announce that a taxi was waiting.

"Jermyn," said his master, "Mr. Corveth has run into a very strange and tragic affair over in Hoboken. I cannot stop to tell you the particulars now, but we are going to need your help in the matter, and I'll inform you later. . . . What time have you?"

"Nine thirty-three, sir," said Jermyn, consulting his watch.

"One minute fast," said Mr. Mappin, glancing at his own timepiece. Jermyn made the correction.

"Say twenty-five minutes to reach Hoboken by tunnel," Mr. Mappin went on, "and ten or twelve minutes for me to look over Nick Peters' premises—to delay longer would not only be dangerous, but awkward to explain. Jermyn, at ten-ten precisely I want you to call up Police Headquarters in Hoboken and inform them that a man known as Nick Peters has been murdered at . . . Write down the address for him, Finlay."

Jermyn accepted this startling order with a matter-of-fact nod.

"Should we be delayed anywhere en route I'll call you up," Mr. Mappin went on. "The police will naturally ask who is speaking, and you are to say that it is Amos Lee Mappin speaking from a pay station, and that they will find me on the premises when they come. That will obviate the necessity of answering any further questions over the phone."

Mr. Mappin made Jermyn repeat this after him. He and Fin then descended in the elevator. During the drive he continued to discuss the case from various angles.

"There must be no camouflage or deception about this visit," he said. "We will drive directly to the door of Nick Peters' store. I assume we will find it locked. You will leave me waiting there while you try to get in through the cellar as you did before. In my opinion there is no danger of finding any of the gang inside the place now. You see, when you ran away from there they could not foretell what you would do. The chances were strongly in favor of your bringing the police back with you, and they could not afford to be caught inside.

"The attack on Nick Peters yesterday was not made at random," he went on. "My guess is that his enemies hired rooms in the neighborhood, probably immediately across the street, where they could watch their man at all hours. If, as I suppose, they were interrupted by your entrance this morning, and if they have not dared return to Nick Peters' room, I hope we may find some valuable bits of evidence lying about."

The arrival of a taxicab in that humble street created a stir of interest, and the elegant figure of Mr. Mappin was regarded as somewhat of a phenomenon by the younger inhabitants. They gathered around, taking him in open-mouthed from the expensive Panama to the smart black brogues. As expected, the two friends found the door of Nick's store locked and the blinds pulled down inside the door and the window.

A lad volunteered: "Nick Peters he opened up early this morning, but he closed up later. I ain't seen him go out, though."

"Did you see anybody go in?" asked Mr. Mappin.

"Not that I took notice of."

Fin descended into the cellar and climbed up to Nick's window by the drain-pipe in the airshaft, just as he had done earlier. This time when he threw his legs over the sill he took his gun in his hand as a precaution. However, all was quiet inside. Everything looked exactly as it had when he left the room two hours before; the still body on the bed that gave Fin's breast a fresh wrench of grief; the door into the hall locked, and the key in the lock. He closed the window and fastened it to guard against an attack from the rear. There were no possible hiding-places in the two bare rooms except under the bed, and Fin made sure of that.

Crossing the store, he admitted Mr. Mappin by the street door and locked it after him to keep out the populace, whose curiosity was rapidly rising to fever heat.

"I'm just as glad to see a crowd gathering," said Mr. Mappin, dryly. "It helps to insure our safety."

"Well, the police will be here in ten minutes or so, anyway," said Fin.

"A lot can happen in ten minutes," remarked Mr. Mappin.

At first glance the store looked just as it had when Fin brought the supper in on the night before. But one little indication after another began to appear. Mr. Mappin made Fin sit down in the customers' chair against the wall so as not to disturb anything. His eye was as bright and quick-darting as a terrier's. He was getting such an obvious satisfaction out of the exercise of his faculties that he felt impelled to apologize to Fin.

"I do not forget that it is your friend who lies dead in the next room," he said, soberly, "but this—this is what I have wished for all my life, a chance to demonstrate my theories."

"That's all right," said Fin. "It's lucky you're here."

The watchmaker's glass was found lying on the floor outside the workbench, which had also served Nick for a counter. Nearer the bench lay Nick's fountain pen, which had been stepped on and partly flattened. Mr. Mappin examined it regretfully.

"I suppose it would not be honest to carry off any of the evidence," he said. "But I could use this! I could use this!"

Suddenly he perceived that Fin was carrying a pen of the same pattern. "I'll replace it later," he said, taking it. He put it on the floor and made Fin step on it. He compared the two damaged pens, and replacing Nick's pen on the spot where he had found it, put Fin's in his pocket.

On the bench or counter lay a little pad that Nick had used in issuing receipts. On it he had started to write: "Received from bearer, one gold watch, Bauer make number 62,3 . . ." The writing ended with a splutter of ink. Beside the pad lay the watch referred to. The back of the case had been removed, and there was the maker's name and number—Bauer, 62322.

Mr. Mappin made a note of it. "A Swiss watch of mediocre quality," he remarked. "It has been carried for at least twenty years. It would be difficult to trace the sale now."

In the doorway leading to the bedroom he found one of the list slippers that Nick Peters had been accustomed to wearing. Its fellow lay a few feet farther along, and the black skull-cap had rolled off the bed. The bed showed indications that a struggle had taken place there, but how much of the disturbance was due to Fin's efforts to resuscitate his friend it was impossible now to tell.

"I wish I could have seen him before you straightened him out," Mr. Mappin said, regretfully, "but of course you did the right thing."

On the bed he found the cord with which Nick Peters had been strangled. "I suppose I must leave this to the police, too," he said, with a sigh.

In addition to the mark left by the cord, Mr. Mappin found other signs on the body; a contusion on the back of the head, a slight abrasion on the forehead, marks of ink about the nose. He then hastily examined the floors of both rooms with a magnifying glass.

"Nick Peters, like most male housekeepers, was not very particular about sweeping," he said. "But the most I can tell is that there were two men concerned in the crime. The actual murderer, who was no doubt known to Nick, sent in an accomplice ahead who was a stranger to the watchmaker. This man offered Nick the watch to repair, and, as he was making out the receipt, struck him over, the head with a blackjack, and Nick fell with his face on the bench unconscious.

"I take it the first man left the store, because I cannot find his tracks in the rear room. The actual murderer then entered. It was he who picked up Nick under the arms, dragged him into the bedroom, flung him on the bed and strangled him. The method of strangling is reminiscent of the Thuggee cult among the Hindus. It is also common in Spain. On the bed a measure of consciousness returned to Nick, and he put up a vain struggle. The murderer must have been interrupted in the very act by your approach, because, as you see, everything was left where it fell."

"That's good work," said Fin, gloomily, "but it brings us no nearer to the actual murderer!" (If only I had been a minute sooner! he was thinking.)

"Well, one must make a beginning," said Mr. Mappin, mildly.

He subjected the dead man's clothes to a further and most painstaking search. In the end an exclamation of triumph escaped him as he held up a tiny triangular fragment of glass he had recovered from inside Nick's vest.

"If we have luck," he cried, "we will hang our, man with this! . . . I must keep this," he added, with a deprecating smile. "It's such a little piece!"

Among the dead man's meager effects there was not a scrap of writing, not a keepsake, no personal belongings of any sort that might give a clue to his past life. Nick had evidently made a practice of destroying everything of the kind.

While Mr. Mappin was still searching there was a knock at the door of the store, and an official-sounding voice was heard demanding admission. Peeping around the blind, Fin saw a uniformed policeman with two men in plain clothes, and made haste to admit them. He again locked the door to keep out the crowd.

The two plain-clothes men flashed their badges with the familiar gesture, and the principal one introduced himself as Detective-Sergeant Ellis, his companions as Detective Dahl and Patrolman Engel. All three were businesslike and very neatly dressed. But all had the hard and covert expression customarily affected by policemen, and the candid Fin disliked them at sight. However, one has to take policemen as one finds them, he reflected. It never occurred to him they might be other than they seemed.

Ellis was a well-built man of forty-five or so with a slight cast in one of his black eyes. Dahl was about the same age, a characterless, self-colored type, evidently accustomed to playing the part of number two. Engel, the patrolman, was a stalwart, stupid-looking lad who kept his blue eyes fixed on Ellis as if he received all his impulses from that quarter.

Mr. Mappin introduced himself and Fin. The Detective-Sergeant's bearing was respectful. He appeared to be familiar with Mr. Mappin's reputation as a writer. Leading the way into the back room, the latter began his story.

"This poor fellow's name is Nick Peters. He is, as you see, a repairer of watches and jewelry in a small way. He was an acquaintance of Mr. Corveth's—that is to say, Mr. Corveth used to drop in on him occasionally for the sake of his talk, which was intelligent and interesting. He appeared to be entirely alone in the world. Yesterday afternoon Mr. Corveth found him lying on the floor in a stupor. He had been beaten and the place partly wrecked, but apparently nothing had been stolen. Peters forbade Mr. Corveth to notify the police, but gave no explanation of what was behind the attack . . ."

During this recital Mr. Mappin and Ellis were standing side by side, looking down on the bed; Fin was a little behind them, with Dahl and Engel on his right. Fin was struck by a peculiar flicker in Ellis's eyes when they turned on Mr. Mappin. The detective-sergeant appeared not to be listening to the story at all, but to be pursuing a line of thought of his own. He seemed to be laboring under an inner excitement. His expression made Fin vaguely uneasy. Before he could act, Ellis interrupted Mr. Mappin with a coarse sneer.

"A likely story!"

Mr. Mappin's eyebrows ran up into two little peaks of astonishment. He stared.

Ellis threw off the decorous mask. He laughed brutally. "It's clear you croaked the guy yourself," he said. "Or this other fellow did. Or the both of you!"

No insult offered to himself could have affected Fin like this. To hear his friend abused brought a red blur in front of his eyes. Still he did not perceive the truth. He had known policemen to act in this manner. "That's a lie!" he cried, loudly. "A damned silly lie! Everybody knows who Mr. Mappin is!"

The patrolman whipped out his club. "Shut your mouth," he cried, "or I'll bean you!"

"Don't you touch me," shouted Fin, "or I'll . . ."

Mr. Mappin laid a restraining hand on his arm. The little man had recovered his self-possession. "Don't aggravate the officers, Finlay," he said, with a marked dryness of tone. "They are only doing their duty."

Like a flash Fin perceived the truth. These were not officers at all. The shock of the discovery paralyzed him for a moment. He could not command his features like Mr. Mappin. "Wh—what! Wh—what!" he stammered.

"Let us discuss this matter quietly," said Mr. Mappin, smoothly.

His coolness did not please the brutal Ellis at all, who wanted to provoke a noisy row in order to save his own face. "Take them along! Take them along!" he shouted.

When he laid rough hands on the unresisting Mappin, Fin saw red again. His hand flew to his hip pocket. Instantly the other two men leaped on him and bore him to the floor. After a hard struggle Fin's gun was taken from him. It was a weird scene there, with the dead man lying on the bed. Mr. Mappin stood perfectly quiet. Whenever he could make himself heard above the racket he kept adjuring Fin not to resist. His words finally reached the young man, and he stopped struggling. He was allowed to get to his feet. Still trembling with anger, he looked to Mr. Mappin for further orders.

"Stick up your hands!" commanded Ellis. "Search him, you two," he said to the others.

Fin obeyed, and they patted his body all over. Ellis did the same to Mr. Mappin.

"He hasn't got it on him," growled Dahl.

"Same here," said Ellis. "Well, you couldn't expect it. . . . We'll make 'em tell where it is," he added, with an ugly grin. "Take them out!"

"Just a moment," said Mr. Mappin, calmly. "Let us discuss this matter." Fin understood that he was simply playing for time.

"Aah, shut up!" shouted Ellis, with the utmost ferocity. "Run them out into the car, boys! If you try to put up a fight, you, we'll beat you to a pulp!"

They were hustled through the store and out on the sidewalk. There were a couple of hundred gaping people gathered there by this time, and Fin marveled at the boldness of the plot. Did they think they could get away with this in the open street in broad day? However, it soon turned out that it was not so bold a scheme as it looked.

There was a closed car, with engine running, waiting at the curb. Mr. Mappin suddenly addressed the crowd in a loud, clear voice:

"These men are not police! That is not a police car, as you can see. They are trying to carry us off! Will you stand for it?"

But the police uniform and the spurious badges overawed the crowd. When Ellis and Dahl drew guns and Engel brandished his club, the onlookers cringed. To a man they sided with the supposed police and began to jeer at their victims.

"Say, that's a new one, all right! . . . You're all wet, Sir Harry. . . . Ain't he the cute little fellow! . . . A ride will do him good. . . !"

It was Fin's first experience of the inhumanity of a mob, and it bewildered him. He was accustomed to having people like him. Meanwhile they were being hustled toward the curb. A feeling of despair seized on him.

"If they get us into the car we're lost!" he cried.

"Then resist! Resist with all your might!" cried Mr. Mappin.

He suddenly lashed out with his fists like a little bantam-weight. Ellis, cursing, aimed a furious blow at his head with the butt of his revolver. Fin, wrenching himself free of the man who held him, flung himself between the two, and caught the blow on his upraised arm. But at the same moment Engel brought his club down with smashing force on Fin's skull from behind, and all turned foggy before the young man. He did not quite lose consciousness, for he heard a clanging bell up the street, and he heard Mr. Mappin's voice clear and controlled to the end:

"Here come the police—the real police! Now you'll see who's right!"

Ellis *et al* dropped their victims as if they had been red hot, and sprang for the car. The car leaped into motion, and knocking aside the onlookers who were in its path, turned the corner of Hudson Street on two wheels and disappeared.

CHAPTER SIX

THE NICK PETERS CASE provided a twice-nine-days' wonder to Hoboken and the five boroughs of greater New York, not to speak of the rest of the country. The murder itself was an insignificant one and might never have got into the newspapers; but the attempted kidnapping of a prominent citizen like Amos Lee Mappin by men masquerading as the police—this was new, and it immediately raised the case to the dignity of a first-class sensation.

Day after day it held the left-hand corner of the front page, and kept the tabloid photographers busy; and during this time there was always a little crowd standing outside Nick Peters' closed store, staring at the curtained windows with blank eyes and open mouths. Fin Corveth wondered what such people did with themselves when there was no murder going, and how they ate if they never worked.

What with hourly newspapers, radio, and news reels, Mr. Mappin and Fin found themselves famous before dinner-time. Thereafter they were followed whenever they ventured out. If they got a quiet moment on the streets, somebody would recognize their oft-photographed faces and the cry would go up:

"There they go!"

"Who? . . . Who?"

"Amos and Finlay!"

"Gee! Lemme get a good look at them!"

"Don't mind us," Mr. Mappin would say, dryly; but the sarcasm was always wasted.

Mr. Mappin bore this state of affairs with dignified unconcern, but Fin found it rather exciting to be blocked by a squatting photographer whichever way he turned. There were solid advantages, too. It was wonderful the way his stuff sold during these days, and the prices he got for it. He even received an offer from the movies, but as it came from a concern of doubtful solvency, he disregarded it. Mr. Mappin dryly advised him not to plan his budget on the basis of his increased income.

In the newspapers Mr. Mappin and Fin appeared alternately as the heroes and the villains of the piece. They were subjected to endless and repeated inquisitions from the police, through all of which they emerged with flying colors, because they stuck exclusively and exactly to the truth—so far as they divulged it. What they did not wish to have known they held their tongues about, and as the police had no other line on what lay behind it all, they were never able to bring it out. The clues of the watch, the broken fountain pen, and the stranger's card led nowhere.

The absence of the brass ball from the foot of Nick Peters' bed was never noticed, because souvenir-hunters promptly stole the other three. The two friends had one moment of serious anxiety when the three small boys of Bloomfield Street and the junk-dealer came forward with their story of the young man who was searching for a brass ball. When Fin was confronted with them, they instantly identified him. Fin did not deny their story, but only laughed at it heartily. "Ridiculous!" he said. Luckily, there were a hundred wild stories, rumors, and hoaxes in circulation at the same time. This story seemed to lead to nothing, and after providing a day's sensation it was forgotten.

In addition to the curiosity-seekers who followed them about, Mr. Mappin and Fin found themselves under keen surveillance at all times. It was impossible to tell whether the spies were in the employ of the police or of "the American" or of "Robespierre"— probably they were of several sorts. At any rate, the two friends went quietly about other business, disregarding them. At this time they took no overt steps of their own to solve the mystery.

"Let the excitement die down," said Mr. Mappin. "We can do nothing while the search lights are playing on us."

The police never stumbled on the track of "the American" or of "Robespierre." They did bring out that a dark man with a cast in one eye (this no doubt was the kidnapper who had called himself Ellis) had hired a front room across the street from Nick Peters' store, presumably for the purpose of watching the intended victim. He had had a number of male visitors, but descriptions furnished by the neighbors failed to tally with either of the striking personages in the case. Clearly Ellis and his helpers were only three more tools in the pay of the real criminals, but which side had hired them it was impossible to say.

During this time Fin looked up Tony Casino. "Well, Tony," he said, "so the old Slovak got bumped off, after all."

"Yeah," said Tony, warily. "I wasn't in on that."

"I know you wasn't," said Fin. "Musta been that guy that hired you to search his place. What like guy was he, Tony?"

"Nottin' doin'," said Tony.

"Aw, come across," said Fin, cajolingly. "You can see by the papers that I'm not in with the police. They got to take their chance with this case. Me, I just want to work it out for the story in it. I protected you, ain't I?"

Tony finally yielded to persuasion. "He was a tall, skinny guy," he said. "Looked like a crazy preacher. Another Slovak."

This piece of information only plunged Fin into a deeper perplexity. If it was "Robespierre" who had hired Tony, how, had the general learned about the brass ball so quickly? That question remained unanswered.

While condemned to a state of inaction, Mr. Mappin was deeply concerned about the situation of the girl in boarding-school who had lost her only friend when Nick Peters was killed. His chief fear was that the mistress of the school might break into print with some story that would reveal the girl's whereabouts to the murderers. Each morning he sighed with relief when he failed to find any item in the newspapers originating in Pompton Lakes. While they were so closely watched, he hesitated to make any move in the girl's direction.

As the days passed and the mystery remained as much of a mystery as ever, the police felt obliged to find a scapegoat to save their faces. Police are much the same the world over—excellent fellows in the main, but frequently forced into a false position by the unpopularity of their trade. In this particular case Mr. Mappin frankly admitted to Fin that they were getting a raw deal. They probably suspected that the author was holding something out on them, but they were no match for him. Was not his brother an Assistant Secretary of State?

The usual clumsy propaganda directed against Mappin and Corveth began to appear in the press. It whipped up interest in the case, and of course the reporters ate it up; that was their business. It was possible by inference to build up quite a strong seeming case against the pair. Even supposing their story to be true, there was a good deal that called for explanation. Why had Corveth, upon discovering the body, run to Mappin instead of to the police? And why had Mappin himself insisted on visiting the scene of the murder before the police were notified? It was simply unbelievable that Nick Peters, having had his place broken into and himself nearly killed the day before, should have forbidden Corveth to notify the police. And so on. And so on.

The attempted kidnapping offered a stumbling-block to this indictment. The police had been excessively annoyed by this incident and would have liked to deny that it ever happened. Unfortunately, there were about two hundred eye-witnesses. It was now suggested that Mappin himself had artfully staged the pretended kidnapping in order to divert attention from his real activities.

The dear credulous public, so easy to lead in any direction, swallowed it whole, and feeling began to run high against Mappin and Corveth. Some of the newspapers asked editorially why they were not arrested. One night when they appeared together at the theater they were hissed. Fin was wildly indignant, but Mr. Mappin merely smiled in a disillusioned manner.

"Put not your trust in democracies," he said.

As a matter of fact, the incident provided him with the opportunity he had been waiting for. He sat himself down that very night and wrote a study of the Nick Peters case in his most brilliant manner.

It was not precisely untruthful, yet it was far from candid. Call it a superb piece of special pleading. Mr. Mappin led his readers just the way he wished them to go. He seemed to prove that the murder was the result of a feud among foreign communists. As such it scarcely concerned good Americans. It was his judicious use of the term Bolshevist that did the trick. Nothing can stand against that. Let the Bolshevists do each other in, he seemed to say.

Of course there was nobody clever enough to cross lances with the brilliant author of *Murder in High Places*, *The Finer Points of Murder*, *The Psychology of Homicide*, etc. in his own chosen field, and Mr. Mappin's view prevailed. As soon as the article appeared in the *New York World* the factitious case against Mappin and Corveth collapsed; moreover, Nick Peters disappeared altogether from the public prints and was never heard of again. Mr. Mappin, who had his private sources of information, learned that the police dropped the whole thing with a sigh of relief the same day.

"Now," he said to Fin, "it is time for us to get busy."

"Well, you do the headwork and I'll be the legs of the combination," said Fin. "I suppose the first thing we have to do is to find 'the American,' and 'Robespierre' again."

"I don't expect we'll have to look very hard," returned Mr. Mappin, dryly. "Unless I miss my guess, they will shortly reappear in our lives. . . . You see, we have the secret."

CHAPTER SEVEN

MR. MAPPIN WAS NOT AT A LOSS for an expedient to throw their spies off the track when the proper time came. He sent Fin with a letter to his attorneys, whose offices were in the Equitable Building. This prominent and prosperous firm occupied an extensive corner suite and, as Mr. Mappin knew, there was a rear entrance for the convenience of the partners in escaping from too-importunate clients. Fin, while his sleuthhounds waited in the main corridor, was shown out this way.

Having escaped from the building unseen, according to instructions he hired a "drive yourself" car, and proceeded through the Holland Tunnel and across the Hackensack meadows on his way to Pompton Lakes. It was a mellow September day with a sky like an inverted turquoise bowl; Fin's heart was lifted up by the sight of the open country and the prospect of adventure.

He found Miss Folsom's school at the end of a secluded side road. It enjoyed a fine site on high ground overlooking a pretty lake nestling among the Ramapo hills. The buildings consisted of a large wooden mansion built in the fancy style of 1897, surrounded by several cottages all painted buff, the whole group suggesting an Orpington hen with her chickens. A driveway lined with stiff maples, all exactly alike, wound up the hill. The place had the deserted air characteristic of schools during the long vacation, and Fin found himself pitying the girl who was obliged to remain there when all her companions had fled.

He inquired for Miss Folsom at the door of the silent house. The maid looked at him dubiously. "Have you an appointment?" she asked.

Fin was obliged to admit he had not.

"Is it important?"

"Oh, decidedly!" said Fin.

"I'll see," she said, leaving him.

Presently she returned to say that Miss Folsom would be down "in fifteen or twenty minutes." Fin marveled at the ways of head-mistresses. The president of the Steel Trust himself, he thought, would scarcely have the crust to send out such a message. He failed to take into account that it was the hour when ladies of a certain age retire for a siesta.

Finding the drawing-room stuffy, he was tempted out through the open door. Behind the house there was a flower-garden gay with zinnias, marigolds, phlox. Beyond it on the highest point of the hill stood a rustic summerhouse embowered in vines. Guessing that it commanded a fine prospect of lake and hill, he strolled in that direction.

He discovered that the summerhouse was tenanted by a tall girl of sixteen, all doubled up in an impossible graceful attitude over a book. She was at the stage of "letting her hair grow out," but she was one who could not look awkward at any stage. Her low-ered face was half hidden behind a screen of fair curls. She had not heard him approach. Guessing that this was the object of his trip to Pompton, Fin studied her with the keenest curiosity. His vanity was slightly disappointed, because sixteen seemed scarcely old enough for him, still he could not have imagined a more charm-ing picture. He decided not to speak of his errand until after he had talked with the headmistress.

"Hello!" he said.

She jerked her head up with a look of resentment. She was pret-tier than he had expected. She was more than pretty. She was at that miraculous moment when the child becomes a woman. She had intense blue eyes of the sort that are generally termed violet, and a complexion of such delicacy as to lend her a look of almost unearthly beauty. A very uncommon girl. The sight of that proud face, expressing such a capacity for pain, struck a sort of ache into Fin's breast that remained there.

"I suppose I should apologize for intruding," he said.

After a brief regard her look of surprised hauteur melted in an enchanting smile. "Oh, it's not my privacy in particular," she said. "You may come in."

He was accepted. There was something quite splendid in the way she brushed aside formalities. Like a great lady. Fin was glad then that she was only sixteen years old. He thought: She's too young for any girl-and-fellow nonsense. I can make friends with her as naturally as if she were a boy. He overlooked the fact that his heart was beating faster than normally. He sat down.

"Must be pretty rotten being left at school in the summer," he said, for an opening.

She considered this. "It is rather," she agreed, "but I'm accustomed to it. They don't bother me much in summer."

"Who don't?" asked Fin.

"Oh, you know—teachers and all that stuffy kind of people."

He laughed. "Sure! I know."

After that all trace of stiffness disappeared. As Mariula said afterward, it was one of those wonderful friendships that start with a bang. As for Fin, he decided she must have had a fairy godmother at her christening, who had exorcised self-consciousness. She appealed direct to the natural, spontaneous, effervescent side of the young man that generally had to be repressed in the business of getting on in the world.

"How do you pass the time?" he asked.

"Oh, in reading and dreaming," she said. "I suppose you think I'm very silly," she added, with a glance through her wonderful curved lashes.

"Not at all," said Fin. "I'm not one of these sensible people."

"I didn't think you were," she said. "There's a sort of a crazy spark in your eye."

They laughed comfortably.

"I used to dream I was a general moving armies around," said Fin. "I never mentioned it to anybody before."

"Nice of you to tell me first," she said, off-hand. "I dream mostly of people. Gracious, intelligent people. Sort of compensation. You don't find them in schools."

"Well, don't expect too much of the world when you get out," warned Fin. "All the stuffy people are not in school!"

"I suppose not," she said. "However, I can stand it if I can find one or two who act human."

"Oh, we can provide that," said Fin, grinning.

"I have to bottle myself up most of the time," said Mariula. "The only one I can really let myself go with is my guardian, and I don't see him very often. He is the only person there is belonging to me. That's why I have to stay here all summer."

This was said with a laugh, but it increased the ache in Fin's breast. She knew nothing of Nick Peters' death, and he must be the one to deal her that blow. He wondered at the relation between them. The shabby little watchmaker and the flower-like young lady! Like everything else about this case, it was inexplicable. Nick may have been one of nature's gentlemen, but he could never have given her that high-bred air.

"What are you reading?" he asked.

"I always carry two books," she said, smiling, "one to read and one to show. For some reason everything that's fit to read is forbidden to girls. Luckily, there's a bookcase full of men's books in the drawing-room, or I don't know what I'd do. Goodness knows how they ever got to this female place. Nobody reads them but me. When I take a book out I put another in its place so the gap won't show. I'm reading my way inch by inch along the shelves like a bookworm. At present I'm reading a book called *Fountains in the Sand*. Do you know it?"

Fin was obliged to confess that he did not.

"The fountains seem to have been rather dirty puddles," Mariula went on, "but I like books of travel better than any. Don't you? I would put up with anything if I could travel. Have you ever traveled?"

"Only in dreams," said Fin.

"Just like me," she said, with her enchanting smile.

"Yet you don't look exactly like an American girl," he ventured.

"I have never been out of America," she said. "But I suppose I am of foreign descent, because Nicky is. . . . Nicky is my guardian."

"Of what country?" asked Fin.

"I don't know," she said, blushing. This was evidently a sore subject, and so she made light of it. "Nicky never mentioned. I have no more background than Topsy. My family history begins with me."

"How romantic!" said Fin.

"Yes," she said, "if you are not tied down by awkward facts you can indulge in the wildest flights of fancy."

Fin's sympathy drew her out. She said with a laugh: "It's easy to talk to somebody right out of the blue."

"Can't you remember your father and mother?" he asked.

She shook her head, making the bright hair dance. "They died when I was a baby. Nicky and Lina adopted me, and gave me their name. For a long time I thought they were my father and mother— I couldn't have had kinder ones—but gradually I got to know they were not. We never talked about it."

"Then how did you know?" asked Fin.

"Oh, by a sort of instinct, I suppose. . . . From watching other mothers with their children. Lina was too respectful toward me. She never smacked or scolded me. I suppose she spoiled me very much."

"Lina was Nicky's wife, I take it."

"Yes, she died when I was seven. Up to that time I was as happy as a child could be. We lived in a little house in a place called Hollis. There were tall locust trees in the yard, with fragrant creamy blossoms in May. . . . Well, she died before I was old enough to understand what I was losing, and Nicky had to put me in a school. I have been in different schools ever since."

"Hard on you," murmured Fin.

"Oh, I'm used to it!" she said, philosophically. "What I don't like I make believe isn't there. I'm good at it. . . . Nicky apologizes to me for the schools because he says they are cheap schools, but such as they are I know he denies himself everything to keep me there. Nicky is poor. He comes to see me very seldom. I believe it's because he thinks he isn't grand enough, and that makes me savage. He has some ridiculous notion of making a lady of me." She laughed merrily, but the dark-lashed eyes were haunted. "What's the good of being a lonesome lady?"

"You're dead right," said Fin. There was a hard lump in his throat. By God! he vowed to himself, I will try to make up to you a little of what you have missed!

He realized that he wasn't making the task ahead of him any less difficult by putting it off. "Aren't you curious to know what I'm doing here?" he asked.

"Well, I didn't like to ask," she said, smiling. "I was afraid you might vanish into thin air."

"I'm a pretty solid phantom," said Fin. "One hundred seventy-five pounds."

"Your manly voice reassured me," said Mariula. "Phantoms have such squeaky voices."

"You seem to know!"

Before he could get any further the maid appeared in the doorway, announcing that Miss Folsom was waiting in the drawing-room. Her tone suggested that it was an unheard-of thing to keep such a personage waiting, and Fin had no choice but to get up.

Mariula, rising, offered her hand to Fin in the forthright manner of a great lady, and said: "Good-by, Mr. Unknown. It's been so nice to talk to you."

"We'll have other talks," said Fin, meaningly.

She smiled, almost pityingly one might have said: "Ah, you don't know them!" she said.

Fin left her quickly. There was a quality in her smile that almost brought the tears to his eyes. At the same time her courage and honesty made his whole heart glad. Nick Peters had not been wrong about her.

He found Miss Folsom in the overstuffed drawing-room, a tall, frigid lady, wearing an elaborately-dressed wig of chestnut hair. A smile of conventional sweetness was fixed in her face, for it was the season when she interviewed parents. But the smile faded at sight of Fin, who was obviously too young to have a daughter of boarding-school age.

"What can I do for you?" she asked, coldly.

"I have come to see you about Mariula Peters," said Fin.

"Ah!" said Miss Folsom, with a sharp look. "Her board is somewhat in arrears."

"It shall be paid tomorrow," said Fin. "I suppose you have read of her guardian's death?"

Miss Folsom, strangely enough, appeared not to have read of it, "Her guardian dead?" she echoed, with raised eyebrows. "How should I have read it? I don't study the obituary columns."

"Well," said Fin, staring in his turn, "it has not been confined to the obituary columns."

"I don't understand you," said Miss Folsom, stiffly. "Mr. Peters . . ." And then comprehension began to break upon her. Her face turned a queer mottled hue and her withered hands trembled. "Nicholas Peters. . . Nick Peters, Good Heavens! Do you mean to tell me that this was the Nick Peters who was murdered!"

"The same," said Fin.

Her reaction was not at all what he expected. "Oh, how I have been deceived!" she cried. "He was represented to me as a reputable business man! I addressed him in care of the Hanover National Bank!"

"What has that got to do with it?" said Fin.

Miss Folsom wrung her hands. "A tradesman in a poor mean neighborhood!" she cried. "Hoboken! *Hoboken!* An humble watch-repairer! Why, the child is less than a nobody!"

This sort of thing was new to Fin. "Is that all it means to you!" he said, hotly.

It is doubtful if she heard him. "Oh, what a blow! What a blow!" she cried.

Fin wondered if she were still thinking about her bill. "I assure you Mariula does not lack friends," he said, stiffly. "All bills will be paid . . ."

"Don't talk to me of bills," she interrupted, with an attempt to recover the dignity of the headmistress. "I am thinking of the reputation of my school!" She partly broke down again. "To be connected with a low, brutal murder like this! It's unfair! It's unfair! To think that this should happen to me! The girls will be coming back in a fortnight. It is sure to leak out! I shall be blamed . . ."

"Good Lord, madam!" cried Fin. "You didn't commit the murder!"

"How could I have let myself be so deceived!" she mourned.

"I reckon it was because you wanted his money," said Fin, grimly.

She paid no attention. "The child must leave here instantly," she cried. "You must take her away with you."

Fin had not foreseen this contingency. His heart sank. "Madam, what are you saying?" he protested.

"Instantly! Instantly!" she repeated.

"But I'm a bachelor," stammered Fin. "I have made no arrangements to have her cared for. . . ."

"That's nothing to me. You must take her away."

"Give me a day or two . . ."

"Not an hour! I do not intend to be left with her on my hands!"

Fin's face turned red and his resolution stiffened. "All right," he said, shortly, "I'll take her. You're not fit to be trusted with anybody's daughter!"

Miss Folsom was already pressing the bell.

When the servant appeared she said, "Where is Mariula Peters?"

"In the summerhouse, 'm."

"Send her here."

The maid went out.

A rush of compassion for the unfortunate girl overcame Fin's anger for the moment. "She does not know yet that Nick Peters is dead," he said, pleadingly. "Let me break it to her gently. Give me a few moments alone with her."

Miss Folsom merely smiled disagreeably.

So they waited, the elderly woman pacing up and down, struggling to conceal her ugly feelings under a cold sneer, and Fin staring at her with fiery eyes that expressed all he would not allow his tongue to utter to a woman. Though she affected to ignore it, she could not bear the young man's look, and she presently left the room.

She came back, accompanied by the wondering Mariula. The girl's face lighted up at the sight of Fin.

"Oh, have you got anything to do with me?" she cried, eagerly. "Are you a friend of Nicky's?"

Fin took her hand. "A friend of Nicky's and a friend of yours," he said. "I hope you will accept me as such."

"Why, of course I will!" she said, instantly. Then her sensitive nature was warned by a premonition of disaster. "What is wrong?" she faltered.

Fin retained her hand. "Bad news, Mariula," he said, simply. "Nick Peters is dead."

No sound escaped from the girl. She lowered her head and the curved lashes lay on her cheeks. Fin, watching, saw her breast rise and catch, again and again as she fought back the sobs. She clung desperately to his hand. I ought to have told her while we were alone together, he thought. That horrible woman makes it worse for her.

"You will go and pack your trunk while this gentleman waits for you, Mariula," said Miss Folsom, coldly. "You are leaving with him."

Mariula raised a white, dismayed face. Her eyes looked enormous. It was of Fin she was thinking, not of herself. "Is she forcing you to take me?" she demanded. "I have no claim on you."

"No! No!" said Fin, quickly. "I am your friend. I want to take care of you. I promised Nick that I would."

Mariula turned and ran from the room. When she returned, carrying her satchel, the tragic face was quite composed. In her little silken skirt and jacket and plain hat she had more than ever an air of distinguished breeding. Fin suspected that she had given tone to the whole school. It was little wonder that Miss Folsom had been deceived as to her social status. The young man's heart was freshly touched by the way she slipped her hand through his arm and looked in his face.

"I am ready," she said.

"You are sure you're not afraid to come with me?" whispered Fin.

"Afraid!" she said, with a level glance at Miss Folsom. "Leaving this place is like getting out of prison!"

"This is what I might have expected," remarked Miss Folsom, acidly.

"Come on," said Fin. "We have nothing to say to her!"

"I will have the trunk put in the back of your car," said Miss Folsom, "though, since the bill has not been paid, I should be justified in holding it."

"You will receive a check tomorrow," said Fin. He thought he saw a way of getting back at the lady. "Mariula has very powerful friends," he added.

The suggestion found its mark. "Who are they?" demanded Miss Folsom. "If they are willing to acknowledge her I might . . ."

Mariula squeezed Fin's arm. "Don't leave me here!" she whispered.

"Not for a million dollars!" said Fin.

It was Mariula herself who unconsciously administered the *coup de grâce* to the headmistress. "It's terrible to have to live with a person like that," she whispered to Fin.

Miss Folsom overheard, and turned slightly greenish. She could think of no retort; she only bit her lip. Fin and Mariula left the house without the formality of good-bys.

In the car the tragic girl, still putting a bold face on it, said with a smile: "Here I am going away with you, and I don't even know your name!"

"Finlay Corveth, commonly known as Fin or Fish."

"Where are we going, Fin?"

"Blest if I know, my dear. We'll call up Mr. Mappin from the first pay station for instructions."

Tears gathered in Mariula's eyes and rolled one by one down her pale cheeks. She struggled hard to master them, essaying to smile and to match Fin's jesting tone. "It's like an elopement, isn't it Fin? . . . Only, there's nobody after us!" . . . The big tears continued to gather and to fall in silence.

Fin's breast was wrenched by the sight. "Cry! Cry!" he besought her, "Don't try to hold it back. Cry out loud!"

"If only I could be sure that you wanted me!" she whispered.

Such a rush of emotion overmastered the young man that he was forced to pull up at the side of the road. "Listen, kid," he said, huskily. "The moment I laid eyes on you I fell in love with you. See? With all my heart! . . . I never had a sister. I love you the way a fellow ought to love his sister, but rarely does. For ever and ever. Get that? for ever and ever!"

With a little cry of relief Mariula hid her face on his shoulder and wept unrestrainedly. "Oh, now I can cry!" she murmured. . . . "Oh, my darling Nicky! If I could only have seen him before he went away!"

The tears gathered in Fin's eyes, too. He scowled fiercely as a young man does, and blew, his nose into his handkerchief with one hand while he patted Mariula's shoulder with the other. "Fire away! Fire away!" he said. "Let it all come out! You'll feel better for it!"

Half an hour later they drew up in front of a drugstore. Mariula remained sitting in the car while Fin went in to telephone. When Mr. Mappin heard his story he whistled in astonishment or dismay, and no suggestion was immediately forthcoming.

"I suppose I cannot bring her to your place," said Fin.

"There's a man watching in the street," said Mr. Mappin.

"What if I hired a motor-boat," suggested Fin, "and brought her to the yacht-landing in the basement. I could get her into the house that way without being seen from the street."

"No good," said Mr. Mappin, gloomily. "I have been aware for several days that the doorman in this house was spying on me."

"Good God!" exclaimed Fin. "Why do you stand for it? Why don't you have him fired?"

"That wouldn't do me any good," returned Mr. Mappin, calmly. "I feel safest when I know where the spies are."

"Then what am I to do?" said Fin.

"I will arrange something," said Mr. Mappin. "Call me up in half an hour."

Fin drove on across the meadows and through the tunnel, and called up from another pay station in lower Manhattan.

"Take Mariula to the Pennsylvania Hotel," said Mr. Mappin, "and meet my sister, Mrs. Gherardi, there. My sister cannot take Mariula into her house, because she has a dozen chattering servants and a hundred gossiping friends. But she will stay with her tonight, and tomorrow will find her another and a better school."

Fin's heart sunk. "But, Mr. Mappin," he protested, "how can we leave the poor girl among strangers when she is grieving so for the loss of her friend?"

A series of odd snorts came over the wire. "Hm! . . . Ha! . . . Ha! . . . Well!" Mr. Mappin always affected to be annoyed when his feelings were touched. "Well, anyway, let me sleep on it," he said, finally. "Perhaps I shall think of something better before morning."

About this time that band of the faithful who made a point of going over to Hoboken every week to see "After Dark," discovered that a new bit had been added to the show without announcement. In the barroom scene, and later in the Germania Garden scene, a ragged newsboy was introduced mutely offering a bundle of rumpled papers. He had not a line to speak, but the wistful beauty of the girl who played the bit made an instant hit. Nearly every night she got a round of applause all to herself.

None of the company were informed of the circumstances except Mr. Christopher Morley, the impresario, and a discreet lady named Angela Dare, who played the second lead in "After Dark." Mariula, rechristened Mary Dare for the time being, was brought forward as the latter's sister. She instantly became the darling of the company, but they could not spoil her, because self-consciousness had been omitted from her composition. After Miss Folsom's school her new life was like heaven, she confided in Fin.

Fin, too, found the arrangement an admirable one. As one of the press representatives of the show he enjoyed the freedom of the stage at all hours, and was able to see his young friend at every performance without exciting remark. On the occasion of their first meeting behind the scenes they pretended to make friends all over again. Mariula, like most of her sex, was a born conspirator.

CHAPTER EIGHT

THE FOUNDRY IS AN OLD BRICK BUILDING of a pleasing quaintness of design, faintly German in flavor. It stands on River Street, facing the Hoboken steamship piers and the broad stream beyond. At this time it had not been altered from its original state beyond what could be accomplished by sweeping and scrubbing. No mere scrubbing could really clean up a place in which the grime of decades of iron-founding was ingrained. As fast as one layer of dirt was removed, another slowly exuded. Walls and rafters were covered by innumerable coats of whitewash which flaked down like snow; and the windows bore a sulphurous patina that had so far refused to yield to soapsuds. Nevertheless, the members of the Three-Hours-for-Lunch Club loved their unconventional clubhouse. It was in keeping with the spirit of the organization.

Inside, the building spread out in a most unexpected and inveigling fashion. A great central hall with a gallery all around, and the mighty traveling crane still hanging overhead; and room after room of different sizes and shapes, and all on different levels. The members never tired of conducting visitors through the endless, empty rooms, running up and down the odd steps, and climbing the casual ladders while they pointed out the future library, the billiard-room, the private dining-room etc., etc. There was a purer pleasure in planning these improvements than in possessing them.

The affairs of the Three-Hours-for-Lunch Club and the Hoboken Theatrical Company were inextricably commingled, and the two organizations shared the Foundry between them. In the rear there was an odd little separate building like a tower, connected with the main structure by a sort of bridge. The upper part was allotted to the press department, and here Fin Corveth had his own particular hang-out, where he worked by snatches at all hours of the day and night.

The bridge had an inexhaustible fascination for him. It commanded, only a few yards away, the rear of a wide block of tenement houses with rank above rank of windows—kitchen windows. In warm weather all these windows were flung up, and particularly at dusk, when the lamps were first lighted, anybody crossing the bridge might share in vicarious intimacy with a hundred households. Within those windows people laughed and cursed and whistled and cried; they ate and fought and kissed and yawned and scratched themselves, all with inimitable naturalness.

All those households invisible to one another were within the view of one standing on the bridge, like God. Fin, a little abashed, would not linger on the bridge, for fear his motives might be misunderstood, but merely in passing across it he received a grand sense of the richness of life and of his kinship with all mankind.

It was the occasion of one of the club lunches. Somebody had presented the Foundry with a set of elaborately carved and lacquered Chinese Chippendale for the dining-room. This was arranged at the rear of the wide gallery upstairs, partly inclosed by handsome screens that matched the furniture; and in the little room thus formed a small company was gathered for the usual midday rites. They were drinking cocktails while they waited for a guest. A cold collation had been sent in from the Continental around the corner.

The contrast of the elegant furniture with its rude surroundings tickled the fancy of the members. They rejoiced in such humorous incongruities, and the Foundry was full of them. Over on the other side of the gallery the costume department of the Theatrical Company functioned amid a fascinating confusion of filmy garments and colorful accouterments. Downstairs the stage properties of the same concern made a quaint litter in every corner, including such diverse objects as the furnace from the last act of

"Where the Blue Begins," the hideous dragon that made too brief an appearance in the "Black Crook," and the famous locomotive from "After Dark," which had been brought over from the theater for a little touching-up after a run of two hundred nights.

Among those present, the principal figure was naturally that of Mr. Christopher Morley, who modestly describes himself as steward *in perpetuum* to the Three-Hours-for-Lunch Club, but is really the whole works. It is impossible to imagine a meeting without Chris. He is the mercury that causes many disparate elements to fuse. With his opulence of physique and temperament he seems to belong to a younger age than ours. His heartiness, his nimble play with words, his penchant for the theater, all stamp him as a belated Elizabethan.

He was flanked at the moment by Captain Felix Reisenberg and Captain David Bone. The Three-Hours-for-Lunch Club has always enjoyed a generous infusion of salt which goes far to explain its vigor. Besides the two doughty skippers there were present former Chief-Engineer William McFee, and Mr. Oliver Perry, the eminent yachtsman. For the rest poetry was represented by Bill (Endymion) Benét; architecture by Frank Abbott; belles-lettres by Amos Lee Mappin; and philosophy or whatever, you like by Don Marquis, the father of Archie and the Old Soak. There were one or two others less well known, and the company was completed by Fin Corveth, very attentive to the jests and ready with applause and laughter. Such, as he conceived it, was his function amid a gathering of wits.

The conversation had to do with crime. The club, naturally had taken a special interest in the case of Nick Peters, since two of the members had been so closely connected with it, and had even, at least by implication, been accused of the murder. This was the first meeting since the case had fizzled out, and Mr. Mappin had to submit to a good deal of joshing.

"Amos, you were always crying for a little murder of your own, and when we provided it you let it die on your hands! How come? How come?"

"It was unworthy of you to put it off on the Bolsheviki. That's Rotary Club stuff. We expected something more original from you."

"Sure! As criminologist in extraordinary to the Three-Hours-for-Lunch Club you have failed to measure up to your office."

All this made Fin uneasy. How they would open their eyes if they knew the truth! he thought. He longed to drop a hint that the case was far from being dead, but of course his lips were sealed. As for Mr. Mappin, he merely raised his glass to the light and squinted through it with a smile.

When they were tired of the subject, Chris said: "Where's your guest, Frank? I can't hold out much longer."

"We don't have to wait for him," said Abbott; "he's not the sort of fellow you have to stand on ceremony with."

"Well, we'll give him one cocktail more," said Chris, proceeding to fill the glasses.

"Who is your guest, Frank?" asked another.

"A real character," said Abbott; "one of a race that is disappearing from the earth. A soldier of fortune. His job is to produce two wars where only one grew before. But he says the bankers are taking the bread out of his mouth. War follows the coupon nowadays."

"What's his name?"

"General Diamond."

"Ha!" said Chris. "I wish I had thought of that first."

"Where did you pick him up, Frank?"

"He came into the office with a letter from somebody who had had a letter from somebody, and so on; one of these chain letters of introduction. He flattered me by asking if I had any little war that I wanted carried on. I had no war to give him, but we started a beautiful friendship. After several meetings it came out that one of the dreams of his life was to attend a session of the Three-Hours-for-Lunch Club, so I told him to come along."

A moment or two later the stairs creaked, and everybody said, "Here he comes!"

Looking down the gallery, they saw a massive figure rising into view at the end; a figure of truly heroic proportions—length, breadth and thickness. He approached at a lively gait, slapping his feet on the board floor. Fin caught Mr. Mappin's eye. His lips shaped the words, "It's 'the American.'" Mr. Mappin got it.

The man's appearance was much changed, but it was impossible for such a one to disguise himself completely. Fin, being young, was one great gulf of astonishment inside, but Mr. Mappin had fewer illusions; his face was as bland as a baby's. Fin was struck with awe at the speedy fulfillment of his friend's prophecy. What a man he was! Fin copied his bland air as best he could.

While General Diamond hastily swallowed a couple of cocktails and was introduced all round, Fin had a good opportunity to size him up. As befitted his present character, the General was now cultivating a rough-and-ready style—baggy tweed suit, thick-soled shoes, and immense fawn-colored wide-awake that he tossed aside with a flowing gesture. The spiked mustache and the monocle had disappeared; in his cheeks a hardy tan replaced the purple flush of high living; but the hard, protuberant blue eyes were unchanged. While he exchanged persiflage with his hosts his eyes traveled around, taking everything in. Fin stiffened inwardly. A dangerous man!

They seated themselves around the table, apparently at haphazard, but Fin observed that Mr. Mappin maneuvered for the seat at the General's left and got it. In his unobtrusive way Mr. Mappin was laying himself out to be agreeable. For a man who gave it out that he lacked physical courage, Mr. Mappin was doing pretty well, Fin thought. The elegant little man and the huge soldier of fortune made a curious contrast sitting side by side.

It was not at all difficult to draw out General Diamond. Like many clever schemers before him, he talked all the time to keep people from observing too much. There was a gobbling note in his bass voice which seems to be characteristic of the braggart. Munchausen probably talked that way. Fascinating place names larded his conversation: Essequibo; Orinoco; Amazonas.

"Yaas," he said, "I know the Amazon better than I do Broadway. Made four trips from Ecuador into Brazil by the headwaters, and back again. Once I was acting as scout for a Peruvian force which had been sent to clean up a nest of headhunters. I was really in command of the bunch, but technically I had to defer to some dusky don who got the honor while I drew the pay. We were camped on a sandbank in the Marañon near the mouth of the Huallaga, and just as it was growing dark I was walking about to stretch my legs after a long day in the canoe, when I came across a track or furrow in the sand that I give you my word was nearly a yard-wide. Anaconda. I confess it took even my well-seasoned breath away.

"I got my Winchester and a lantern, and I followed that track. None of the Peruvians would accompany me when they saw the size of it. I followed it until I came upon the monster sleeping in the sand about a hundred feet from the water. Gentlemen, he was piled in a mound of coils higher than my head. In his thickest part he was bigger round than I am in my thickest part. It was like an obscene nightmare. Holding the lantern above my head, I walked around and around him, looking for his head. Finally I found it. I fired point-blank and then ran to get between him and the river. He came at me, hissing like a locomotive. It was the most awful sight I ever hope to see. My heart turned to water, but I stood my ground, and the anaconda was more terrified than I was. He only wanted to escape. As I blocked his way he turned aside, and when I headed him off on that side he turned to the other. There we were dodging back and forth like a couple of boys playing prisoners' base. But I kept pumping lead into him whenever I saw a chance, and finally he collapsed and expired in the sand with frightful struggles. I had nearly blown his head to pieces. In the morning we straightened him out and I paced him off. . . . Fifty-six feet, gentlemen!"

A low whistle of astonishment went around the table. "Some snake!" they said, politely, and, "Some liar!" they thought.

"It was the biggest anaconda ever known!" said the General, impressively.

"My God!" said Mr. Mappin, agitatedly polishing his glasses. "I hope you saved the skin, General."

The General spread out his big hands deprecatingly. "I did my best," he said, "but what could you expect amid the hardships of a campaign in the jungle? I sent the skin out by a returning convoy, but it never arrived. It was a year later before I got out myself, and the bearers said my snakeskin had been eaten by ants. I expect the truth of it is, they chucked it in the river."

"What a loss to science!" murmured Mr. Mappin. "Go on, General, do!"

The General proceeded to tell how the headhunters had eventually wiped out the Peruvian detachment. He alone had been spared, and was adopted into the tribe, who looked on him as a sort of superman because of his size. However, as he was unable to bring himself to share in eating the Peruvians, a coolness arose and he was obliged to fly for his life. After unparalleled hardships he succeeded in reaching the nearest Brazilian settlements, six hundred miles away.

Other stories followed; of guerrilla warfare in the Gran Chaco and fighting along the disputed boundary between Guatemala and Honduras. Boundary disputes seemed to be the General's specialty. "You can get up a boundary dispute 'most anywhere," he said, with a grin.

Mr. Mappin listened to all this with an expression of innocent wonder that was highly flattering to the storyteller. The General had undoubtedly come to the Three-Hours-for-Lunch Club for the express purpose of scraping acquaintance with Mr. Mappin, and he was charmed by his success. He gobbled with self-satisfaction. Fin, watching from across the table, thought: Well, if he's playing a deep game, Mr. Mappin is playing a deeper one!

One of the General's best stories dealt with the chase and final capture of Rosati, a famous Macedonian brigand. He described how he had painstakingly collected evidence of the man's crimes in the face of a hostile countryside, and had eventually convicted Rosati, though he was the hero of the peasantry.

"Now that's what I call detective work," said Mr. Mappin, turning to his fellow-members. "You had better elect the General in my place."

"Hey! what's that?" asked the General, who did not understand the allusion.

"The club has passed a vote of censure on me because I fell down on the Nick Peters case," said Mr. Mappin, blandly. "They want an official detective who will add luster to the organization, and so I am recommending you for the post."

"No! No! No!" said the General, wagging his hand. "I am not in your class, Mr. Mappin. I have read your books, sir."

"But I am only a theorist, General, whereas you have had the advantage of experience in the field!"

The compliments flew back and forth. Finally Mr. Mappin said, casually, "By the way, what is your opinion of the Nick Peters case, General?"

Fin held his breath while he waited for the answer.

The General never turned a hair. "Oh, I know no more than any other newspaper-reader," he gobbled. "But with all due respect, Mr. Mappin, I think you were mistaken in ascribing the murder to foreign plotters. To me it bears all the marks of the native thug. It seems that Nick Peters did quite an extensive business in his small way. Well, it evidently occurred to some local bad man that being a Slovak, Nick would have his hoard concealed under the floor or somewhere, and he went after it, that's all. Not finding it the first time, he came back again, and in the rage of his disappointment he strangled the poor Hunk."

Fin glanced with inward horror at the General's powerful hands. Were those the hands?

"But how about the three men who attempted to carry off me and Corveth?" said Mr. Mappin.

"Oh, those were the murderer's friends," said the General. "They would only have taken you for a ride. There was evidently some evidence in there they didn't want you to stumble on."

"Very likely you are right," said Mr. Mappin, sadly. "I confess I was completely baffled. The newspaper article, of course, was simply to save my face."

"The case wasn't worthy of your talents," said the General.

"I'd like to talk it over with you further," said Mr. Mappin. "Will you lunch with me at my apartment tomorrow?"

Fin gasped at the little man's daring.

"I should be delighted!" said the General.

Leaving the Foundry in a body, they waited for taxicabs on the sidewalk below. The General, who was describing how he had raised the Riffs in rebellion in 1910, was still the center of attention. Suddenly he stumbled in his speech, and Fin saw him change color unpleasantly. He instantly recovered himself and went on with his story, but Fin, following the direction of his glance, was in time to see a lean, black-clad figure slink behind one of the stone posts that marked the gateway to the steamship piers across the street. So it appeared there was one man even the fire-eating soldier was afraid of. From the excessive blandness of Mr. Mappin's face Fin guessed that he had observed the incident. Fin's heart beat fast.

Mr. Mappin carried Fin over to New York in his taxi. "Gosh!" said Fin when they were alone. "For a timid man you have your nerve about you!"

"I am a timid man," said Mr. Mappin, plaintively. "I hate excitement! But I can't stop now."

"That old boy would murder us as easily as he'd turn over in bed!"

"Of course he would."

"Yet you ask him home!"

"He won't do it there," said Mr. Mappin. "Too difficult to make a getaway. Much safer to shoot us down in the street."

"Gosh!" said Fin again.

"It's because I'm afraid that I must seem to make friends with him," said Mr. Mappin. "I have to keep an eye on him. I hope you will see me through this, Finley."

"What the hell!" growled Fin. "This is my case, isn't it?"

Mr. Mappin patted his shoulder. "You had better come live in my house," he said, "so I won't seem to be sending for you every time I have the General there."

"I'll move up tonight," said Fin.

"The General is a practical man," Mr. Mappin went on, thoughtfully. "He will not try to put us out of the way until he thinks we are dangerous to him. Our job must be to satisfy him we are harmless."

"But he knew you were lying when you let on you had given up the case."

"Quite so. On the other hand, it would have aroused his suspicions if I had exposed too much of my hand. I'll feed him more tomorrow."

"You saw 'Robespierre' watching him—or us?"

"Yes," said Mr. Mappin. "I will now engage McArdle to watch our watchers. We will see what we can learn about these worthies. We must try to make friends with 'Robespierre,' too. He's a more dangerous man than the General. Much, much more dangerous."

"Why?" asked Fin.

"Well," said Mr. Mappin, "according to my observations, the General is working for money, but 'Robespierre,' like his great prototype, is working for an idea!"

CHAPTER NINE

IT WAS A FAR CRY FROM A FURNISHED ROOM south of Washington Square to the unobtrusive luxury of Mr. Mappin's apartment; however, luxury is never incongruous, and Fin accepted his translation with a sigh of content. This is what I was made for, he told himself; this suits me.

He had been bidden to lie late. When he awoke he had only to stretch his hand to the bell button, whereupon Jermyn entered with the morning papers and a cup of ambrosial coffee. Jermyn, who possessed his master's entire confidence, was Mr. Mappin's only servant.

He bade Fin a cheerful good morning. "Breakfast at nine-thirty, sir. Please ring again when you're ready, and I'll come draw your bath. Or perhaps you would prefer a shower?"

Fin had only to raise himself a little in order to look out over the river. "Jermyn," he said, with a serious air, "this is too good to be true!"

"I wish you could stay here always, sir," said Jermyn. "Mr. Mappin enjoys having you so."

"No, no, Jermyn!" said Fin. "It would soften my fibers!"

Jermyn laughed discreetly. "About the bath, sir . . . ?"

"I'll take the whole works," said Fin.

A couple of hours later Mr. Mappin and Fin were in the former's workshop with the much-creased square of white paper pinned to a drawing-board before them. So far it had refused to yield its secret. A square of about seven inches; a thin, hand-made paper very tough and resilient. Not made in America, Mr. Mappin had said. The only blemish on its white surface was a black dot near one corner. A magnifying glass revealed that it had been made with a lead pencil.

The two friends had approached that dot from every angle. Fin opined that, after all, it might have been made by accident, but Mr. Mappin would not have it so.

"The whole thing has been too carefully prepared to admit of any accident," he said. "That dot is our key if we only knew how to apply it."

Since the commonest sorts of sympathetic ink yield their secret to heat, they had first tried holding the paper over the flame of an alcohol lamp, but without results.

Mr. Mappin produced quaint bits of information from out-of-the-way corners of his richly-stored mind. "The oldest formula of all is to write with milk and let it dry," he said. "The writing may then be deciphered by dusting a colored powder over the paper. A certain amount of it will stick to the dried milk."

He had plenty of dry pigments at hand that he used in painting his little ships. They had tried dusting vermilion over the paper, but none of it stuck.

"Then it must be an acid which will only yield its secret to another acid," he said.

"Do you know the formula?" asked Fin, eagerly.

"My dear fellow!" said Mr. Mappin, ruefully. "There are a hundred formulas! . . . In the Indian Mutiny, when General Sales wished to advise his superior officer of his danger, he wrote a dispatch in rice water with the single word 'iodine' for a clue. When iodine was applied to the paper it turned the writing bright blue.

"That's only one," he went on; "the old books are full of recipes for making sympathetic ink. If you write with solution of Saturn, as they used to call it—we know it under its more matter-of-fact name of acetate of lead, and treat it with sulphuret of potassium, the writing turns brown. Or you can write invisibly with a solution of gold in hydrochloric acid and turn it purple with tin in the same acid. Or nitrate of bismuth which yields its secret to an infusion of nutgalls. Or iodine again. If you write with colorless iodine it will turn brown under a wash of chloride of lime. And so on, *ad lib.* Any chemist could think up a new one."

"Good God!" said Fin. "How would we know where to begin?"

"Ay," said Mr. Mappin, "that's the rub. If we applied the wrong acid it would be at the risk of destroying the message forever!"

"If there is a message," said Fin.

"There must be a message," said Mr. Mappin. "Nobody would go to all that trouble to hide a blank piece of paper."

"If we daren't experiment, we're licked before we start!" cried Fin.

"I wouldn't say that," said Mr. Mappin, cautiously. "I have an idea it is not acid writing at all, but some other device. Something that would account for the pencil dot."

"Well, what the devil are we going to do?" said Fin, helplessly.

Mr. Mappin, sunk in a deep study, did not answer immediately.

There was a tap at the door, and Jermyn's voice was heard saying: "Telephone from down stairs, sir. General Diamond is calling."

Mr. Mappin jerked his head up. "Ask him to come up," he said. He glanced sideways at Fin with a curious grin. "Let us see what we can extract from him," he said.

Fin gaped at him.

They locked everything in a drawer, and, furthermore, locked the door of the shop behind them. Mr. Mappin dropped the keys in his pocket.

"But what are you going to do?" demanded Fin, breathlessly. "What line are you going to take? Give me the dope so I can play up to you."

"I'm going to confide in the General," said Mir. Mappin, with his peculiar smile.

"Confide in him!" echoed Fin, in dismay. "Confide in an anaconda!"

Mr. Mappin chuckled noiselessly. "Oh, I shall only confide a few things that he knows already," he said, dryly.

A moment or two later General Diamond, clad in the same shaggy brown homespun suit, came striding into the big living-room, slapping his feet on the floor in his characteristic fashion. He was of the lusty type that can grow fat without sacrificing vigor.

He must have weighed near three hundred pounds, but every ounce of it was instinct with strength and energy. It was hard fat. A rhinoceros of a man, thought Fin, and with the same wicked look in his eye.

Notwithstanding the hearty camaraderie that issued from his lips, the General's eye was both wicked and watchful. He did not know what awaited him in Mr. Mappin's apartment, and he was ready for anything. He could not be sure yet whether or not they were on to him. Fin was forced to respect the man. It must have required courage of the first order to venture alone into his enemies' stronghold in such a state of uncertainty.

"How are you? How are you?" he cried, sailing in. "Certainly is good of you to have me here, Mr. Mappin. How are you, Corveth? Mighty glad to see you again."

"Corveth is stopping with me," said Mr. Mappin. "We are engaged in a very delicate operation, and I want him right at hand."

"That sounds interesting," said the General.

"I'll tell you about it later," said Mr. Mappin. "First I want to show you my view." He led the way out on the balcony.

The General raised his hands in a kind of benediction. "Superb! Superb!" he cried. "You may say all you like about the beauties of nature, but there's nothing so inspiring as a broad view of the works of man! Ships, bridges, docks, and towers!"

When he had exhausted his enthusiasm they came in for cocktails. "By God! Mr. Mappin, you've got a comfortable dugout here!" cried the General. "Luxury and good taste! It makes an old campaigner envious!"

"Anybody can buy comfort," said Mr. Mappin, deprecatingly, "but adventurous spirits are rare. We envy you your adventures, General."

"Well, in one way I have it on you," said the General. "I can appreciate your comforts better than you can because you've never been right down to hard pan. . . . Take this beautiful room, for instance, it recalls to my mind by force of contrast a certain moment during the winter of 1919 in Russia."

"Were you serving in Russia, General?"

"Yaas. I was a kind of liaison officer with one of the White armies. . . . We were licked and licked again. The Whites were always licked. It was an error of judgment on my part. Imagine winter in the heart of Russia. It was like the end of the world after the sun had gone out. An army of ten thousand men and almost as many refugees and camp-followers streaming blindly across the frozen plains. No proper clothes, no shelter, no food. On one occasion I stole the commander's potatoes at the point of my gun— However, that's another story.

"The whole army had to cross a deep river filled with running ice by a single narrow bridge. While we were still huddling our way across, the Red cavalry came up. They simply made a ring around that struggling mob and shot them down, laughing. Hundreds threw themselves into the river and were drowned. Dead bodies heaped the bridge from rail to rail. Of those who remained on the wrong side of the river only the strongest got across."

"Of whom you were one?" put in Mr. Mappin.

"Yes, sir, I don't hesitate to admit that I crossed that bridge on the necks of weaker men." The General tossed off his cocktail. "And none too soon," he went on. "While a third of his force was still on the wrong side, our commander blew up the bridge."

"Good God!" said Mr. Mappin.

"Well, he had to sacrifice a third of his men in order to draw off with the other two-thirds," said the General.

"What a ghastly experience!" said Mr. Mappin.

"It served me right," said the General. "I don't deserve any sympathy. A man of sense has no business to be fighting on the wrong side."

"Well, have another cocktail, General."

"Thanks. I get your point, sir."

"I expect you had many adventures during the Great War, General," said Mr. Mappin.

"Oh, yaas, yaas," said the General, carelessly.

"In France?"

"O God, no! Mr. Mappin. France offered no field for a man of my peculiar talents. . . . But around the edges of the great conflict, the doubtful areas, that was where profitable negotiations might be carried on—South Russia, China, Persia, North Africa."

"I get you," said Mr. Mappin.

In the dining-room to which they presently repaired General Diamond did full justice to the excellent meal that Jermyn put before them. It was better than the commander's potatoes, he averred. Even while he ate he managed to relate snatches of his adventures, ranging from Archangel to Tierra del Fuego. Fin's feelings toward the old scoundrel were curiously mixed. Quick-witted, humorous, and cynical, he put on such a good show it was impossible not to feel a sneaking fondness for him. But as soon as you began to like him that dull, wicked eye pulled you up short. Remember Nick Peters! it seemed to say.

Upon returning to the living-room the General was somewhat in advance, and Mr. Mappin whispered to Fin: "Sit with your back to the windows and watch his face. I must not appear to do so."

Down at the end of the big room stood a vast davenport upholstered in a gay chintz and facing the French windows that opened on the balcony. Mr. Mappin waved his guest to the place of honor in the corner, and the General spread himself among the down cushions with a groan of satisfaction.

"To hell with Russia!" he said.

Mr. Mappin sat beside him on the davenport and Jermyn placed a stand before them bearing coffee, liqueurs, and cigars. Fin, according To instructions, sat down facing them. He was very glad to have his own face out of the light during the grim comedy that followed.

"And now by your leave, General," said Mr. Mappin, lighting a cigar, "I'm going to relate our little adventure."

"I am all ears!" said the General.

"Corveth and I are working on the Nick Peters case."

"What!" said the General, with a well-simulated start. "I thought that had been given up."

"Not by me," said Mr. Mappin. "That newspaper article I wrote was simply to befog the real issue. I could do nothing as long as we were being watched and followed and questioned by the police."

"Ah, you're a deep one!" said the General, jocosely. But Fin was aware of a tenseness behind. The big man did not know what was coming next. He was ready to spring.

"As soon as I heard you talk yesterday," Mr. Mappin went on, "I made up my mind that you, with your experience, were the very man to help us . . . that is, if you are free?"

"Free as air," said the General, with a wave of his hand. . . . "Did my remarks on the case give you a lead?" he asked, innocently.

"No," returned Mr. Mappin, coolly. "You were 'way off!"

"What!"

"It was natural," Mr. Mappin explained, politely, "since you are unaware of the facts of the case. The true facts have not been published."

"You amaze me, sir!"

A grim comedy! While they sat with their liqueurs and cigars, conversing so urbanely, Fin could feel lightnings in the air. A single wrong word or look would transform the fat man into a wild beast. Fin regretted that he had not a pistol in his pocket; the General had, undoubtedly. But it had not occurred to him to arm himself against a luncheon guest. Fortunately, the General, sprawling among the cushions, was in an awkward posture for attack. I could jump on his stomach before he could draw, thought Fin.

"The man who first attacked Nick Peters," Mr. Mappin went on, "was after an emerald pendant. He tore up the place, looking for it. When Peters came to, the thief snatched a brass ball off the foot of the bed and cracked him over the head with it. The emerald was hidden in that ball. The thief carried it away without knowing that he had it!"

"Good God! What a story!" murmured the General.

"The brass ball passed from the hands of the first thief to a second thief," resumed Mr. Mappin; "and from the second thief to some boys who sold it to a junkman. Corveth recovered it by a clever piece of work."

"And you have it?"

"We have it safe."

"I suppose the emerald is worth a fortune."

"They were not after the emerald."

"What was it, then?"

"I don't know," said Mr. Mappin. "Nick Peters refused to tell Corveth what was behind it all unless he brought back the brass ball. If it was lost the whole thing had better be forgotten, he said. When Corveth brought him the brass ball he was dead."

"Well! Well! Well!" said the General.

Fin took note of the slight breathlessness in his voice. Under his suave air he was violently agitated. He might well be. He had his features under perfect control—except his eyes. Joy and suspicion contended there. He dared not let himself believe that Mr. Mappin was playing directly into his hands.

"We opened the brass ball," Mr. Mappin went on, "and the emerald, which was in the form of a locket. Inside it . . ."

"Well?" said the General, excitedly.

"There was a blank piece of paper."

"My God!"

Fin saw that this was trumped-up surprise.

He knew well enough that the paper was blank.

"It probably carries some sort of a message in invisible ink," said Mr. Mappin. "If I can find the right acid I'll bring it to light."

The General started up. "No! No! Mr. Mappin," he cried. "Don't put an acid to it! You'll destroy it!"

That's genuine, anyhow, thought Fin.

"Then what am I to do?" said Mr. Mappin, plaintively. "Will you help me?"

"Why, sure!" cried the General, with a crooked grin. "This is the most interesting case I ever . . ."

"I ought to warn you that it is dangerous," interrupted Mr. Mappin. "The men who want this emerald or this paper so desperately, know that we have it. Corveth and I find ourselves followed everywhere."

"So!" said the General. "Have you ever had a glimpse of the principal?"

"How can we tell?" said Mr. Mappin. "The faces of the spies change continually."

"He must be rich," remarked the General. . . . "Are you willing to show me the emerald and the paper you found in it?"

"Why, of course!" said Mr. Mappin. "If you're going to help us you must see the evidence. They're in my safe-deposit vault. I dare not keep them here. I'll have them here when you come again."

"Now, look ahere, Mr. Mappin," cried the General, with hearty confidence, "don't you go to tamper with that paper until we know where we are. We must have better information. As I see it, there are two lines for us to take. We must watch the men who are watching you, and get behind them and find out who is hiring them."

Fin smiled inwardly at the idea of intrusting this job to the General.

"Are you willing to stand for the expense?" asked the General.

"Surely! Any legitimate expense!" said Mr. Mappin.

"Good! Then the second thing to do is to investigate Nick Peters' antecedents. They called him a Slovak. That only means that he came from one of the countries in southeastern Europe. Well, I know those countries. I speak their dialects. There's a Bulgarian revolutionary committee right here in New York. Beside Czechoslovakian clubs and Jugo-Slavs. I know them all and they know me. You couldn't have come to a better man than me. I will mix among them, and it will be a funny thing if I can't find out who this Nick Peters was and what sort of a secret he was hiding."

"Splendid!" cried Mr. Mappin.

The dangerous comedy proceeded.

Soon the General heaved himself out of the davenport. "I'll start to work this very afternoon," he said. "I'll keep in touch with you. You just leave this to me for a while."

When the door closed behind him, Mr. Mappin sank back into the davenport and mopped his bald head. "My God! what an ordeal!" he murmured. "I am trembling like a leaf!"

Now that the danger was past, Fin himself was a little shaky, but he would not confess it. He poured Mr. Mappin a stiff drink of Scotch.

"Fin," said the latter, sipping it, "I vow if I come through this alive I'll stick to my books hereafter. I am not fitted by nature to perform in the General's field. The sheer bulk of the monster overwhelms me!"

"You hid it damned well," said Fin.

"Thank you, my boy, thank you. . . . Well, what have we gained by it? You were watching his face."

"In the first place," said Fin, "his fright when you suggested treating the paper with acid was perfectly genuine. He is as much afraid of having the message destroyed as we are."

"Good!" said Mr. Mappin. "Then we won't tamper with any acids. . . . What else?"

"He is not yet satisfied that this is not, well, just what it is, a deep-laid scheme to entrap him."

"We could hardly expect anything else," said Mr. Mappin. "The General is not exactly a greenhorn. . . . That means we must go on and better our performance. We must appear to take him further into our confidence. O my God! my stomach turns over at the prospect of facing him out again! However, there's no help for it. Give me another drink. . . . Will you see me through, Fin?"

"I can stand it if you can," said Fin.

CHAPTER TEN

EVERY DETAIL OF THAT LAST TALK with Mariula was etched on Fin's recollection as with an acid. It was heartbreaking to remember her sweetness when he had lost her. Her delicate beauty was rendered more piquant by the ragged clothes she wore in her stage part. Seated on a trunk backstage with her cheeks grimed, a boy's cap pulled over one eye and under her arm the ragged papers she never put down, fearing to mislay them, she made him laugh with the most delicious pleasure—and swallow hard. Her life of semi-conventual seclusion made her seem younger than she was. She was in no hurry to grow up.

In his anxiety to have it appear that their relation was merely a casual one, Fin had never visited her at the boarding-house where she lived with Miss Dare, nor did he ever accompany her to and from the theater. Their only meetings took place backstage. As far as Fin knew, there were no spies inside the theater, and he had hoped that their friendship was completely unknown to those who followed him about outside.

Nearly an hour elapsed between Mariula's first and second appearance in the play, and this was Fin's innings. She would wait for him sitting on this empty trunk behind the scenes. At intervals during the play the lid of the trunk was slammed down to imitate the closing of a door off-stage; that was why it was there. Fin would happen along as if by accident, and while the actors spoke their lines and the house laughed, clapped, hissed, and otherwise comported itself in the obstreperous fashion expected of an "After

Dark" audience, the two of them sitting side by side confided to each other in whispers all that had happened during the past twenty-four hours.

From the first Fin's guard had been down with Mariula. He persuaded himself she was only a child and there was no penalty attached to loving a child. Having reached the great age of twenty-five himself, he was a little ashamed of letting stuffy people see how completely he could play the kid with her; so he lowered his voice when there were others about, and they held in their foolish laughter until they nearly burst. Mariula's supposed childishness covered everything. It was blessed to love a child; he told himself there was nothing to be got out of it and no ritual to be observed. On both sides it was as free as the wind blowing. Fin never realized how deep it went until he was stabbed by her loss.

This particular performance was a midweek matinee and Mariula had not expected him. How enchantingly she lowered her lashes and smiled and made room for him on the trunk.

"I wouldn't let myself hope you were coming," she whispered, "but just the same I was listening for the squeak of the stage door. What do you think, Fishy darling? I can't keep it in! Mr. Morley has promised me a speaking part in the next show!"

"Lovely!" said Fin. He did not add that he thought the impresario knew a good thing when he saw it. Nothing like cynicism must be allowed to breathe upon the lucent Mariula.

"It's going to be a Civil War play," she went on, "and I'm to be a drummer boy. A real veteran is to teach me to drum."

"Like pretty Polly Oliver," murmured Fin.

"Who was she?"

He sang under his breath:

> "*I cannot live single, and false I'll not prove;*
> *So I'll list for a drummer boy and follow my love!*"

"Pooh!" said Mariula. "I don't think much of her! . . . I'll be a real drummer boy and drum for my side. A real boy. It's more fun to be a boy, anyway."

"Girls are nicer," said Fin,

"You may think so because you're a big softy. You can't see through them."

"Is that so?"

"I wish you'd promise me never to commit yourself with a girl without giving me a chance to look her over first."

Fin laughed delightedly. Mariula didn't mind.

"Of course it doesn't matter much when you're young," she went on. "It's much the same being a girl or a boy. But think of growing up to be a miss. That's what I dread."

"Misses have gone out of fashion," said Fin; "except with the Miss Folsoms and that lot."

"The old-fashioned kind has," said Mariula; "like Eliza in the play. That's why she's so funny and dear. But the modern ones are worse. It makes me tired the way they begin to wiggle when a man comes around."

"Only the second-raters," said Fin. "The first-raters don't wiggle. They make the men wiggle."

"I'll think that over," said Mariula. "Some of your funny sayings are quite sensible."

"Go on!" said Fin. "That's taffy."

"I only said some of them."

"Of course," said Fin, "I would much rather have you just as you are for ever and ever." "Why?" she asked, curiously.

"Because you like me now. We are a great comfort to each other ..."

Mariula gave his hand a little squeeze.

". . . But when you finish growing up you'll be somebody else again. You may not like me then."

"Well, if you think I'm that kind of a person," she said, affronted, "I'm not going to swear any oaths."

"It will be a sad day for me when you become a young lady," Fin went on. "I'll have to share your society with dozens of fellows then. And as a competitor I'm a washout. I have no advertising value, no ballyhoo. You will overlook me in the crowd."

"When you talk like that it's just a kind of false modesty," said Mariula, calmly. "I don't pay any attention to it."

How Fin wanted to hug her.

She soon climbed down from her high horse. "Listen, Finny Tribe," she said, giggling, "and I'll tell you something funny. There's a new boarder come to Mrs. Balcomb's and his name is Mr. Goldfogle. Isn't that priceless? If you say it rapidly to yourself the funniest combinations come out. Try it!"

Fin tried it, and Mariula tried it.

"Listen," she went on. "All the other boarders call him Mr. Old Fogie, of course. That was foreordained . . ."

"*What?*" said Fin.

"Foreordained," she faltered. "Isn't that right?"

"Absolutely," said Fin. "But it startled me from those infant lips."

"Oh, go on!" she said. "Pay attention to what I'm telling you. . . . I've got a better name for him. I call him the dear little Ogo-Pogo, after the song. And listen! Mr. Ogo-Pogo is bowlegged in one leg only. It's unique! Look! he walks like this." Mariula illustrated with two fingers on her knee, and they rocked in silent laughter.

When she got her cue and jumped down from the trunk, she said, offhand, "Coming over tonight, Fish?"

"Sure!" said Fin. "I've got a press story to get out." They maintained a fiction that it was business brought him to the theater.

"I'll see you then." She hesitated a moment. "I wish we lived in the same house," she said, with a sigh.

"Maybe we will," said Fin.

As she went around the corner of the set she looked back at him with her luminous smile. That was his last sight of her.

At half past seven Fin and Mr. Mappin were beginning dinner in the latter's apartment when Jermyn entered to say that Mr. Corveth was wanted on the telephone. Jermyn looked rather queer and Fin said:

"Who is it?"

"Didn't give any name, sir. A lady. Seems very agitated."

"O Lor! what have I been and done now!" said Fin, lightly.

It was Miss Angela Dare. So extreme was her distress she could scarcely articulate. "Oh, Mr. Corveth . . . Mary . . . gone!"

"What!" cried Fin.

"Gone! . . . gone!" she repeated.

"When? Where?" cried Fin, with a terrible sinking of the heart. "For God's sake tell me a plain story!"

Miss Dare succeeded in pulling herself together. "I had a rehearsal with Mr. Rich this afternoon. I took her home after the matinee and returned to the theater. She never goes out in the streets alone. While I was at the theater somebody telephoned to the house in my name and told Mary to meet me in Hudson Park. She went out and . . . and she never came back!"

"O my God!" groaned Fin. "I'll be right over!"

"What is it?" cried Mr. Mappin, running out into the hall.

Fin pressed his bursting head between his hands. "Those beasts!" he muttered. "Mariula . . . they've got her!" He snatched up his hat.

"Eat a bite as you go," urged the practical Mr. Mappin.

"It would choke me!" cried Fin, making for the door.

"I'll follow you in a few minutes," Mr. Mappin called after him.

In a taxicab Fin tore downtown and through the Tunnel, suffering agonies of impatience. As he ran into the theater a wild hope filled his breast. Perhaps she had come back! A glance in Miss Dare's face destroyed it. The poor woman was trying to make up before her mirror with the tears running down her cheeks. The entire company was distraught, but as good troupers they had to go on with the show.

Miss Dare could add but little to her story. A woman had called up the boarding-house at six o'clock and, representing that she was speaking for Miss Dare, had asked the servant to tell Mary to meet her in Hudson Park, so they could get a little fresh air before dinner.

"Has anything been done?" cried Fin.

"I went to the park to look for her," faltered Miss Dare.

"Why didn't you call me up before?"

"We were hoping every moment she would come back!"

Fin ran to the nearest police station. As soon as he had told his story the lieutenant at the desk said:

"Yes, we know about that."

"Where is she?" cried Fin.

"Oh, I can't tell you that, mister. All I know is that at six-fifteen this evening a boy came out of Hudson Park and reported to Patrolman Clausen that he had seen a young girl hustled into a black sedan car at the corner of Hudson and Fifth. The car went north in Hudson."

"What measures have been taken?"

"We can't do nothing without a complaint," said the lieutenant, blandly. "You can't place no reliance in what them kids tell you."

At this point ex-Senator Corwin, Mr. Mappin's attorney, arrived, and took full charge of the search for Mary Dare. By this means both Mr. Mappin's name and Fin's were kept out of it. Thus they avoided reviving the Nick Peters' case and dragging the whole thing through the press again. Miss Dare appeared as Mariula's sister and nearest relative, and Fin with his breaking heart was relegated into the background.

No means that could possibly aid in finding the girl was neglected. The police were aroused to action and an army of private detectives engaged. The police of other cities were notified. The news of the kidnapping was announced in the press and broadcasted by radio. Before midnight the net was spread over the entire country—but nothing fell into it.

The black sedan was said to have borne an Illinois license, and the police were in possession of the number. Two telephone conversations with Chicago proved that the plates were false ones. The kidnappers must have had other license plates in reserve, for no abandoned car was found. The only clue to their destination was furnished by a guard in the Holland Tunnel, who stated that at 6:30 that night he had been forced to warn a speeding black sedan bearing an Illinois license plate. As the car had slowed up at the sound of the whistle, he had not taken its number. This merely indicated that the child had been carried to New York, catch basin for so many crimes.

Fin spent the entire night walking the streets in a fog of pain and despair. He could never give any clear account of where he went. At one time he found himself at 168th Street, and some hours later he was stopped by the Battery sea wall. His only object was to read the license plates of all the cars that passed him. He was dimly aware of the uselessness of such a quest, but he had to be doing something. Occasionally he hired taxis to get him over the ground quicker, but he soon had to get out and walk again. It was impossible for him to sit still even in a speeding cab.

The last editions of the evening papers and the first editions of the morning papers, which quickly followed, alike informed him that there was no news.

At eight o'clock in the morning he staggered into Mr. Mappin's apartment, a haggard ghost of himself. Old Jermyn led him in with the tact and tenderness of a woman and sat him down without tormenting him with questions. Jermyn put food before him and he ate, and immediately fell asleep with his head on the table. Jermyn let him stay there.

When he awoke, a couple of hours later, Mr. Mappin was looking at him compassionately. "Is there any news?" asked Fin, hoarsely.

Mr. Mappin mournfully shook his head.

"There wouldn't be," muttered Fin, "They've got her! . . . And it's all my fault!" he cried, brokenly. "I must have led them to her! I should have stayed away from her!"

"Now come, old fellow!" said Mr. Mappin, patting his shoulder. "It's bad enough without tormenting yourself uselessly. . . . Our enemies may have known long ago that Mariula was at Miss Folsom's. Why couldn't they have followed Nick on one of his visits to the school?"

"If the General's hand is in this, the error of judgment was mine," Mr. Mappin went on, pacing up and down the dining-room. "If he knew of the existence of Mariula he knew we had taken her under our protection. I ought to have included the child in the story I told him. My not saying anything about her would make him suspicious of us. Half measures are always fatal!"

"Why should they carry her off just at this time?" groaned Fin.

"That I cannot tell," said Mr. Mappin, gravely. "But I am confident they will not harm the child."

"Why?" said Fin.

"Because the secret they are after is still locked in our safe."

Fin was too wretched to follow his reasoning. "They've got her! They've got her!" he groaned, beating the table with his fist. That fact obscured everything.

"It was providential that we decided to keep the child in ignorance," Mr. Mappin went on. "She knows nothing of the emerald or of the paper it contained. She has never heard of the General or the other. That may be the means of saving her life now."

Fin could take no comfort from his words.

"The General is coming here to lunch today," Mr. Mappin reminded him.

Fin scrambled to his feet, breathing hard. This appointment had been made for several days, but he had forgotten it. "Just let me get at him!" he said, hoarsely. "I don't care how big he is! . . . The foul brute! To strike at a child!"

"Easy! Easy!" warned Mr. Mappin. "We don't know that the General did it."

"He's capable of it!"

"Quite so. But that's no proof."

"I couldn't keep my hands off him if I were to see him," said Fin, brokenly.

"Sure, sure!" said Mr. Mappin, soothingly. "You keep out of the way and I'll receive him."

Fin almost quarreled with his patron then. "You mean you will pretend to be friends with that beast!" he cried.

"What I have started I will carry through," said Mr. Mappin, firmly. "It would be fatal to let him see that we suspect him of having a hand in this."

"What's the use?" cried Fin. "What's the use of anything, when Mariula is gone!"

"We will get her back again," said Mr. Mappin. "And we will win her inheritance for her, too."

"What will you say to him?" asked Fin.

"I will frankly let him see our distress. I'll tell him the whole story of the child. I'll ask his help in finding her."

"What a ghastly farce!" sneered Fin.

"Just the same, it's the best way of getting her back safe," said Mr. Mappin, firmly.

Fin was too done up to oppose him further. He dropped back in the chair and pressed his head between his hands. After a moment or two the thought of the danger to his friend penetrated his pain-befogged understanding. "You can't receive him here alone," he said, raising his head. "That would be too easy for him."

"Jermyn will be here," said Mr. Mappin.

"Jermyn and you together would be no match for the General. The chance would be too good for him to lay you both out and ransack the place at his leisure."

"That will not happen," said Mr. Mappin. "We will both be armed."

Fin resumed his weary, aimless plod, plod through the streets, glancing at the numbers on the automobiles and searching the faces of the passers-by. So many streets, so many cars, so many people, there was no end to them. Millions of windows, and behind one of them Mariula was confined. He had taken a horror of the town which spread to infinity before him whichever way he turned. How could one poor pair of legs cover it? Yet he could not stop walking. It was like a nightmare from which there was no awakening.

The frequent editions of the newspapers kept him informed as to the progress of the search elsewhere. No news!

He returned to Mr. Mappin's after dark in a state of exhaustion. His patron was out. Jermyn put food before him again, but he could not eat now.

"Was that beast here today?" he muttered. Jermyn nodded.

"What happened?"

"Nothing, sir. Mr. Mappin told him of the trouble you were in, and he appeared to be most sympathetic. As soon as they finished eating he hurried away to see what he could do."

"Laughing in his sleeve," muttered Fin; "laughing in his sleeve! He's making a monkey of Mr. Mappin!"

Just then the telephone rang. Fin sprang up, but halfway to the door he stopped.

"You answer it, Jermyn," he faltered. "I'm not up to it."

After a murmur in the hall a loud cry came from Jermyn. "Mr. Fin! Mr. Fin! Good news!"

Fin quickly found the strength to snatch the receiver out of his hand. "Yes? Yes?" he said, breathlessly.

It was Miss Dare. She was now as inarticulate with joy as she had been heretofore with grief. "Oh, Fin! Fin! . . . Mary! . . . She's back!"

"Where?" cried Fin.

"At the theater!"

"She's all right?"

"Oh, quite! quite! She's making up to go on."

"Who found her?"

"Nobody. She was brought back in a car just like she was taken away."

"Where was she taken?"

"Oh, I can't tell it all over the phone."

"Sure! Sure! I'll be right over."

"No! Mary says please don't come until after the show. She's afraid you'll break her up."

"Oh . . . all right," groaned Fin. "Damn the show! . . . You're sure she's quite all right, Angie?"

"Oh, quite! She says she was well treated. She's the calmest one among us over here."

"Oh! . . . Take care of her until I get there!"

"Don't you worry about that! The whole company is guarding her."

Fin hung up with a groan. Three hours to wait! However, he fell right there on a sofa in the hall and slept like a dead man. Jermyn covered him with a rug.

CHAPTER ELEVEN

MR. MAPPIN AND FIN rode over to Hoboken together. Fin was jumping with impatience. He had telephoned again, and Mariula was all right, but he could not rest until he saw her with his own eyes.

"How can we best take care of her from this time on?" he said. "There's no longer any reason for keeping her in hiding."

"I've been thinking about that," said Mr. Mappin, in his calm way—but he was perhaps not as calm as he made out. He polished his glasses frequently. "If as a result of this uproar Mariula's connection with Nick Peters becomes known to the public, there is no further reason for keeping her under cover. . . . But I'm hoping we may keep that secret. In that case she must continue to be known as Mary Dare, and should go on playing her part in 'After Dark.'"

"I shan't know a moment's peace," muttered Fin.

"Think it out," urged Mr. Mappin, soothingly. "Where could we find a safer place for her? It would be impossible to turn the same trick twice. In the Rialto Theater she has the whole company to watch over her. Moreover, I will get McArdle to supply me with one of his best men who will always be armed. Chris can give this man a walking part in the show, and he can board at Mrs. Balcomb's. Thus he can have Mariula under his eye at all times without making the child conscious that she is under guard."

"I wish I could have the job," said Fin.

"Sure!" said Mr. Mappin. "But you agree, don't you, that it would quadruple our difficulties to take Mariula into the house

102

with us. It would be a dangerous place for her. We have the secret there that is the main object of our enemies."

"You are right," muttered Fin. . . . "But I wish I could be with her!"

When they got to the theater the show was over. According to custom, the set had been struck and the curtain raised, and as they entered the empty house they saw a throng on the stage, all pressing around Mariula, perched on her trunk—actors, policemen, newspaper reporters, and such of the general public as had been able to get by the doorkeepers. All the women were trying to embrace Mariula, and all the men were asking her questions. Mr. Mappin and Fin made their way through the boxes. The first person they ran into on the stage was Chris Morley.

"There's been a riot ever since she came on the scene!" cried the warm-hearted impresario, laughing and wiping his eyes "God knows how we got through the show!"

Fin made no attempt to address Mariula. They exchanged a poignant glance, and he dropped into the background. What a lot she understands! he thought. He watched her wonderingly. She had removed her make-up and was dressed for the street. She was pale from strain, nevertheless she kept the too-affectionate women at arm's-length and answered the men's questions intelligently. Who is this strange lost girl? Fin asked himself for the hundredth time. Where did she get such poise? She has been nowhere and seen nothing.

He heard her tell her story. "This woman came up to me in the street and started talking. She was a nice-looking woman and I didn't want to be rude. So I let her talk. I didn't notice the automobile standing by the curb until she swept me into it quick as a wink and slammed the door."

"Didn't you scream?" asked a voice.

"I'm sorry," said Mariula, apologetically. "I ought to have screamed, but I couldn't. I always get quiet when I'm frightened. . . . I wasn't *very* frightened," she went on, "because the woman didn't seem to want to harm me. I thought she must be a little cracked. I thought perhaps she had lost a daughter and just snatched up the first girl she saw. You read of such things in the paper.

"She pulled down the blinds inside the car," Mariula went on, "so I couldn't see where we were going. But I heard the roar of the Tunnel as we passed through it. We went fast. The woman didn't say much, but her manner was kind enough. After a long drive, more than an hour I should say, we stopped. It was dark by that time and I could see very little. It was a house standing by itself among trees. There seemed to be nobody living in it but this woman and her servants. I planned to make friends with the servants as soon as she was out of the way. We had supper. She talked all the time."

"What did she say?" asked some one.

"Nothing in particular," said Mariula. "It was silly talk, the way a person talks to a young child. She was always trying to smooth me down. But I wouldn't have anything to do with her. To everything she said I just answered, 'You had no right to take me away from my friends.' But you couldn't pin her down to anything. Her talk wandered. She was certainly cracked. After supper she took me up to a bedroom and locked me in it. The windows were very high above the ground, and there was nothing to climb down by, so I thought I had better wait quietly until morning.

"All day today it was just the same. I never got a chance to speak to the servants alone. The woman was always coming to the room, trying to make friends in her crazy way, but I wouldn't. At last when it got dark she suddenly said, 'All right, I'll take you back.' And back we came. She put me out at Hudson and Fifth Streets, just where she had snatched me up, and the car whisked away like lightning."

Fin heard her repeat this several times with slight amplifications. She is not telling the whole story, he thought, anxiously.

Meanwhile Mr. Mappin had been consulting with Chris. The manager now made his voice heard above the babel. "Please, ladies and gentlemen, I must ask you to clear the stage. Mary has told you everything she knows. She must be allowed to go home and sleep."

The crowd, shepherded by Mr. Morley, moved very reluctantly toward the stage door.

Mr. Mappin joined Fin. "We are to go on ahead to Mrs. Balcomb's," he said. "Chris will bring her."

They waited for Mariula in her own room. Even the faithful Angela Dare was excluded from this interview, for they dared not tell her all they knew. Fanciful tales concerning Mariula were circulated among the "After Dark" company; Mr. Mappin didn't mind as long as they were far enough away from the truth.

Mariula cast herself headlong into Fin's arms and burst into tears. "Oh, my blessed Fin! my blessed, blessed Fin!" she gasped. "I can cry on you! You are my wailing wall!"

"Sure! Sure!" said Fin, laughing and crying both. "Let it all come! You kept a stiff upper lip too long!"

But Mariula soon dried her eyes and decorously retreated from Fin's knee. "What a fool you must think me," she said, suddenly the maiden. "I always cry when the trouble's over."

"You didn't tell them the whole story?" Fin said, anxiously.

Mariula shook her head. "I told enough for the newspapers," she said, coolly. "It is horrible to think of everything about you being talked over on the street corners."

"Hear! Hear!" said Mr. Mappin, suddenly. "I wish more people felt like that!"

"Besides," Mariula went on, "I felt I ought to tell you and Mr. Mappin before I told anybody else. You know more about me than I know myself."

"Very little," said Mr. Mappin.

"Tell us more about this woman," said Fin, eagerly. "What was she like?"

"A youngish, prettyish kind of woman," said Mariula. "Nothing in particular. She wasn't really a lady. There was a man in the car, too. A rough-looking fellow. He never opened his mouth the whole way. He was just there to control me if I struggled. She told me so. I said I wouldn't struggle if she sat between us, because I couldn't bear to have him touch me. I wasn't so awfully afraid then. The woman wasn't bad to me. Only kept looking at me so strangely."

"Go on," said Fin, breathlessly.

A shudder went through Mariula's slender frame. "There was another man in that house," she said. "That is what I didn't tell them. I heard him whispering with the woman behind the door. My instinct told me that he was back of it all. The woman and I had supper together, but the door into the hall was open and I knew he was listening there. She made out that she was a friend of my dead mother's and had a hunger to see me, but she couldn't come openly because of her enemies, so she had yielded to a sudden impulse to carry me off.

"But this was all acting, of course—and not very good acting, either. I know my mother never had any friends like *that!* The woman was just trying to find out how much I knew about myself. I told her right away I knew nothing, but of course she didn't believe me. She talked and talked and tried in a hundred ways to entrap me, but she couldn't, because I really did know nothing. She kept asking me about an emerald pendant and what had become of it, but I told her that was news to me. And all the time pretending that she loved me so. It was disgusting.

"After a longtime she went out into the hall to the man. I could hear them whispering there. They got excited and I caught a word or two. I think she was telling him that I knew nothing, and he was saying I was only fooling her. Afterward I heard her say quite plainly: 'You promised me you wouldn't hurt her! You promised me!' Oh, I was afraid then! . . . The man ran into the room. He was like a horrible picture. A tall thin man dressed in black. His body twisted. . . ."

"'Robespierre,' by God!" murmured Fin.

". . . His hair hung over his face and his eyes glared at me. He had a silk scarf in his hands and I thought . . . I thought he was going to strangle me with it like poor Nicky . . ."

"What's that?" cried Fin, sharply.

"Oh, you wouldn't tell me," she said. "But I soon found out. Everybody in Hoboken knew."

"Go on!" he said, hoarsely.

"He jabbered at me in some foreign language, then English. It was about the emerald pendant. I could only say: 'I don't know! I don't know! I don't know!' The silk scarf fascinated me. I couldn't keep my eyes off it . . ." She paused.

"What happened?" gasped Fin.

"The telephone saved me," she said, simply. "I heard it ring, and a moment after the woman ran in and whispered something in his ear. It made him stop. His face turned quite green.

"'It's too late,' he said, looking at me. 'She has seen me now.'

"'But if you send her back unharmed they can do nothing to you,' she said. She was so excited she forgot to whisper. 'It's a trap! It's a trap!' she kept saying.

"He said, 'I'll make sure of that!' and he ran right out of the house. I heard the door slam.

"I never saw him again. The woman slept in the room with me that night. I couldn't sleep. In the morning I knew he had come back, but nobody told me. The woman said it was all right. She said it wasn't safe for them to take me back by daylight, but as soon as it grew dark they would. She seemed quite pleased about it. She wasn't a bad sort. Sure enough, when it got dark they put me in the car and brought me back."

"What does it all mean?" cried Fin, springing up. "I can't make sense of it!"

"A feud between our two adversaries," said Mr. Mappin, soberly. "It is the only hypothesis that fits the facts. . . . One is cunning, one savage. Suppose the cunning one caused information of Mariula's whereabouts to be conveyed to the savage one, hoping to profit by the result in two ways. Luckily the savage was informed of the trick in time."

"Very likely! Very likely!" cried Fin. "They are capable of it! They must both be arrested now. Such brutes can't be allowed to remain at large."

"That is the decision we have to make tonight," said Mr. Mappin, gravely. "Easy enough to arrest them with the information in our hands. But dare we risk the chance that the secret of Mariula's identity may be lost in the subsequent confusion?"

"Who could take the responsibility for such a decision!" cried Fin, clapping his hands to his head.

"One thing is clear," said Mr. Mappin, "we can no longer sport with Mariula's fate while she remains in ignorance. We must tell her everything we know now."

He told her. Mariula listened in still amazement. "An emerald pendant, mine?" she murmured. "A secret about me that men are fighting over? What does it all mean?"

Mr. Mappin shrugged. "That is what we must find out."

"Which is it to be?" Fin demanded, agitatedly. "Shall we drop the whole thing and enjoy a little peace and quietness once more, or shall we go on until we have discovered the truth?"

There was nothing of the child about Mariula then. Sitting on the edge of the bed, leaning against one arm, she lowered her head with the familiar gesture, letting the bright hair screen her eyes. "I think," she said, slowly, "we must go on. I'm sure you and Mr. Mappin can take care of me." She flung the hair out of her eyes. "How can a person stop when he has once started a thing?" she asked. "It would torment us as long as we lived."

"So be it," said Mr. Mappin. "We will guard you well, my dear."

CHAPTER TWELVE

AT BREAKFAST MR. MAPPIN TOSSED a typewritten sheet across the table to Fin. "First report from the McArdle Agency," he said. "These fellows are damned ingenious."

Fin read:

> Being assigned to pick up any or all of the men who are trailing Mr. Amos Lee Mappin, and trace them back to their employers, I did not show myself around Mr. Mappin's residence, but took up a stand at First Avenue and Fifty-second Street, where anybody leaving the said house would have to pass me. My partner (No. 19) let his cab stand across the street from Mr. Mappin's with the flag down, so nobody could hire him.
>
> Mr. Mappin issued out at 2:30 yesterday afternoon, and was immediately picked up by a man with a black mustache who was loitering against the railings at the end of the street. Mr. M. hailed a taxi from the regular rank in front of the house, and the black-mustached man got one at the corner where it had been waiting for him. They passed through Fifty-first Street, and my partner picked me up and we followed.
>
> Mr. Mappin already knows where he went, so I need not describe it. He returned home at 3:45.

Shortly afterward the black-mustached man was relieved by a fellow with sandy hair. The black-mustached man then hailed a taxi in First Ave. leaving
his own taxi stand there, and was driven south. My
partner picked me up as before and we followed him
to No. — West Forty-second Street. I followed him
inside the building and up in the elevator to the offices of the L'Aiglon Agency where he is employed.

This is a pretty shady concern. They let it be
known in a discreet way that they will take anything
the reputable agencies turn down, so they have
plenty of business. An operative who was formerly
employed by our agency and got into trouble is working there now. I knew he was crazy to make good
with us again, so I got in touch with him at his home
last night, and I told him I was after the name of the
man who was having Mr. Mappin watched. After
some talk he agreed to get it for me.

This morning I met him in Forty-second Street,
as agreed, and he told me that the name of the client
who was having Mr. Mappin watched was General
Diamond; address, Hotel Madagascar.

Number Four.

Mr. Mappin had in the meantime finished reading another typewritten page. "Report number two from the same operative," he
said, handing it over.

Fin read:

I had no trouble picking up General Diamond at the
Madagascar. I understand he's already known to Mr.
Mappin, so I needn't describe him. He's well known
around the hotel. Seems to want to establish himself in his present character and makes friends with
everybody. But all his friends are recent ones. He
seems to have turned up there about a month ago.

Further back than that I have not yet been able to trace him.

He makes out he has no regular business and hangs around the lobby most of the time, but I notice that he does a lot of telephoning from the booths. It is impossible to trace such calls. I engaged a room almost directly opposite his and squared the chambermaid. When I satisfied her who I was, she left the door of his room unlocked as if by accident, and I went in there and made a search while the General was having lunch with some of his chance acquaintances.

He is evidently an old hand, because I found no letters or papers or proofs of identity of any sort. He brought with him to the hotel a leather suitcase, a new steamer trunk, and an old-fashioned leather-covered trunk, small and much worn. No marks on it. You could see where the different labels had been soaked off. The suitcase and the steamer trunk were unlocked and empty, and all the stuff in the bureau, closet, etc., was just what a man of his sort would carry. No marks on anything but laundry marks.

The leather-covered trunk was locked, but it was a simple kind of lock. I opened it with a piece of wire, and locked it after me again. This trunk contained four outfits for a complete disguise, also a make-up box and several colors of false hair. The outfits were for (a) a fashionable gentleman, (b) a general's uniform, (c) another military uniform, (d) worn, rough clothes as for a workman. I was unable to give these clothes a detailed examination, because I could only allow myself about half an hour while he ate. But I will enter the room again if desired.

I made notes of the two uniforms and looked them up in the library later. The General's uniform is Peruvian. The other, which was badly worn and

stained, I could not find in any of the illustrated
books, but it came closest to the Russian ones.

Number Four.

Mr. Mappin handed over a third report without comment.

Having received further instructions to try to pick
up a party who had been seen following General Diamond on two occasions, I got my man on Forty-second Street today. The General come out about 10:30
and this other fellow was laying for him in the street.
He is known to Mr. Mappin, so I won't describe him.
The name he goes under is Nipperg. The General
turns west and this Nipperg takes after him. He's a
clumsy tracker and the General soon gets on to him
and is scared. The General goes into a lunchroom,
though he just had his breakfast, and after a while
he come out and returned to the hotel again. Nipperg
hung around for awhile and then he made up his
mind the General wasn't coming out, so he hopped
on a Fourth Avenue car bound south. I was on the
platform. At Grand he changed to an eastbound car
and finally entered a house at — East Broadway.

This is a long-established rooming-house kept by
Mrs. Caroline Emmett for professional men who
have to live on the East Side. A very respectable
house. I watched it from under cover for a couple
of hours, and while I was waiting I telephoned the
office from a drugstore for another man, and Number 11 joined me. Nipperg come out again about one,
and after eating his dinner in a restaurant took a taxi
uptown. I left it to Number 11 to trail him while I
entered the rooming-house.

The landlady was a talkative woman and I
learned everything she knew easy. It was she who

told me the man's name. He rents her best room from her, second floor front. She don't like him much because, though he's lived with her near a year, she can't find out anything about him. She thinks he's some kind of an anarchist and I reckon she charges him double for it. He never speaks to anybody in the house and has no visitors.

I made out to be looking for a room, and hired the one over Nipperg. He has his own telephone in there. I made a hasty search of his room, but he's another wise one. No writing left about anywhere. There was a couple of family photographs, but the photographers' names and addresses had been scratched off. They looked foreign. There was a tin dispatch box locked with a brass padlock that I could not open without busting it. I can make a key for it later if desired.

Nipperg come in late and started telephoning. By putting my ear to the floor I could hear him talking, and I judged it was some foreign language by the inflections. Even if I knew the language I couldn't hear what he says, because he talks too cautious. He has a dial phone which makes it impossible to trace local calls.

Number 11 reported to the office that he lost Nipperg in a traffic jam in Thirty-seventh Street. The way the streets are it is impossible to prevent this sometimes. When they got out of the jam he was still following Nipperg's taxi, but the man was no longer inside it. But we know his hang-out now and can pick him up any time. I'll try to make up to him inside the house, but can't promise certain results, because the thing he's most suspicious of is anybody trying to make friends with him.

Number Four.

Mr. Mappin's comment on these reports was, "Interesting, but not very instructive."

He led the way into the living-room. Lighting a cigar, he paced thoughtfully up and down the long room, while Fin dropped into an easy chair with a cigarette.

"It's the best espionage money can buy," said Mr. Mappin, still referring to the reports, "but it won't get us anywhere. All espionage is useless when the watched man is on his guard—it is worse than useless, because he can drop false clues for his spies. . . . No, we must rely on our own efforts, Finlay."

"Shall you try to get in touch with 'Robespierre'—or Nipperg, as he calls himself?" asked Fin.

Mr. Mappin slowly shook his head. "I see nothing to be gained by it. The man is armed with suspicion like a porcupine with quills. . . . The General is still our best bet."

"He's suspicious, too."

"Yes, but he is also conceited. He is willing to fraternize with us because he is sure he can overreach us in the end. Overconfidence may betray him."

Mr. Mappin took a turn up and down. "On the other hand, it is quite on the cards that the General may overreach me," he resumed. "Nobody is infallible. It bothers me a good deal. We are too dependent on the General. We ought to have other lines out—collateral lines."

"Have you anything to suggest?" asked Fin.

"I've been thinking of the woman who carried off Mariula. Seems to have been a well-disposed sort of woman, though weak. It isn't likely she knows the whole plot, but we might get something out of her. We might even induce her to betray Nipperg."

"How can we find her?"

"That won't offer insuperable difficulties," said Mr. Mappin. "We will question Mariula more closely. . . . In the mean time," he added, coolly, "I have asked the General to come and stop with us for a few days."

"What!" cried Fin.

"Well, he gave me an opportunity to do so, and it fitted in very well with my plans."

"Would you be able to sleep while that ruffian was here in the apartment?"

"All the bedroom doors have very good locks on them," said Mr. Mappin blandly. ". . . He'll be here at lunch-time, bag and baggage."

"I'd like to have a look inside that leather-covered trunk of his."

"So should I," said Mr. Mappin. "I hope he doesn't bring it."

"Why?"

"One has such ridiculous scruples! I couldn't possibly open it in my own house, but if he leaves it outside I shouldn't mind."

"What do you suppose is his object in coming here?" asked Fin.

"He hopes to get a chance to steal the precious paper."

"Well, we can easily block that."

"If we wish to do so," said Mr. Mappin, quietly.

Fin stared, not quite getting his drift. Mr. Mappin did not enlighten him then.

"Have you studied the paper again?" asked Fin.

"No," said Mr. Mappin. "Having examined it thoroughly, there is nothing to be gained by looking at it again. I have deposited the result of my examination with my subconscious, which will prompt me at its own good time."

"Eh?" said Fin.

"Man's subconscious," Mr. Mappin went on, smiling, "is his own best oracle. Ask of your subconscious and it shall be given you. Every man has a subconscious, but few know how to use it. Most of us rely on reason, a very imperfect faculty. Your reason tells you what you want it to tell you, but your subconscious is never deceived."

"I don't quite get you," said Fin.

"Well, to put it in the vernacular," said Mr. Mappin, with a wider smile, "I am waiting for a hunch."

"Oh!" said Fin.

"At the same time," Mr. Mappin went on "you must not neglect to feed your subconscious with every bit of information available.

. . . This paper was presumably prepared by Mariula's parents, who died when she was an infant. Tragic deaths are indicated. It is hardly questionable but that their deaths were brought about by the same evil influence that is now trying to recover the paper. That would make it about sixteen years old. I try to project myself back into that time. The beginning of the Great War, when man's inventive faculty was enormously stimulated by the desire to wipe out his fellowmen. . . ."

Mr. Mappin fell into a study, and Fin, leaving him alone with his subconscious, drifted out on the balcony. A hum high in air caused him to throw his head back. He saw an airplane so far away that it appeared like an insect busily spitting out letters of smoke against the blue. Forward and back and around and back, spreading its flat tail, working as real birds never work. The result of its labors drifted lazily across the sky:

DRINK
SARVIS

As Fin watched idly, Mr. Mappin came to his elbow. "Ah, a sky-writer," he said.

"Effective way of advertising," said Fin.

"It is as long as people will look up," said Mr. Mappin. "But I notice they are getting accustomed to it."

Suddenly Fin's wrist was caught in a nervous grip. "By Gad!" said Mr. Mappin, excitedly. "By Gad! he's given me an idea! Those flowing letters, that line which must not be broken. I believe I have it, Finlay!"

"What is it? What is it?" cried Fin,

"Years ago when I was young," said Mr. Mappin, "a certain firm of famous pill-makers who covered the earth with their advertising used to hand out blank pieces of paper—just like that which we have in our safe, just like it! And each had a dot on it, too. That was to show you where to start. You touched fire to the dot and a spark began to travel through the paper spelling out the words, 'USE MINCHIN'S PILLS.'"

"Hey?" said Fin staring.

"Come on! Come on!" said Mr. Mappin, pulling at his wrist. "Let's try it!"

Jermyn was warned not to admit anybody to the apartment. They shut the windows of the shop to keep any vagrant breeze from interfering with operations, and spread the precious square of paper on the workbench. Mr. Mappin's usual calm had deserted him. His spectacles glittered, and his well-kept hands trembled a little.

"Something black should be put under the paper," he said, breathlessly, "so the letters will show up better."

Fin fetched a book for the purpose. "Should I put a match to it?" he asked.

"A spark is better. Blow the ashes off your cigarette and touch the lighted cone to the dot."

Fin started to obey, but his hand hung suspended. "I hate to do it," he said. "Suppose we destroy it."

"If we are wrong it will only scorch a little hole in the paper."

Fin touched the point of his lighted cigarette to the dot. Instantly there was a little sputter and a spark began to eat its way through the paper, up and back again and around, the same evolutions of the sky-writer on a miniature scale. The letter B took shape.

"Thank God, we have it! We have it!" cried Mr. Mappin.

They watched the moving spark with fascinated eyes. It progressed like a little creature with a gentle hissing sound; a disembodied intelligence shaping human letters and words. It had all the effect of a spirit voice speaking of the unknown, and the two watchers were filled with awe.

CHAPTER THIRTEEN

MR. MAPPIN THREW OPEN the windows of his workshop. With a common impulse the two men leaned their elbows on the bench and let the river breeze cool their damp foreheads. It was a relief to forget the cause of their excitement for a moment. Far below them the river panorama ceaselessly unrolled itself; tugs, lighters, rowboats, and boys in swimming; millionaires' speedboats scuttling downstream to the landing at Twenty-sixth Street. A little to their left the Queensboro Bridge flung itself high across the stream, while immediately in front lay the point of Blackwells Island—or Welfare Island, as they call it now. (Welfare! with those ugly prisons!) The whole scene was bathed in the sparkling sunshine of a September morning.

"Well, it's nice to see that business is going on as usual," remarked the older man.

Finally he recalled himself to the matter in hand. "Let these words impress themselves on your mind," he said to Fin, pointing to the paper, "and I'll destroy it. Now that we have read its secret, there's no object in keeping it. . . . Besides, the General will be here shortly."

"I couldn't forget those words if I wanted to," said Fin. "Don't you need the paper for a copy?"

"I've already made a copy to fool the General, and from that I'll make a better one."

"'Behind Dazbog's House,'" murmured Fin. "We solve one puzzle only to find ourselves faced with another. Of all the houses in the world, which is Dazbog's?"

"I don't think it's a house at all," said Mr. Mappin, thoughtfully.

"Eh?" said Fin.

"I think the message has a figurative meaning. It is obviously meant as a guide to the spot where something is hidden. But behind a house! A house is such a large object. At what point behind it would you start looking and how far behind? I cannot believe that anybody would take all that trouble to give such a vague direction."

"Then what does it mean?" said Fin. "Who is Dazbog?"

"Well, I have heard of one Dazbog," said Mr. Mappin. "In the ancient Slav mythology Dazbog was the god of fire. Dazbog's House, therefore, may conceivably refer to some fireplace or stove. When you say behind the fireplace or behind the stove, you have an explicit direction."

"By God! yes!" cried Fin. "But where? Where?"

"Ah, that we have to find out," said Mr. Mappin. "Presumably the General knows. We must try to make him lead us to it."

"How?" said Fin.

"I propose to make a perfect copy of the paper, hidden message and all—only, of course, the message will be a different one. We will then give the General a chance to steal it and will try to find out what use he makes of it."

"But you don't know any of the circumstances," objected Fin. "How can you fake up a message that won't give the snap away as soon as the General reads it?"

"I can but try," said Mr. Mappin, blandly. "Logic must aid me. The real message indicates a house. Now what is there that is common to all houses in all parts of the world?"

Fin could only shake his head, and Mr. Mappin proceeded to answer his own question. "A kitchen. . . . I propose to let my message read, 'Under Kitchen Floor.'"

"Sounds good to me," said Fin, grinning.

"I have a friend that I can trust who is a chemist," said Mr. Mappin. "I will go to him at once. If the General comes before I get back, make my apologies."

Mr. Mappin, fully accoutered in hat, gloves, and stick, went out, and for the next two hours Fin mooned restlessly about the apartment, unable to settle down to anything. It was cruelly hard to be condemned to inaction at such a moment. The different factors in the situation turned and shifted in his head like the bits of colored glass in a kaleidoscope: Nick Peters; Mariula; the emerald pendant; General Diamond; Nipperg and Nipperg's woman; Dazbog's House; what could be hidden behind it of such importance that even the superb emerald was as nothing beside it? Mariula again. . . .

Fin violently shook his head and went out on the balcony to look at the view. He had a young man's healthy distrust of useless brooding, but he could not stop it. Always his thoughts came back to Mariula. There was such a rare quality about her that even had her lot been cast along the most humdrum lines he would have feared for her, because fate always seems to threaten the rare and the lovely ones. Actually, however, the girl was surrounded by dangers that made him tremble. And there was something else that tormented him. As the possibilities loomed greater and greater he feared that the outcome, whatever it might be, was going to part him from Mariula. How could a poor devil like himself expect to share in such great matters?

The sound of the General's gobbling voice at the door of the apartment drove away these gloomy fancies. Here was something definite to fight against. The General brought a sense of danger with him that braced Fin's nerves. He went out in the hall to meet him.

"Ha, Corveth!" cried their guest, with the ample smile in which his hard eyes took no part. "Grand weather, my boy! Much too fine a day for the young fella to be hanging round the house."

Nothing he would enjoy better than to split my skull! thought Fin, looking at those evil eyes. It bucked him up. "Morning, General!" he said, grinning. "I just stayed in to greet you."

"Damn decent of you," gobbled the General. "Damn decent of Mr. Mappin to ask me here."

Apparently he had brought nothing but a suitcase with him. "You travel light," said Fin.

"Well, I didn't want you fellas to think this was a visitation," said the General. "Left my trunks at the hotel."

"Not at all," said Fin. "Mr. Mappin is very glad to have you here for extra protection. This spying business is getting on his nerves. He suspects that even the doormen in the house and the elevator boys are in the pay of those scoundrels."

"That's bad! That's bad!" said the General, with heavy concern.

Mr. Mappin himself returned at this moment, and the General gobbled fresh greetings. At the same time his eyes were sharp with curiosity. "Any developments?" he asked, as they all entered the living-room.

Mr. Mappin gloomily shook his head. "I've just taken the paper to a friend of mine who is a chemist," he said, with sly intent.

In spite of self-control, the General changed color unpleasantly. "By God! I hope you didn't let him tamper with it!" he cried.

"He refused to experiment without having some clue to the formula," said Mr. Mappin.

"That's what I told you!" cried the General. . . . "By the way," he added, "you said you'd show me the paper."

Mr. Mappin took the much-creased square from his pocketbook and handed it over. "Nothing much to see," he said. Fin knew this to be merely a piece of plain paper with a pencil dot on it.

They were standing within one of the French windows. Mr. Mappin on one side and Fin on the other watched the General's fat hands while they held the paper. They trembled ever so slightly. Well, it must have been maddening to come so close to the secret without possessing it. Fin was reassured by these signs of excitement. We are a lap ahead of him, he thought. He doesn't suspect that this is a trick paper.

The General took a tiny rule from his vest pocket and measured the paper. Fin saw him silently counting the creases in it. Planning to make one to leave in its place, he thought.

The paper was handed back. "Aren't you afraid to carry this through the streets unattended?" asked the General.

"No one would expect me to do such a thing," said Mr. Mappin, blandly. "I thought there was safety in that. . . . However, I confess I was nervous," he added. "I shan't do it again."

They seated themselves.

"Have you made any progress?" asked Mr. Mappin.

"Well, I have and I haven't," said the General, heavily. "Nothing definite yet. Not what I hoped for."

Mr. Mappin looked his question.

"I've had a glimpse of your enemy," said the General—"of our enemy, may I say? He calls himself Nipperg, and he lives in a rooming-house on East Broadway. Tall, lanky fellow with his hair in his eyes; looks as if he might be toting a bomb in each pocket."

Fin concealed his surprise. The General was certainly a shrewd player. He always made the unexpected move. "Sure!" cried Fin. "I've had a glimpse of that fellow two or three times."

"Well, if you ask me, you've done pretty well, General," said Mr. Mappin, blandly.

The General wagged his hand, deprecatingly. "I have no idea what his game is," he said. "Nor have I been able to open up anything concerning Nick Peters. None of the Slav circles I am in touch with ever heard of Nick Peters. Whatever his game was, he played a lone hand. Nipperg likewise."

"How can we approach him?" asked Mr. Mappin.

"We can't," said the General, bluntly. "At least, not openly. He has the look of a madman to me. One of these nihilists who would blow all creation to hell, and himself with it, at the drop of the hat."

"Good gracious!" said Mr. Mappin.

"Not openly," the General said for the second time, with meaning.

"What do you suggest?" asked Mr. Mappin.

"Well, I might seize him on the street and fetch him here," said the General, casually. "I'd make sure, on the way, that he wasn't carrying any explosives."

"Seize him on the street!" cried Mr. Mappin.

"Easy enough," said the General, coolly. "I'd load him in a motor-boat and bring him to the yacht-landing."

"What for?" gasped Mr. Mappin.

"Once we got him here we could force him to tell all he knows," said the General, with a truly fiendish grin.

What's his game? thought Fin. He doesn't want Nipperg to tell what he knows. And then the answer flashed before him—Nipperg would be murdered there, before he could open his mouth, and Mr. Mappin fatally compromised. It was a settled policy with the General to let others bear the brunt of his murders.

Mr. Mappin evidently reached the same conclusion. "No! No! No!" he said, waving his hands.

"Why not?" asked the General, with a falling face.

"My interest in this case is purely that of an investigator," said Mr. Mappin, piously. "There is a limit to the lengths I am willing to go. My private home must not be dragged into it."

"Well, if you've anything better to suggest . . ." said the General, a little sulkily.

"I'll think it over," said Mr. Mappin.

Jermyn announced luncheon.

AFTER THE MEAL the General announced with many apologies that he had an engagement to keep, and he presently departed, energetically slapping his feet. Mr. Mappin and Fin looked at each other.

"He's gone to prepare the paper that he means to leave for the one he steals," said the latter.

"Quite!" said Mr. Mappin, with a dry smile. "And I'm going to get the paper that I mean to let him steal. The chemist promised to have it ready for me at three."

"It's a curious game," said Fin.

"When he gets our paper we must be prepared to watch every move," Mr. Mappin went on. "While I'm out I'll arrange to have plenty of men planted up and down First Avenue, and in the side streets."

"Intelligent men are hard to find in a pinch," said Fin, dubiously. "He may give us the slip, anyhow."

"Oh, surely," said Mr. Mappin, philosophically. "We can only do what we can."

"It's matinée day," said Fin, very offhand, but with a delicious warmth stealing around his heart. "I'll just run over to Hoboken to see if everything is all right."

CHAPTER FOURTEEN

THE THREE MEN DID NOT COME TOGETHER AGAIN until they sat down to dinner. While they ate, General Diamond related his further experiences in Amazonas and on the Orinoco. He gobbled and gesticulated with his fork and shook all over with laughter at his own jokes. It was all very friendly and jolly, but Fin was conscious of a strain. He knew that Mr. Mappin had in his pocketbook a paper that was ready to yield its false message to the touch of a spark, and he suspected the General had another false paper in *his* pocketbook.

In the living-room later the General, while his thick fingers toyed with a delicate liqueur glass, related anecdotes of wild days in our own country. "Most folks think that the West was cleaned up sixty or seventy-five years ago," he said. "But it ain't so. There was plenty of fun going in Colorado right up to the last days of the century. Yaas, I mind I was in Gunnison and there was a girl there, an actress in the local theater and a friend of mine, and she was put on trial for half shooting a fella's hand off. It was a big sensation.

"She had a good case, too," he went on, "that fella ought to had both his hands shot off for what he was doing with them, but you know how it is with the law. The case seemed to be going against her and my friend got sore. She pulled her gun and started to clean out the courtroom. It's the truth! Judge, lawyers, constables, jury, and spectators! She cleared the room and decided the case in her own favor."

"Good gracious!" said Mr. Mappin.

"Of course I helped her some," the General added, modestly, "but I didn't want to spoil a good story, so I kept myself out of it. It made her famous."

It might have been considered a big jump from Gunnison, Colorado, to the business in hand, but the General cleared it neatly. "Speaking of actresses reminds me of your little friend over in Hoboken," he said. "I didn't neglect her business when I was out today. Went to see an old pal who's in the paper business now and got him to tell me a lot about paper. If you'll let me have another look at that paper, Mr. Mappin, maybe I can tell you where it was made."

"Why, surely," said Mr. Mappin, producing his pocketbook.

All Fin's faculties sprang to attention. The General studied the paper closely. Suddenly he affected to find that the light was not good enough where he sat. He looked around him and, heaving his body out of the settee, walked rapidly to a tall lamp at the back of the room. It was about ten paces away, and while he as taking them his back was turned to the other men.

Fin followed him up as quickly as possible because he did not want the General to think they were careless of the paper. When he reached him the General was attentively studying it under the floor lamp, but there was a button on his vest undone, and Fin was very sure he had slipped Mr. Mappin's paper inside on his way to the lamp and had abstracted another that he had ready.

His face was almost too innocent. He continued to study the paper, holding it this way and that, turning it over. Finally he shook his head sadly. "I guess it takes more than one day to learn about paper-making," he said. "This tells me nothing." He returned it to Mr. Mappin.

"We might ask your friend here to look at it," suggested Mr. Mappin, mildly.

"Good idea!" said the General.

By-and-by, Mr. Mappin noticing that the General's cigar had gone out, offered him a fresh one, but the General held up his hand in negation.

"To tell you the truth, Mr. Mappin, your cigars are too good for me, sir. An old campaigner is accustomed to a coarser weed." He felt of all his pockets. "I'm all out of my own sort," he said. "If you'll excuse me for five minutes I'll run down to the street and get some."

"Let Jermyn go," said Mr. Mappin.

The General wouldn't hear of it. "It will do me good to stretch my legs after so hearty a meal," he said.

Fin thought, This is where he is counting on making a get-away.

But, as usual, the General surprised him. "If you'd like a breath of air, come along with me, Corveth," he said.

"Sure," said Fin.

On the way the General took Fin's arm and kept up an amiable flow of anecdote. Fin's flesh crawled with repulsion at his touch, but he had to submit to it. In the cigar store the General bought a handful of the sort he favored and lighted one. As they were leaving he affected to be struck with a sudden recollection.

"Half a moment, Corveth; there's a pal I ought to call up while I think of it."

Along one side of the store there was a row of four telephone booths, none in use at the moment. The General entered the first one and shut the door. This was like a challenge thrown in Fin's teeth, but what was he to do? If he had entered the adjoining booth the General would only have lowered his voice and chuckled at him. Fin felt frantic in his helplessness. Suddenly a crazy plan popped into his head. At any rate, it would do no harm to try it.

He entered, not the adjoining booth, but the one at the other end of the row, and dropped his nickel in the slot. To the operator he said in a curt, hard-boiled voice:

"This is detective Finlay, New York police. Get me the number asked for from booth number one and what he says over the wire."

The girl said in a scared voice, "Sorry, we're not allowed to . . ."

Fin caught her up quickly. "Step on it, girl!" he rasped. "A man's life depends on this!" The scared voice faded.

Fin had to wait for a whole minute, quivering with impatience. The General came out of his booth and cast a sharp look at him

through the glass. Whereupon Fin grinned at the receiver in a foolish fashion, and made believe to be talking. The scared voice came
back.

"He called for Mott Haven 0109. A man called Harvest answered. He told him to tell Mike to meet him at Harvest's place
between eleven and twelve tonight."

A surge of gratitude made Fin's voice warm. "Thanks, sister.
Tell me your name and I'll . . ."

"Oh, we're not allowed . . ." said the voice more scared than
ever, and the connection was broken.

Fin came out of the booth with the same foolish smile. "Thought
I'd call up a girl while I was waiting," he said to the General. "I
kinda hate to do it from Mr. Mappin's."

"Sure," said the General, sympathetically. "Did you date her
up?"

"Sure," said Fin.

They retraced their steps to the apartment house. Fin could feel
almost friendly toward the General now because he had got the
better of him. He wondered what excuse the General would make
to get out again later.

The answer was forthcoming shortly before eleven. They were
still sitting in the living-room when there was a ring at the door-
bell and Jermyn presently entered with a telegram for the General. A snort of disgust escaped from that worthy when he read it.

"It's too bad this should come just now," he said. "A pal down
in Baltimore has sent for me. A phosphate ship has come in there
and the captain has a communication that I must receive in person. . . . It has to do with Peruvian matters," he added, mysteriously.

"We'll be sorry to have you go," said Mr. Mappin, blandly.

"I'll take the sleeper down," said the General. "Then I can come
back in the morning."

He finished the story he was telling, and followed it with another before he arose. "Well, I'd better amble over to the station,"
he said, "or all the lowers will be gone. . . . This is more traffic than
an upper berth will bear," he added, patting his belly complacently.

Mr. Mappin laughed politely. His spectacles glittered brilliantly. Fin reflected that eye-glasses were a great help to a man in concealing his true feelings.

When the General and his suitcase went down in the elevator Mr. Mappin said, "The rest is up to McArdle's men."

"Not altogether," said Fin, grinning. "I've got a line on him myself." He described the incident in the cigar store.

"Good boy! Good boy!" said Mr. Mappin, patting his shoulder, while Fin swelled with gratification.

They made haste to consult the telephone-book, and discovered that one William Harvest sold cigars and stationery at 125 Wilson Street. His phone number was Mott Haven 0109.

"Well, in the words of the General, I'll amble up there," said Fin.

Mr. Mappin looked dubious. "Hadn't you better let me telephone to McArdle for a man to help you?" he suggested.

This was not at all to Fin's taste. "It would double the risk," he protested. "I got the brass ball back all by myself."

"All right," said Mr. Mappin. "After all, this is your case. . . . Don't take any unnecessary risks," he went on. "You cannot hope to overhear what passes between the General and this Mike. The important thing will be to learn what becomes of Mike when he leaves the General. Keep in touch with me by phone as well as you are able."

Fin changed to his old clothes and set out.

Mott Haven lies along the north bank of the Harlem River. Once upon a time it promised to be a fine suburb, but the capricious city in its progress northward jumped over it, leaving only a sluggish and forgotten backwater among the yards of two great railways. It is not a pretty place at midnight.

Fin dismissed his taxi at the Manhattan end of the bridge and walked across. The oily black tide swirled underneath, suggesting suicides, wharf rats, and river pirates.

Before he got to Wilson Street he was warned of what to expect by the dirty looks the policemen gave him when he asked the way. It proved to be only half a street; that is to say, a single row of crazy little tenement houses, some of brick, some of wood, facing endless railway sidings across the way. A furtive-looking place, much too quiet for the city, and Fin hesitated at the corner. It was cold and the houses were shut up tight. The only humans in sight were two men standing under a gaslight, shoulders hunched, hands in pockets, aimlessly shifting from one foot to the other. Fin thought, Why do they stay there if they've got nothing to say to each other?

However, there was no help for it. He turned up his collar, thrust his hands in his pockets, and slouched by them. He was aware of being examined sharply, but they did not take their hands from their pockets. Impossible to tell if they were pickets of the General's or mere street-corner loafers. Fin was sure he had not seen them before.

Here and there along the row were meager little stores all closed now until he came to number 125, where a light still burned. The little stationery-cigar store was of a type well known to older New York. Such was its anxiety to display its whole stock, you could scarcely see into the store through the clutter in the show-window. Fin wondered how it made a living in such a poor neighborhood until he saw, the little sign reading, "Letter Boxes Rented." Thus the proprietor advertised that he was willing to act as go-between in any sort of shady business. He's got a first-rate stand for that, thought Fin.

As far as it was revealed to the street, the store was empty. Perhaps the General and Mike were already conferring in the back room. However, Fin doubted if the General had had time to get there yet. He had first to give his pursuers the slip. There was one feature of this ugly street that Fin strongly approved of—the strings of freight cars on the sidings provided a perfect observation post.

He proceeded for a block further, cut across the street in the dark, climbed over the couplings of the first string, and came back behind it, peeping between each pair of cars until he found himself opposite the little stationery store again. Here he took up his stand between two cars. On so dark a night there was no possibility of his being seen. Peeping out, he found that the two loafers were gone from under the lamppost. No matter, he thought, they couldn't possibly have seen him cross the street below.

It never occurred to Fin that so excellent a point of lookout might have been preempted. He *heard* the blow on his own head that he never felt. For the time being it ended everything.

CHAPTER FIFTEEN

WHEN HIS SENSES RETURNED, Fin found himself lying between the freight cars on the spot where he had fallen. His first blind terrified impulse was to roll clear of the rails, though there was little danger of those cars being moved at night. He lay on the ground, shivering and nauseated, trying desperately to gather his wits together. His first conscious feeling was one of thankfulness that he had any wits to gather. It was more than he might have expected. Fin didn't want to die until Mariula grew up.

He got to his feet and leaned against the car. His head had grown too small to hold its contents. The pressure was terrific. However, upon gingerly feeling of his bruised crown, it appeared to be whole. His thoughts as they became clearer were very bitter. What a fool to walk directly into their trap! He found he had been stripped of watch and money, but this, of course, was only to make it appear that he had been set upon by footpads. He was not deceived.

The little stationery store was dark now, and he went away from there. Whatever had happened, the birds had flown long ago. He did not venture out on the street until he had come to the end of the string of cars. His sense of direction was somewhat confused and a long time passed before he stumbled on the Harlem River again. The dawn was breaking then. He crossed the bridge and had to walk to 125th Street before he picked up a taxi.

The sun was up when he got home. He borrowed money from the night watchman to pay his taxi. Upstairs, Mr. Mappin was so overjoyed to see him able to navigate under his own power that he pooh-poohed Fin's confession of failure.

"What the deuce, my boy," he said, patting him on the shoulder just as if he had come flushed with triumph. "It might have happened to anybody. It's only in stories that the hero invariably gets his man. We ordinary fellows have to take plenty of kicks among our ha'pence."

Fin began to feel better. Mr. Mappin wanted him to go to bed, but he refused. "I've got to be doing something else in order to forget this bonehead play," he muttered.

While they were at breakfast the first mail brought more bad news. Number Four reported that while he was eating his dinner the night before, Nipperg had suddenly paid his bill and fled from the house on East Broadway. Something had alarmed that queasy soul. He had been heard to tell the taxi-driver to take him to Grand Central, but that was a stall, of course. The plain fact was that Number Four had lost him.

They had no more than read his report when McArdle himself called up to say that Number Seven had phoned from Baltimore to say that General Diamond had given him the slip. Numbers Seven and Nine had trailed him to the Pennsylvania Terminal, and while Seven was buying a ticket, Nine had seen him aboard the train. Seven followed him aboard a minute or two later, but in the morning there was no General. This was scarcely news to Mr. Mappin. McArdle asked for further instructions.

"Call off all your dogs for the present," said Mr. Mappin, with the utmost good humor. "I am planning a new campaign." He returned to his breakfast with unimpaired appetite.

"You seem to take it pretty well," grumbled Fin.

"I dwell on the bright side of the picture," said Mr. Mappin. "We are relieved of the General's society."

"He may come back today," said Fin. "He has gall enough."

"He won't come back as long as he thinks he has stolen our secret."

"When he discovers he's fooled he may come back with a bullet."

"No," said Mr. Mappin, calmly. "The General is ever a practical man."

"We gained nothing by having him here," said Fin, gloomily.

"I wouldn't say that," returned Mr. Mappin. "I have secured his trunks."

"What!" cried Fin. "How?"

"By a piece of rather sharp practice, I am afraid," said Mr. Mappin, with a deprecatory wave of his hand. "But one cannot be too particular with the General."

He refused to specify further. "Let us go over to see Mariula this morning," he said, to divert Fin.

Two hours later the three friends were sitting in the last row of the Old Rialto Theater while a rehearsal was taking place on the stage. In the obscurity under the balcony Mariula slipped her arm through Fin's, and the young man sat silent and blissful, all his troubles forgotten. Nothing had been said about the events of the night before, but Mariula divined that he had need of comfort. Amid the somewhat jaded atmosphere of a morning rehearsal she was as fresh and fragrant as a sweet-pea blossom, Fin thought.

In the daylight which filtered through various apertures the old theater, so jolly when the footlights were on, showed its age. They were rehearsing the old play that was to succeed "After Dark" in due course. It was called "The Blue and the Gray," or "War is Hell"— the sub-title undoubtedly a Morleyan embellishment. It was a first rehearsal and the worried-looking actors, one eye on their typed parts and the other on the director, moved stiffly back and forth on the stage like automatic chessmen at the voice of command. In the medley of spoken lines, directions, and arguments nobody could have made head or tail of what was going on.

The director sat on a temporary platform set up in the middle of the auditorium, with a table in front of him and his minion, the stage manager at his side. Other actors and hangers-on generally were scattered in couples and little groups among the seats, whispering together when the stage manager was looking elsewhere, and eating sandwiches. The impresario, Mr. Morley, warm and disheveled, moved here and there, always followed by a little train of satellites seeking instructions. When the poet could get a few seconds to himself he scribbled lyrics for the new show on the back of a grimy envelope. Under such difficulties must the Muse of the theater function.

Away at the back under the balcony the three friends whispered softly together to avoid attracting the irascible eye of the director. Mr. Mappin was questioning Mariula with a view to establishing the location of the house where she had been kept prisoner—endless patient questions that elicited a nugget of information every once in so often.

Mariula said when the kidnapping car issued from the Tunnel on the New York side it turned sharply to the left and never made another turn until they almost got to their destination, an hour later.

"That's important if you can be sure of it," said Mr. Mappin. "It indicates that you were carried due north. An hour's swift driving you said, with only a few pauses for traffic lights. You were evidently carried up the western edge of the island to Inwood or across the Harlem River to one of the villages beyond."

Mariula added that when they were almost there they had turned sharp to the left again, had climbed a steep hill on second gear, had made several more turns, and had then descended a driveway to the house door. She had heard the brakes squeak.

"That helps narrow it down," said Mr. Mappin. "Not many houses are built below the level of the street."

Mariula described the house as well as she was able. She had had but two brief glimpses of it in getting out of the car and getting in again. It was an old-fashioned stone house she said, with wooden trimmings painted yellowish-grayish. It had a fancy wooden veranda running around the back. Everything about the outside was pointed—pointed front door, pointed windows, steep pointed gables.

"Excellent!" said Mr. Mappin. "You have exactly described the domestic Gothic style so fashionable in the 'sixties and 'seventies.

And yellowish-grayish was the favorite color for trim in those days.
. . . How about the inmates of the house?" he went on. "You needn't
say anything about the man, because we know him. He calls himself Nipperg. But can you give me a better description of the
woman?"

Fin felt a little shiver go through Mariula. Evidently this had
been a much more terrible experience to her than her pride had
allowed her to confess. He pressed her arm warmly against his ribs.

"It's hard to describe her," said Mariula, "she was so usual-look-
ing. I think she had been a pretty girl, but she was beginning to
run together. She looked as if she were sorry for herself. She
dressed in a showy way that made her look worse than she was."

Questioning was interrupted at this point by an explosion of
profanity from the director on his little platform. This was regarded
as part of the routine of rehearsal. Perfect silence descended upon
the theater for a moment or two, then the whispering recommenced
like mice behind the wainscot.

"You were confined in an upper room all day long," Mr. Mappin
resumed. "What did you see from the windows?"

"Not much," said Mariula. "The windows of my room looked to
the front—that is, toward the drive we had come down in the car.
This drive turned among the trees and disappeared. The trees were
very thick and I could not see where it went. Everything had been
allowed to grow as it liked. It was almost like a wild woods."

"And what was behind the house?"

"I couldn't see," said Mariula. . . . "But wait," she added. "I could
hear trains passing; behind the house and lower down. Many
trains."

"Ha!" said Mr. Mappin. "Now we're getting warm! If you were
carried north those must have been the New York Central trains
along the river."

"Yes," said Mariula, "there must have been a river behind the
house, because at night when it was very quiet I could hear the
little waves lapping."

"Were they freight trains or passenger trains?" asked Mr.
Mappin, with glittering eyeglasses.

"Why . . . what's the difference?" said Mariula.

"Freight trains are pulled by steam locomotives. They move slowly with heavy puffing," said Mr. Mappin. "And the cars rattle and jerk. . . . Passenger trains are pulled by electric engines. They move swiftly and make no sound above a low rumble."

Fin imitated both sorts *sotto voce.*

"Perfect!" said Mariula, with a clap of her hands. "I can hear them now. . . . There were both sorts. And many of them."

"Then we have it!" said Mr. Mappin, with solemn satisfaction. "You were carried above the Harlem River because the freight tracks and the passenger tracks divide at Spuyten Duyvil. But not far above, because you were only an hour on the way. It must be Riverdale." He stood up and buttoned his double-breasted jacket.

"Where you going?" asked Fin.

"I'll motor over to the Newark flying-field and engage a plane for a couple of hours," he answered. "It ought not to be difficult to spot that house from the air. You stay here and take it easy. I'll pick you up some time this afternoon."

"Righto!" said Fin.

Mr. Mappin went out softly, and Fin slumped down in his seat and relinquished all care. How utterly delicious it was just to look at Mariula!

"Make me some more imitations, Finny Tribe," she whispered, cajolingly. "If there's anything I love, it's imitations!"‘

Fin obliged with a whole zoological garden—muted, of course. But when he got as far as the wart-hog, Mariula uttered a snort that caused the stage director to turn around squarely in his chair and glare in their direction. So they were forced to behave.

"Berenice is going to be wonderful in this part," said Mariula. "With those big eyes of hers. No one would believe she could be such a cat?"

"Is she?" said Fin, idly.

"Absolutely. And the worst of it is, you never can get back at her, she looks so hurt. The only thing that would make Berenice natural is a good hard slap."

"Well, give it to her," said Fin. "I'm with you."

"If we only lived in a state of nature!" said Mariula, with a sigh.

"That means undressed," said Fin, teasingly.

"It's not what I mean," said Mariula, with dignity. "I mean behaving naturally. As it is, the sly ones profit by all the rules for good behavior."

"Hear! Hear!" said Fin, sleepily.

"You never came over last night," remarked Mariula.

"I had to help the chief entertain a guest."

"Oh."

In his perfect sense of well-being a numbness began to steal over Fin. With Mariula beside him filling all his senses, it was sweeter than music. He floated away.

"Why, you're nodding!" she said. "My poor Fishy! I don't believe you went to bed at all last night!"

"Didn't," murmured Fin.

"What were you doing?"

"Business of the chief's," he murmured. (And of yours, he might have added, but did not.)

"Poor darling!" she whispered. "Put your head down on my shoulder and snatch forty winks. I won't be called for until the second act and they may not reach it at all today."

Fin was in no condition to resist anybody. While he was still protesting she gave his head a little pull and it sank on her shoulder. This was not sleep; it was enchantment.

CHAPTER SIXTEEN

AT ONE O'CLOCK THE ENTIRE COMPANY adjourned to the Foundry, around the corner, where a picnic lunch was had in by Mr. Morley. Such amenities did wonders in smoothing the prickly path of theatrical relations. Even the director became human for the time being. Chris Morley had a special affinity for picnics; they suited his large and careless style. He insisted on mixing mighty pitchers of shandygaff, a drink that will be forever associated with his name. Nobody quite shared his enthusiasm for it, but nobody would have hurt his feelings by saying so.

Mariula belonged to the light-hearted, slangy, hard-working crowd without being exactly of it. In spite of all outside influences, she remained her individual self. Even Mr. Morley treated her with an affectionate and half-quizzical deference that set the style. Why was it? Fin asked himself. Far from expecting it, Mariula was inclined to resent the way they conspired to look after her. He speculated on the mysterious nature of personality.

They returned to the theater after lunch and rehearsal resumed its snail-like course. Fin and Mariula sat under the balcony, whispering and smothering their laughter. Time was nothing to them.

At three Mr. Mappin turned up with his spectacles shining. In response to their questions he said: "Yes, I found the house. Pointed gables, thick woods, and all. There is but the one house answering to that description anywhere along the river, so I was saved any uncertainty. I thought Finlay and I might motor up there now, and prospect around the neighborhood from ground level."

Mr. Mappin's taxicab was waiting outside the theater. They had a fifteen-mile drive before them. Fin wondered if he would ever reach the point where he could drive around in taxicabs all day without watching the meter.

As they roared through the Tunnel, Mr. Mappin said, "Have you noticed that we are not being followed today?"

"I didn't pay any attention this morning," said Fin.

"It is very convenient," said Mr. Mappin. "I hope it may continue. When we find that we are being followed again, we will know that the General has discovered the trick we played on him."

"The hiding-place we are all looking for may not be in America at all," said Fin.

"Quite," said Mr. Mappin, "but it makes little difference in these days of quick communications. We could reach any part of Europe by ship and plane within a week."

Money is as good as Sinbad's magic carpet, thought Fin.

They sped up Eleventh Avenue, across the railway yards at Thirty-third Street, through Hell's Kitchen, and up San Juan Hill into fashionable West End Avenue, and so into upper Broadway, all without turning a corner. They dipped into the Manhattanville valley, and climbed Washington Heights beyond, where the interminable miles of apartment houses put Fin to sleep again in the corner of the cab.

He was awakened by the grinding of the gears. "This is Mariula's hill!" he exclaimed, sitting up.

"Yes," said Mr. Mappin. "Riverdale lies at the top of it. . . . One of those curious misnomers that nobody notices."

Presently Mr. Mappin ordered the driver to slow down. "We are coming to the place," he said. "I took careful bearings from the sky."

They were then traveling northward on a street that followed the slope of the high hill overlooking the Hudson. New winding streets had been cut down the hill toward the water and suburban houses were rising here and there.

"Great changes hereabouts in fifteen or twenty years," said Mr. Mappin. "The place we are looking for is one of the last of the old estates to escape subdivision. I can't conceive how it came into Nipperg's possession."

They came to an old-fashioned stone wall on the left-hand side, with a dense growth of trees beyond it. There was a formal gateway with a neatly kept driveway winding down out of sight among the trees.

"This is the place," said Mr. Mappin. "One could not possibly be mistaken, you see. . . . I want you to get acquainted with the woman who lives there," he went on, in some embarrassment. "We know that she is left much alone, and Mariula said she was sorry for herself. That . . . er . . . may make your task easier. It is not very scrupulous, perhaps, but . . ."

Fin's heart warmed toward his gentlemanly little friend. "Nobody would think of that but you," he said. "Don't worry. I'll play fair."

They went on for a furlong, and then by Mr. Mappin's orders turned around and came back slowly. As they passed the gateway a woman somewhat showily dressed was approaching it from the other side.

"There she is," said Mr. Mappin. "Observe the justice of Mariula's description. A pretty woman, she said, who was beginning to run together."

"No time like the present," said Fin. "You'd better let me out."

"We'll just turn the first corner out of sight," said Mr. Mappin. He offered Fin a neatly folded packet of new bills. "Take this," he said. "I don't know what your expenses may run to. Hire a lodging in the neighborhood if it seems advisable."

Fin got out in the side street, and the taxi went on. When he turned back into the main road he saw the woman three or four hundred yards ahead of him, walking in the desultory manner of one who is merely killing time. If she was as bored as she seemed to be, there would be no difficulty in scraping acquaintance, Fin judged, but he was in no haste to overtake her. No use risking everything by a false start.

She turned up one of the side streets and made a circuit through the newer part of Riverdale, gazing idly at the big expensive houses. In the course of it she became aware that she was being followed.

Let's see how she takes it, thought Fin. She did not increase her pace, but put on a more elaborate air of boredom. He grinned inwardly. Maybe she comes out every day in the hope of an adventure, and has never had one yet, he thought. She was young enough to give a certain zest to the affair.

She finally came back to the road above the river and headed homeward. In a spot where this road turned around a projection of the hill a thoughtful municipality had placed a bench commanding a wide view. She seated herself upon it with a highly self-conscious air. This was as good as a direct invitation, and Fin slid into the seat beside her. She affected to be absorbed in gazing at the panorama below.

"Beautiful view," said Fin.

She startled and bridled with an indignant glance, but not too indignant. Her eyes confessed that she found him attractive.

"I hope you don't mind my speaking to you," he said, with becoming humility. "You seemed to be lonely just like me."

"I am not accustomed to it," she said, stiffly.

"I can see that," said Fin, cunningly. "I don't see any harm in it if a fellow is respectful."

She began to unbend. "I'm not narrow-minded," she said, "but a girl has to be careful."

"I suppose she has," said Fin. "I never thought of it that way."

"You never meet strangers around here," she said.

Fishing for information! thought Fin. "Well, I like to walk," he said, "and I always look for the out-of-the-way streets to get clear of the automobiles."

"Few men have the time for it," she said.

"I know," said Fin. "I'm a writer, so I don't have to keep office hours."

She melted completely then. "A writer! How wonderful!"

"Oh, I don't know," said Fin.

"I think it's marvelous to write!"

Gosh! what a fool! thought Fin. I must get her on a more natural basis or I can't keep this up!

"What do you write?" she asked.

"Stories. . . . Do you live around here?"

"Yes," she said. "In the old house behind the trees down the street."

"I saw the entrance as I came along. I wondered what was in there."

"Maybe you thought it was a cemetery," she said, with a forced laugh.

"Oh no!" said Fin, politely. "Have you got any family?"

"Only a husband and he's away mostly."

"Gee!" said Fin. "If he travels I should think you'd sooner have an apartment."

"I would," she said. "But he won't let me."

"Ain't that tough!" said Fin. "He must be a funny fella."

"He's a foreigner."

"Is that so? What kind?"

"A Russian."

"No! Can you talk Russian?"

"No."

"How long you been married?"

"Six years."

"It must be funny for an American girl to be married to a Russian."

"Well, it's no treat," she said, with pinched nostrils.

By this time Fin had pretty well taken her measure. A lonely, discontented woman, it was clear he had happened along at the well-known psychological moment. Well, he had a genuinely friendly feeling toward her because she had been kind to Mariula, and might even have been instrumental in saving the child. If in return he could get her out of Nipperg's clutches it would be all to the good. Besides, her excitement in this encounter with a good-looking young man had brightened her eyes and made her lips look youthful. That helped, too.

They talked on according to the well-established ritual of such meetings. She was alternately languishing and haughty. This was what Fin called second-rate tactics, but he could hardly object to a show that was being put on for his benefit. She was clearly enjoying herself. It was charming to see how the cloud of boredom lifted from her pretty face. Every woman is entitled to some diversion, Fin thought.

By-and-by they got to the point of exchanging names. "Mrs. Nipperg," she called herself; "Daisy," she added, with a very self-conscious glance down river. Fin countered with "Ronald Shay," which he thought had a writerish sound. She enlarged upon the married state under a thin disguise of sarcasm. "Are you married?" she asked.

"No," said Fin.

She seemed disappointed.

Finally she said she had to go, but this was merely a lead for Fin to dissuade her. Which he did. Another half-hour passed before she actually arose. Still she lingered.

"Can I call you up?" asked Fin.

"Oh no!" she said, startled. "It's a silent phone."

"But you can give me the number."

"I wouldn't dare," she said, with a nervous giggle.

"Can't I call sometime?"

"No indeed!" she said, in a real panic. "You must never do that!"

"Gosh!" said Fin. "Don't you have your friends in when he's away?"

"He wouldn't allow it," she murmured.

"Why don't you have 'em, anyhow—when he's gone?"

"The servants. They're Russian like him. They'd tell."

"He must be one of these regular old-fashioned husbands!"

"I think he's crazy," she murmured, bitterly.

"Well, anyhow, I'm glad they let you out sometimes," said Fin.

"Yeah, they think my spirit's broke," she said, with a sneer.

"Why don't you show them?" said Fin. "After all, this ain't Russia."

"Maybe I will," she said, darkly.

"Will you be taking a walk tomorrow?" he asked, offhand.

This was the cue for her elaborate hauteur. "Maybe," she said, pulling a curl out from under her hat.

"I'll walk around this way just on the chance," said Fin. "Same time."

"Oh, don't put yourself to the trouble," she said, walking away with swaying hips, but the backward glance she sent him was promising.

Fin grinned fatuously as the young man is supposed to do in such cases, but privately he was thinking: Hm! this affair don't need any speeding up from me. I'll have to be the four-wheel brakes!

CHAPTER SEVENTEEN

THERE WAS STILL AN HOUR OR SO of daylight remaining that Fin desired to put to advantage before he left the neighborhood. What he wanted most was to have a look at Nipperg's house, and he considered walking along the railway tracks below, but gave up the idea on account of the risk of exposing himself to observation from the house. Suddenly he remembered having seen a public boathouse near the Riverdale station as he turned in by the upper road. He determined to hire a rowboat, and proceeded downhill for that purpose.

It was a calm evening, cool enough to make the thought of exercise agreeable. The sun was hanging low over the Palisades, and the steam boats were beginning to appear in their nightly procession upriver. Frequent trains ran swiftly along the shore. Fin took off his coat and applied himself to the oars with a feeling of satisfaction. A fellow doesn't get enough chances to use his back, he thought.

He rowed upstream against the ebbing tide. Gradually the patch of woods opened up, revealing the little old-fashioned villa in its midst. It was built on a natural shelf about halfway up the hill. There was a terrace of grass in front of it, and what had once been gardens falling away toward the tracks below; but the gardens were neglected and overgrown. The main building was of stone, to which had been added an incongruous wooden wing. Above the house and on both sides of it was the thick growth of woods cutting it off from the view of its neighbors.

145

On the north side there was a wild ravine with a stream falling
through it. The whole place had a stark and secret look, like a sur-
vival from simpler times.

At first Fin could distinguish no sign of life, but as he rowed
slowly by, a man appeared at one side of the bare house and, passing slowly across the terrace, disappeared at the other. Fin was
too far away to distinguish his features, but the figure was im-
pressed on his mind by a peculiar-looking skull-cap with a visor
that he wore. Looks like a guard, he thought, idly.

He rowed on out of sight without pausing, and after a few minutes he came back again, loafing down with the tide. Again as he
passed, he saw the man appear on one side of the house and disap-
pear on the other. Now he was sure it was a guard. Lucky for me I
didn't try prospecting around the place, he thought. What the
dickens does Nipperg want guards for?

Fin landed at the Riverside float where he had hired the boat,
and passed over a gangway into the boathouse to pay for it. The
railway tracks were immediately outside the windows. As he
glanced through, his attention was sharply arrested by the figure
of a workman walking up the track, a big man in earth-stained cor-
duroys, carrying a spade over his shoulder. It was the way he gave
slightly at the knees and slapped his feet on the ground that struck
Fin. He looked again and was sure. It was the General. He was dis-
guised by a shapeless felt hat and a sweeping black mustache; he
might conceivably have been taken for an Italian if they ever came
so big; but it was the General, all right, and Fin's head whirled
under the shock of his surprise.

He quickly changed his plan of action. There were refreshments
on sale in the boathouse, and he made out he had come in to get
something to eat. With his hands full of sandwiches and cakes he
got in his boat and pulled upriver again. It was growing dark now
and he had some difficulty in keeping his man in view, though he
rowed close to the railway embankment. His heart beat fast with
hope. If his luck held, he saw a chance of wiping out his failure of
the night before.

At Nipperg's place Fin lost his man altogether. Putting his back to the oars, he made the skiff jump through the water. But in two hundred yards he had not overtaken the walker and he was sure then that the General had left the tracks below Nipperg's place and started to climb up. This was what Fin had expected. The General was aiming to turn the tables on Nipperg, it seemed, and spy upon the spy. Well, two can play at that game, thought Fin.

At the point where the ravine came down to the river there was a culvert under the railway tracks. Fin waited awhile until it was perfectly dark, and then easing his skiff through, beached it on the other side and tied the painter to a fencepost. He had to climb this fence to enter Nipperg's property. He made his way up the stony side of the ravine, carefully feeling his way in the dark, and pausing every few steps to listen. It was only seven o'clock, and he was still within the city limits, but in this wild spot he felt as if he had left the world.

Somewhere above his head he heard a curious sound that he could not interpret—a sort of gentle squeaking. Suddenly there was a soft thud overhead, and earth and stones rolled down and over his feet. Fin turned cold with fear, for it was like a blow aimed at him out of the dark. He made a hasty detour to the right to escape the thing, whatever it was. All became quiet again.

He rose over the edge of the ravine and found himself in the overgrown garden below the house. A tangle of blackberry canes caught at his ankles. A hundred yards above him he could see the pointed gables against the sky. No light showed on this side. Down in the river the Albany night boat was making its dignified way upstream jeweled with a thousand lights, its pistons sighing with every stroke. This belonged to the world that Fin had left. The beating of his heart quieted down and he resolved to find out the cause of the sound that had so startled him. He continued to detour to the right in order to get above it.

The thickly growing trees that marked the edge of the ravine rose before him. When he got among them he proceeded with extra caution, feeling the way before him with exploring hand and foot. Upon stopping to listen he could hear nothing but the distant voice of the city— the trucks, the trolleys, the steamboat whistles, subdued away up here to a mere breath of sound. Suddenly his foot struck something hard, and upon feeling for it he found a plank laid upon the ground. Investigating further, he found it to be one of a line of planks laid end to end like a track. Guessing that this had something to do with what had startled him, he flattened himself on the ground a couple of paces away to wait and see.

After awhile he heard the curious soft squeaking, and again he was afraid because he did not know what it was. When the wheel struck the first plank he suddenly recognized the sound, and his breast was lightened with relief. He had to suppress the desire to laugh then. Nothing more mysterious than a wheelbarrow! It paused for a moment, and a flashlight was turned on a few yards away. A new and more acute fear filled Fin, but it was too late to move; he lay still.

The flashlight was fastened to the front of the wheelbarrow to show the track, and it passed by Fin without revealing his presence to the man who was behind it. The barrow was loaded with a single big sack standing upright. The man was not the General. After he had gone by Fin made out the odd-shaped cap with the visor against the reflected glow of the flashlight. Nipperg's guard.

The barrow stopped again, and presently Fin heard the thud of earth as the sack was emptied, followed by a scrambling sound as the clods and stones rolled down the steep side of the ravine. Questions loomed big in his puzzled mind. What was the man excavating? And why did he have to wait until after dark here in the seclusion of his own place?

In order to see what became of the man on his way back Fin crept to the point where the planks began at the edge of the trees, and lay down again. Nipperg's man presently returned, pulling the wheelbarrow after him. He could feel his way with his feet now, and the flashlight was turned off. He went off up the hill in the direction of the house.

Fin followed with infinite care. He had it in mind that the General was watching these mysterious operations from some hiding-place, and he did not want to run into him. It was evidently one of the old garden paths he found himself upon, for the way was pretty clear. When he had got within a stone's-throw of the house he heard the wheelbarrow coming with another load, and retreated into the shadow of the trees.

When the man came back uphill, Fin was able to follow him by the sound to a point immediately under the wooden wing. Here he put the wheelbarrow down. This wing stuck out from the main building on the left-hand side as Fin faced it. He detoured still further to the left. Progress was slow, because tonight he meant to make doubly sure that the General had not occupied this point of vantage before him.

However, there was nobody there. He snaked himself through the weeds at the end of the house, and peeped around the corner of the foundation. By this time the man had gone with another load, and he had a long wait. He lay still, trying to extend his senses all around him like feelers, to guard against surprise. From under the house he could hear the faintest sounds of digging. So there was another of them.

The man came back with the wheelbarrow. As he set it down he murmured to his unseen companion, "Are you ready with another?"

The answer came from below, "Half a moment." Whereupon Fin received another great shock of surprise, for he recognized General Diamond's gobbling accents. Impossible to mistake that voice.

So the spade over his shoulder had not been mere camouflage. What does it mean? Fin asked himself in a daze. Was it possible, after all, that had happened that Nipperg and the General were working together? It knocked all their theories of the case into a cocked hat.

Fin heard slight sounds of scrambling and panting, and when the General spoke again, it was evident he had heaved himself out into the open air. "I'm tuckered out," he muttered. "I ain't got the figure for this mole work."

"I'll spell you for a while," whispered the other man.

"Nah," muttered the General, sullenly. "I'll do the digging. . . . Just let me get my breath."

After a silence he said: "You ought to grease that wheel. I heard you coming a long way off."

"It don't make no difference," said the other. "It's Paul's night out, and there's nobody in the house but my old woman and the missus. The missus she never comes to this part of the house in the evening."

"That's all right," growled the General. "I'm not taking any chances. You grease it tomorrow."

After a moment he asked, "Where's Nipperg tonight?"

"Damned if I know," returned the other. "We never know when he's coming until he comes."

"Suppose he comes now?"

"My woman will stamp on the floor over your head," answered Nipperg's man. "It's all right. If he comes all we got to do is lay some boards over the hole, and a pile of leaves. He'll be off early in the morning."

From this it was evident to Fin that the General and Nipperg were not working together. Evidently the General had bribed Nipperg's man to betray his master. This was a more credible explanation, and Fin was relieved. His heart began to beat faster as the real truth of the situation shadowed itself before.

From the sounds that reached him it was evident the General was letting himself down into his hole again. "I have to dig a regular goddam cave," he grumbled, "in order to get through myself. It would be a cinch if I could only pull up the kitchen floor!"

The kitchen floor!

"We couldn't conceal that," said the other man. "You never know when Nipperg will take a fancy to nose around inside."

"Pass down the spade, Mike," said the General from below.

So this was Mike! As in a lightning flash Fin saw the whole truth. This was the house where the mysterious secret was hidden. Or at any rate the General believed that it was. Under the kitchen floor! It was Mr. Mappin's fake message that had started all this digging.

Fin stole away without waiting to hear any more. Let them dig! Let them dig! he thought. Let the General sweat off some of his surplus fat! It was too rich a joke. He felt as if he must laugh or strangle.

After making a wide circuit, he ran down the old garden path, chuckling. He struck into the woods beyond the place where the planks led in, and knowing that the man with the wheelbarrow was far behind him now, let himself slip down the side of the ravine, careless of the stones he displaced. Casting off his boat, he pushed it under the culvert, and applied himself to the oars. His chest was puffed out with triumph. I've got it! rang like a song in his inner, consciousness. After his humiliating failure of the night before it was very sweet.

It was still something short of nine o'clock when he burst into Mr. Mappin's apartment with his story. His friend solemnly polished his glasses while he listened.

"Well, I'll be damned!" he said. "I'll be eternally damned! Nipperg has it in his own house and he can't find it!"

"Well, the General thinks so," said Fin.

"The General must know," said Mr. Mappin. "He wouldn't wage this whole expensive campaign on a guess." He adjusted his glasses. "If I were a proper criminologist," he went on, with a quizzical grin, "I would make out that I knew all the time. But I cannot deceive you Finlay . . . I'll be damned!"

He sent Fin off to bed to make up some of his lost sleep. But presently he came to the door of Fin's room with his spectacles glittering.

"Finlay," he said, solemnly, "this clears up one point that has bothered us from the beginning."

"What's that?" asked Fin, sitting up in bed.

"Why, if Nipperg's confidential man has been in the General's pay all the time, it explains how the General learned so soon about the brass ball."

"Sure!" said Fin . . . "and Nipperg is the murderer!" he added, scowling.

"Looks like it," said Mr. Mappin, mildly. "But you go to sleep now."

CHAPTER EIGHTEEN

IN THE MORNING Mr. Mappin stuck his head inside Fin's door to bid him lie in bed until noon. He had to do a little preliminary spade-work he said, before they made their next move together. So Fin turned over and went back to sleep.

After an early lunch the two of them set out for Riverdale in another taxi. There were no loiterers in the street below, and no other car undertook to follow them. It appeared that Mr. Mappin had been making inquiries among old friends for one who might know something of the history of Riverdale, once the country retreat of wealthy New Yorkers. He had been furnished with an address, and they were on their way to look it up.

Fin was somewhat surprised when they drew up before one of the cheaper apartment houses that line Broadway in Kingsbridge. With its chain stores on the street level, the up-to-the-minute young wives doing their shopping, and the extremely new children roller-skating on the pavements, it did not seem a likely place to obtain information as to bygone days. However, "You never can tell," remarked Mr. Mappin.

The door of the four-room apartment, second floor rear, was opened to them by a little old gentleman somewhat threadbare as to clothes, but with charming manners. An air of having seen bet-ter days lent a grace to his white hairs. This was Mr. Harold New-bold, of whom they were in search. Mr. Mappin understood such a one perfectly.

"Are you in the real-estate business?" he asked.

The old gentleman turned pink with gratification. "Why . . . yes!" he said. "Come in, gentlemen. You must excuse me if I appear a little surprised. I have been somewhat inactive in business lately. May I ask you who gave you my name?"

"An old friend who used to live in Riverdale," said Mr. Mappin. Mr. Newbold led the way into a little parlor, like its owner, well bred and shabby. A fragile old lady bowed and retired.

"When Kingsbridge and Riverdale were still country villages I did a very nice little business in real estate," said Mr. Newbold. "I represented the old families in the neighborhood. . . . But one by one they moved away," he went on, smiling, "and the war finished the real-estate business. When the boom started up afterward it seemed to require a new type of man. And so you see . . ."

"It is the common fate," said Mr. Mappin. "You are fortunate in having preserved your chief treasure." He glanced toward the inner room.

Mr. Newbold was intensely gratified. They bowed to each other. "What can I do for you?" he asked.

"It is very simple," said Mr. Mappin. "I was coming down the Hudson in a friend's yacht a few days ago, and I happened to notice an old neglected estate among the new developments of Riverdale."

"Ah, you mean Slav Castle," said Mr. Newbold. Fin pricked up his ears.

"Slav Castle? How odd!" said Mr. Mappin.

"A popular name that has been applied to the old place," said Mr. Newbold. "Please go on."

"Well, I merely thought there might be an opportunity in developing the place, and I called to inquire if it could be purchased."

"I'm afraid not," said Mr. Newbold. "At any rate, not at a bargain. Others have noticed, like yourself, what an opportunity it presents, and several offers have been made to the owner. So far he has refused to sell."

"Who is the owner?" asked Mr. Mappin.

"A person named Nipperg. Quite a mysterious character. Nobody in Riverdale is acquainted with him. In fact, he is never seen around the place. All those who inquire are received by his wife, who merely says the place is not for sale at present. It is all the more strange because I happen to know it is mortgaged up to the hilt. A heavy burden. One wonders why they should continue to carry it when they seem to get so little out of it. I understand that none of the ladies of Riverdale have ever called on Mrs. Nipperg."

"Nipperg, I presume, is a Slav," suggested Mr. Mappin.

"He may be," returned Mr. Newbold. "I really don't know. The place was called Slav Castle long before he became the owner. It has a very curious history, sir."

This, of course, was the point at which Mr. Mappin had been aiming. "Really!" he said. "You pique my curiosity. Do tell me the story. May I offer you a cigar, sir?"

Mr. Newbold accepted it thankfully, and the two gentlemen lighted up and settled themselves comfortably, one on each side of the radiator. It was clear Mr. Newbold enjoyed nothing better than telling a story.

"It is the old Howland place," he began. "Before the war it was owned by Miss Lavinia Howland, the last of her family, who had refused all temptations to sell. However, like other persons with a small, fixed income, she was cruelly pinched at the outbreak of the war and the result was, she had to offer it for sale at a time when there were no buyers. She made a sale even more difficult by the restrictions she put upon it."

"What were those?" asked Mr. Mappin.

"A buyer was obliged to agree not to subdivide the property for twenty-five years, and not to cut down any trees."

"Ah," said Mr. Mappin, "such amiable eccentricities were commoner formerly."

"I see you understand, sir," said Mr. Newbold, with a look.

"Pray go on, sir."

"In the end a buyer was found who agreed to her restrictions. This was a young foreign gentleman, a Mr. Duborov."

"Ah, Slav," said Mr. Mappin.

"Yes; that was how the place got its name. He was reputed by the neighbors to be a count in his own country, but I do not know that he ever laid claim to such a title. He got the place for a low figure and paid cash for it. In the beginning he was certainly well supplied with money. He put the house in good order, furnished it handsomely, and he and his wife established themselves there with an unusual retinue of servants of their own race."

"It was the many servants, perhaps, who got them the name of being of noble blood," suggested Mr. Mappin.

"Undoubtedly," Mr. Newbold agreed. . . . "They lived entirely to themselves," he went on. "To all who ventured to call they were politely not at home. An exceedingly handsome and aristocratic young couple said to be passionately in love with each other and to have been exiled from their own country by the war, you can imagine the crop of legends that sprang up around them, both romantic and sinister."

"Such as . . ." prompted Mr. Mappin.

Mr. Newbold shrugged. "Well, for one thing," he said, "somebody remembered that in looking at the house Mr. Duborov had paid particular attention to the cellar. It appeared he wanted an old-fashioned cellar without any windows or other openings on the outside. From that, as you can readily imagine, the neighbors had everything buried in that cellar from human bodies to treasures of gold."

"What other stories?" asked Mr. Mappin.

Mr. Newbold shrugged. "Oh, they were called German spies, of course, though they were obviously not German. One hardly listened to such gossip."

"A strange tale!" said Mr. Mappin.

"I have not yet come to the strangest part, sir."

"Do go on."

"It was said that they had been married but a short time," Mr. Newbold resumed, "and while they were living in that house their first child was born to them."

Mr. Mappin's spectacles glistened. "When would that be?"

Fin's heart was already beating fast when the answer came. "About sixteen years ago."

"Of which sex was it?"

Fin knew the answer before it came. "A girl."

"And what did they call her? . . . You see how interested I am."

"The child was christened in the house by a priest or pastor of their own faith," said Mr. Newbold. "Consequently the neighbors learned nothing. Somebody had sufficient curiosity to consult the Bureau of Vital Statistics, and there it was learned that the child had been christened Mariula Duborov. . . ."

Fin sprang out of his chair in uncontrollable excitement. It was the first real clue . . . the first clue! All the blood seemed to rush to his head. Both the elder gentlemen looked at him in astonishment, and he immediately recollected himself. "My—my foot went to sleep," he stammered, blushing.

"Walk around and stamp on it," said Mr. Newbold, kindly.

"Do continue, sir," said Mr. Mappin.

"Now comes the tragic part," said Mr. Newbold. "The young father and mother disappeared."

"Disappeared!" echoed Mr. Mappin.

"Oh, I do not mean that they were made away with!" Mr. Newbold hastened to add. "Presumably they left of their own free will, leaving the infant in the care of the nurse and other servants. Indeed, a story was circulated later to the effect that they had been seen driving away in a car with sad and tearful faces. However that may be, they never came back again. The household was so well screened from observation, you see, that nobody knew just when they had gone. It was just realized by degrees that they were no longer there."

"How strange!" murmured Mr. Mappin. "What happened next?"

"For a month or two all went on as before. The servants seemed to have plenty of money to carry on with. Then it was noticed that the establishment was being cut down. The servants seemed to drift away one by one. By-and-by it began to be rumored that the nurse was living there alone with the infant. She was said to have been seen weeping in a heartbroken fashion while she trundled it up and down the veranda."

"How did she get food?" interrupted Mr. Mappin.

"Oh, the tradespeople called as usual. But their orders had fallen away to almost nothing. That was how they kept tab on the household. About this time the young woman was seen taking the child into the Subway, and it was reported she was supporting herself by carrying small objects downtown to the pawnshops. She could speak very little English."

Once more Fin's feelings got the better of him. "My God! What a frightful situation for her!" he cried.

"Your young friend has a tender, heart," said old Mr. Newbold, beaming at him kindly.

"Quite," said Mr. Mappin dryly. . . . "How did it all turn out?"

"Oh, quite a pretty ending," said Mr. Newbold, innocently. "It seems the young woman picked up a follower, a beau of her own race, a superior sort of young workman. He married her and came to live in the house with her and the baby. Nobody knew, of course, where or how they had met."

"If unhappy innocence could always find a champion!" murmured Mr. Mappin.

"Yes, yes," said Mr. Newbold.

"Do you remember this man's name?" asked Mr. Mappin.

"Petrovich or Petrovsky or some such name," said Mr. Newbold. "A Slav name that suggested Peter."

"And then what happened?" asked Mr. Mappin.

"For a while they got along all right. A circumstance of this time that I recall was reported by a doctor who was called in to attend the baby for some minor ailment. He said she had a heart-shaped emerald hanging around her neck that was worth a fortune. That was one object that had escaped the pawnshop."

"So?" said Mr. Mappin. "And then?"

"It began to be reported around that the couple had been threatened by ruffians of their own race," said Mr. Newbold. "I don't know if there was anything in it or not. They lodged no complaint with the authorities. However it may be, one day they were found to be gone and the house shut up, and they've never been seen since. Not any of them."

"Strange! . . . Strange!" murmured Mr. Mappin. "Was no investigation ever made?"

"It was to nobody's interest to make an investigation. Mr. and Mrs. Duborov had no friends. On the other hand, they left no debts behind them. People just wondered and talked, and after a while they forgot about it. But when the house was broken into, the Riverdale Association took action."

"So the house was broken into," said Mr. Mappin.

"Yes, it was discovered that tramps from the railway had forced an entrance into the empty house and had partly wrecked it."

"How did they know it was tramps?" asked Mr. Mappin, mildly.

Mr. Newbold spread out his hands. "Who else would break things up out of sheer vandalism?"

"What did the Riverdale Association do?"

"They advertised for the owners, but without result. They then engaged a respectable couple to live in the house rent free, and protect it."

"I see," said Mr. Mappin. "Where does Nipperg come into the story?"

"Oh, he first turned up while the caretakers were in the house," said Mr. Newbold, "and offered to rent it from the Association. But they couldn't take rent for something that was not theirs, of course. You see, it was a peculiar situation. Moreover, I understand that this Nipperg made an unpleasant impression. He wasn't considered a desirable addition to the community, and they declined his offer."

"But he got the house eventually?"

"Yes. When it was sold for taxes a couple of years later he bought it in. He paid a good price, too, though he didn't start living there until he married some years later. Everything about the place is cloaked in mystery! It is Riverdale's House of Mystery!"

Mr. Mappin joined with Mr. Newbold in sympathetic exclamations of wonderment and mystification. The old gentleman had no suspicion that his caller had any concern in the matter beyond that of any listener to a strange tale.

When the subject appeared to be exhausted Mr. Mappin said: "Mr. Newbold, I want you to keep an eye on that property for me. But do not let it be known that you have a client who is interested."

"You may depend on me, sir," said the gratified old gentleman.

Mr. Mappin took out his pocketbook and abstracted several of the crisp bills of high denomination that always seemed to be on tap. He offered them to Mr. Newbold. "Pray accept this as your retainer, sir."

The old gentleman turned pink to the crown of his head. "My dear sir! My dear sir!" he protested. "Nothing that I can do for you is worth such a sum as this!"

"Take it! Take it!" said Mr. Mappin, adding, quite truthfully, "I assure you I have often paid more for services of less value to me."

"You overwhelm me, sir," murmured Mr. Newbold, in a flutter of pleasurable excitement. One could see in his eye the joy with which he anticipated showing this windfall to the old lady in the next room. "Please give me your name and address."

"No," said Mr. Mappin. "I don't want my name to appear in it. You just keep your eye on the situation, and I will communicate with you from time to time."

"You can depend upon me, sir. . . . You can depend on me," stammered the old gentleman.

They finally succeeded in bowing themselves out. On the stairs Mr. Mappin grumbled, half ashamed of his own emotion: "Hm! Ha! One of the rare occasions when one can do a little good with the filthy stuff!"

In silence they lined up on the curb to wait for a taxi. Mr. Mappin looked at Fin, and Fin looked at Mr. Mappin. They understood each other. The older man glanced at his watch. "It is almost time for you to meet your lady friend."

"I'll walk up the hill," said Fin.

"I won't attempt to advise you how to deal with her," Mr. Mappin went on, with an embarrassed smile; "I expect that your experience in that direction is greater than mine. *And you know what we have to do next!*"

Fin nodded with compressed lips.

"Take your time!" Mr. Mappin said, earnestly. "Consider every step before you take it! Remember the secret is still in our possession. If it has eluded them all these years, it is not likely they will stumble on it within the next day or two."

"I get you," said Fin.

A taxi drew up at the curb, and their hands instinctively shot out toward each other and gripped. It was the only expression of feeling they permitted themselves. Mr. Mappin drove away.

CHAPTER NINETEEN

SHE CAME SAUNTERING UP to the bench with an elaborate affectation of indifference. "Oh, you're here!" she said, almost insultingly. Yet it was clear that she had gotten herself up with particular care to please.

Fin was used to such tricks. "Sure! What did you expect?" he asked, grinning.

The grin displeased her. "I can't stay out to-day," she said, stiffly.

"Well, sit down while you're here," he said, moving over to make room.

"It's too near the house. Somebody might see."

"Then let's go some place else."

A demon of perversity seemed to possess her. "That would be worse," she said, scornfully. "Walking through the streets with you! It would start all the old cats in town whispering."

"Well, you don't know them," said Fin, thoughtlessly.

"Why shouldn't I know them?" she demanded.

"I mean," he said, correcting himself, "what do you care about the old cats? Whatever you did or didn't do, they would have it in for a good-looking girl like you."

She lowered her lashes and a slow color crept under her rouge. Fin guessed that, though she was a pretty woman, she had not had much admiration from men, and it was balm to her soul.

"Where can we go?" he said, standing up.

She said, "Let's stay here," and sat down.

Fin never reminded a woman of her inconsistency. He sat down, too. He felt a little sorry for her, her tactics were so poor. That's not the way to get a fellow going, sister, he wanted to tell her; but he knew it only made matters worse to try to be honest with such a one, so he laid himself out to play the cheerful fool.

"I dreamed about you last night, kid."

"Yes, you did!" she said, scornfully.

"Yeah, on the level. Seems I was down by the railway yonder, and a freight train come along and there was you sitting on a flat car all dressed up like the Queen of the May, with straw sticking in your hair."

"Straw in my hair!"

"Yeah. You know, coocoo, sort of. Maybe it's Ophelia I'm thinking of. Anyhow, you looked swell. You were holding a cat-tail in your hand for a what's-this, you know, what queens always hold."

"A scepter?"

"Yeah, a scepter. So I swung on by the handrail and they made me king because I could play the jew's-harp. Seems they wanted music for dancing. But the gang all got splinters in their feet from the car floor, and had to walk home on their hands. You and me flew back to the castle in a tri-motored plane."

Daisy was melting fast. "Crazy!" she said, with a sidelong look.

"Sure!" said Fin. "It runs in all the old families." He concluded with an obligato on an imaginary jew's-harp.

There was method in his idiocy. He turned it off and on as the occasion seemed to demand. Daisy still affected to scorn him, but it carried no conviction. On the contrary, a helpless look had come into her eyes that suggested he had laid a spell upon her. Fin recognized the symptoms. It won't do her any harm if I play fair, he told himself.

"Brr! It's cold!" he said, after a while. "We won't be able to meet out-of-doors much longer."

"Who said we were?" said Daisy, bridling.

"I bet it's cold in that old house of yours in the winter," said Fin.

"What do you know about that house?" she asked, suspiciously.

"Only what you told me."

"Well, it is cold," she said, spitefully, "and I'm fed up with it."

"How do they heat the dump?" asked Fin, in his scatterbrained style.

"Hot air."

"Pretty good," he said, laughing.

"No, I mean it," she said. "There's an old-fashioned hot-air furnace, and it's out of order. It sends coal gas through the house."

"Why don't Nipperg have it fixed?"

"He won't let anybody go into the cellar."

"What!" said Fin.

"I mean," she said, hastily, "he's too close to spend the money."

"Haven't you got any stoves to help out?" he asked.

"Only the kitchen stove, and that don't do the rest of the house any good."

Fin thought. Nothing valuable would have been hidden in the kitchen, because that part of the house is built of wood. Aloud he asked, idly, "Any fireplaces?"

"All the rooms have fireplaces," said Daisy, "but my husband don't like to burn the wood."

Dazbog's House must refer to the furnace, thought Fin. "Have you ever looked at the furnace?" he asked.

"No," said Daisy.

"Aren't you allowed to go in the cellar?" he asked, slyly.

No answer.

"Gosh!" said Fin. "What do you suppose he's got hid down there?"

"Nothing at all," she said scornfully, "it's just his crazy way."

"I bet I could fix it," he said. "I know furnaces."

She laughed. "Do you think you'd ever be let in the front door, not to speak of down cellar?"

"I'll charm them, honey," he said, grinning.

"Yeah!" she said with a painfully curling lip. "What is charm to a lot of Hunkies?"

"I'll show you," he said, boldly. "I'll call tomorrow aft."

"Don't you do it!" she said, instantly becoming panicky. "Don't you dare to do it! If you was ever to come there I'd deny you to your face! You don't know . . . you don't know . . ."

"Don't know what?"

She lowered her head. "Well, never mind," she said, sullenly. "Don't fool with things you don't know about, that's all."

"Aw, Daisy," he said, cajolingly, "I gotta come. We can't go on just meeting on this bench."

That helpless glance fluttered to her face. "I told you there were three servants to spy on me," the sullen voice said; "two men and a woman. How can you get around that?"

"I'll put something over on them," said Fin. "That's my specialty, putting things over."

"All the putting over in the world can't get around the fact that I'm Nipperg's property," she said, bitterly.

"Just wait and see," said Fin. "You should introduce me as your relation. Have you got a brother?"

"Yes," she muttered. "He'd be about your age. But I haven't seen him in ten years. I don't know where he is."

"So much the better. Does Nipperg know you have a brother?"

"Yes."

"Has he ever seen him?"

"No."

"Good! Then it's all set! Nipperg could hardly do less than ask me to stop awhile!" Fin of course, had no intention of letting Nipperg see him. All the testimony was to the effect that Nipperg never showed himself around Riverdale by day.

"It's too dangerous," whimpered Daisy; "I couldn't get away with it."

"You don't have to," said Fin. "That's my job."

"How would you explain how you found me?"

"Easy. Where were you living when Nipperg married you?"

"In a boardinghouse on East Seventeenth Street."

"That's all I need. . . . What's your brother's name?"

"Bill Zell."

Fin thought, Mustn't get my aliases mixed.

When darkness began to gather they were still sitting there, heads close together, careless of the cold. Fin had not realized the fatal power of sympathy from one of the opposite sex, consequently he was a little appalled suddenly to discover how far they had got. After he had been listening to the tale of Nipperg's neglect for an hour he said:

"How did you come to fall for this bird in the beginning?"

"I was down on my luck," she muttered; "ready to jump at any chance."

"Yeah," said Fin, "I reckon many a girl gets caught that way. Why don't you leave him now?"

"Got no place to go. He made me drop all my friends when I married him."

"He certainly is a lulu!"

"And I got no money," she went on. "He never gives me any."

"Gee! that's tough!"

"I'm afraid of him," she murmured. "He would kill me if he knew. And those Hunkies would help him do it. They have always hated me."

"He's only trying to terrorize you," said Fin. "It's a jealous husband's regular line."

She shook her head. "You don't know him, it's in his eye—you can't mistake it—the killing look."

Fin knew that this was only too true. It brought danger near. He drew a long breath to steady himself. "You'll have to get some other fellow to help you out," he said, lightly.

The look of breathless eagerness she gave him made him long to take to his heels. He had had to fly from that look before. "Would . . . would you?" she murmured.

He faced it out. "Sure!" he said, boldly.

"Young fellows never have any money," she said, in tones of scorn, while her eyes wistfully searched his face to see if he was in earnest.

"I'm no exception," said Fin, "but I have a friend who has plenty."

"Would he help you out?"

"Sure! To any extent."

"He must be a friend!" she murmured, incredulously.

"One of the best!"

She lowered her eyes. "Do you . . . do you really care?" she whispered.

This was like a cold shower upon Fin. He knew he could not keep up the part of the rapturous lover unless his heart was in it, and after a moment's hesitation he resolved to tell the truth. "Sure I'm crazy about you," he said. "But if you mean the real knock-down-and-drag-out kind of love, why, no! I wouldn't lie to you."

She moved a little away from him. "Then what did you want to make up to me for?" she demanded, breathing fast. "Why are you hanging around me?"

"Aw," said Fin, "every time you cross eyes with a pretty girl, does it have to be for life? We're not living in the dark ages any more!"

"You'd better go away from me," she muttered.

However, he perceived in her stormy glances that he had not lost any ground. On the contrary, a repulse had caused her to incline even more strongly toward him. Such is human nature.

"Sure, if you mean that," said Fin, threatening to go.

"I didn't mean it," she murmured, unhappily.

He sat down again. He was sorry for her, but he couldn't let that stop him. She was only a pawn in the game. And, anyhow, he thought, she'll be amply repaid later for any slight hurt she takes.

"How did we get to be so serious?" Fin rattled. "It's all wrong! All wrong! . . . Listen, did you ever hear the story of the little Welshman who was married to a woman three times his size? One day she took after him with the rolling-pin and he crawled under the bed, which was the only place he knew where she couldn't follow. She stood beside the bed, shaking the rolling-pin and yelling: 'Come out of that! Come out of that and I'll learn ye!' But Davy he pounded his fist on the floor and he yelled out: 'No, by Cot! I will be master in my own house! I will not come out!'

"Huh!" said Daisy, bridling elegantly. "You don't hate yourself, do you?"

Fin whooped with laughter. That was a corner turned on two wheels.

"I don't see anything so funny," said Daisy.

"You must excuse me, honey," said Fin, wiping his eyes. "I just got to laugh. It's a nervous affection, as the circus man said every time he stuck his head in the lion's mouth."

"Oh, you!"

CHAPTER TWENTY

FIN SPENT PART OF THE FOLLOWING MORNING in laying in an outfit for the part of Bill Zell. In his mind's eye he saw Bill as a breezy young sport who had had a bit of luck lately, and to carry this out he bought a plum-colored suit with a fine green stripe, a green ensemble comprising shirt, tie, handkerchief, and socks, and a purplish Fedora described by the salesman as "our dregs-of-wine model." For a finishing touch he had a pair of freckled pigskin gloves turned down over the hands. The whole effect was exceedingly sprightly.

All this preparation was perhaps unnecessary, but it helped to work Fin up to the point of what was, when he stopped to think of it, the hardest thing he had ever had to do in his life—*viz.*, to march up to Nipperg's door and ring the bell. He well knew with what joy Nipperg would blow him to pieces if he caught him inside. Fin was going armed, to be sure, but what was one gun against three or four?

It was about three o'clock when he turned in at the formal gateway, whistling and swinging his arms. As soon as he started down the winding driveway the trees closed in behind him, giving him the feeling that he had lost touch with all his kind. The driveway was neatly kept, but the trees pressing up close on either hand and arching overhead were choked with a dense wild growth of creepers and briers, almost like a green wall. Awkward if I had to make a dash through that, thought Fin.

When the sharp-gabled house opened up before him he was almost suffocated by the beating of his own heart. Such a strange

168

old house, so secret and shabby, standing there enveloped in its own atmosphere like something separated by a half a century from our life. In that house Mariula had first seen the light; in that house her parents had mysteriously deserted her; under that house lay the terrifying secret of her identity.

It stood in the middle of a narrow lawn with the dense growth pressing up close all around except at the back where the neglected gardens went down. On the left-hand side there was a veranda disappearing behind: on the right was the wooden wing partly screened from this side by a tall growth of ragged shrubs. There was no sign of life about the place. Fin made haste to press the bell before his courage failed him altogether.

The door was opened by a woman short and squat as a worker in the fields. She had a dull, heavy face of the Slav type. "What do you want?" she demanded of Fin, scowling. She spoke good English.

Fin grinned in vacant good nature, according to the character he had assumed "Mrs. Nipperg live here?" he asked, briskly.

"What do you want of her?" grumbled the woman. "She don't see no canvassers."

Fin laughed and slapped his thigh. "Canvasser! That's good! That's good! Why, I'm her brother! You just tell her it's Bill Zell and see what she has to say."

The woman looked him up and down with insolent deliberation and closed the door in his face. This was disconcerting. Suppose she never came back, what a fool he would look! . . . What a crazy scheme this was anyhow, he thought, with a sinking heart. He shook the thought away. He whistled between his teeth, and taking out a cigarette tapped it on the back of his hand and lit it with an air. After all, it was a great help to be Bill Zell and not himself.

While he waited on the step a man appeared to the left and stood some twenty paces away, staring at him with dull animosity. Fin recognized the visored cap and stiffened himself. So this was Mike. It was possible he was the man who had hit him over the head in the railway yard, but even so he could scarcely have had a good look at him in the dark. Fin faced him out, grinning. He had the stupid little eye of a bear. Fin was thankful to see no sign of recognition there. After a prolonged stare Mike disappeared the way he had come. Pleasant household, thought Fin.

Soon the door opened beside him. "You can come in," the woman muttered, sullenly.

Fin's heart leaped up. He threw away the cigarette. The house was more spacious inside than one might have expected. He entered a wide dim hall that ran through to the other front. It was paneled and ceiled throughout with a dusty blackish wood so fantastically carved and molded there was not a square foot without its ridges and bumps. Gothic gone mad. At the back rose an elaborate heavy stairway lighted on the landing by a mullioned window filled with little panes of purple and green glass that cast a nightmare glow on the scene. It smelled cold and stuffy. There was no furniture except a single carved black chest like a funeral casket.

The Slav woman moved through the dimness without a sound. Fin saw that she was wearing felt slippers. She stood by an open door and jerked her head inside. "In there," she said.

It was a dining-room, stark and foreign-looking, very little furniture. In here there was plenty of light from a pair of French windows opening on the front drive, light which showed up every stain on the sad-colored walls. It was one of the rooms Mariula had described.

Daisy was standing by the table, pale and shaking with agitation. She looked tawdry in the bare room. Fin's thought was, If she wasn't such a light piece of goods she'd have gone off her nut long ago in this dump. His breast tightened with apprehension. Was she going to let him down? He glanced at the nearest window. I could burst out there if they turned on me, he thought. The servant stood watching them from the door with hardy insolence.

"Hello, sis!" cried Fin, heartily.

She came running to him with little steps, and caught him by the elbows. Tears of pure nervousness were running down her cheeks. "Oh, Bill! . . . Oh, Bill!" she stammered.

Fin gave her a brotherly kiss. "Gee! it's great to see you!" he cried. "You're not changed any. What you crying for?"

"Oh, I'm so glad to . . . it's so long . . ." she murmured.

He relaxed a little. After all, it was not such bad acting. She put her tears to good use. "You never wrote," he said.

"I didn't know where . . ."

"I know," said Fin. "All my fault. I was down on my luck, and I hated to let anybody know it."

The Slav woman passed noiselessly through the room, and out by a door near the other end, leaving it slightly ajar. She was listening, of course. Daisy did not miss it, for she said in a voice meant to carry:

"How did you ever find me, Bill?"

"Oh, that was no trouble when I set out to do it," said Fin. "I went to that boarding-house where you used to live on Seventeenth Street, and the woman told me you had married and moved up to Riverdale. So I come up here and asked around at the stores, and somebody soon told me." Meanwhile he moved to the pantry door and coolly closed it.

"Oh, don't do that!" whispered Daisy, trembling. "She'll only tell him when he comes."

"Sure," said Fin. "That's why I did it. It's a natural thing to do. If we let them spy on us without saying anything, they would suspect we were playing a game."

"You got to get out of here!" she said, a little wildly. "I can't stand it. If you don't go I'll tell them!"

Fin was not alarmed by this threat. It was too late to tell them now. He had perceived before this that Daisy was the sort of woman who cannot resist a man's dominance. He had mastered her now, just as Nipperg had mastered her years before, and she would have to do what he told her.

"Come, pull yourself together!" he said, peremptorily.

She obeyed, though she still complained. "What good is it?" she whimpered. "They'll never leave us alone for a minute!"

"Watch me bluff 'em, kid," said Fin, airily. "I ain't got in my stride yet."

"You can't do anything against a man like Nipperg. He ain't human. . . . I'll suffer for this when he comes."

"Well, if it gets too bad I'll help you get away from here," said Fin, coolly. "That's understood."

His eye was on the pantry door. It opened a crack and he went on in Bill Zell's hearty voice without a pause, "You're pretty well fixed here, eh, sis?"

She instantly fell in with his changed tone. "We haven't got much furniture," she said. "He don't buy any because we're going to sell here soon."

Fin took a package of chewing-gum from his pocket. Gum was naturally a part of Bill Zell's equipment. To chew a good wad of it helped to produce the slatternly style of speech he affected. "Have some?" he said to Daisy.

Daisy chewed also.

"But at that," Fin went on, still for the benefit of the ear at the pantry door, "there ain't many folks in New York City has a whole house to themselves. I bet the place is worth a pot of money. Let's take a look around, sis."

Daisy protested with mute, terrified eyes, but Fin had no mercy on her. It was necessary for him to get the lay-out of that house. "Come on, let's take a look around," he said.

She followed him apathetically out into the hall. "What's the good of it?" she muttered.

"It's a natural thing to do," returned Fin. "I got to make them think I feel at home here, ain't I?"

On the other side of the hall was a suite of two drawing-rooms with bay windows opening on the encircling veranda. Strange, oppressive rooms filled with rich old-fashioned furnishings slowly falling to pieces as a result of dampness and neglect. The wood veneer was peeling off the handsome cabinets, the draperies were rotting where they hung; rats had gnawed great holes in the upholstered chairs. Apparently the windows had not been opened in years; the smoke from thousands of railway engines had deposited a sulphurous film on the panes.

"All this stuff came with the house," remarked Daisy, indifferently. "I never come in here."

Mariula's family possessions! Fin thought, looking around him with extraordinary interest. Suddenly he bethought himself that he must not neglect to play the part of Ronald Shay for Daisy's benefit.

"Gee! what a dump!" he murmured, sympathetically.

Tears of self-pity came into her eyes.

When they returned to the hall they found the Slav woman hanging about, making an absurd pretense of dusting while she watched and listened. Dusting was obviously not in her line. "Let's take a look upstairs," said Fin.

Near the foot of the stairs they passed a door on the same side as the dining-room. "What's in here?" he asked.

"His study," said Daisy. "It's locked."

May be valuable evidence in there, thought Fin. Must get in.

The woman followed them upstairs and disappeared through a door on the right. "That's her room," murmured Daisy.

She showed him into the room over the dining-room, a cheerless, sordid chamber without curtains or pictures, and having two tall old-fashioned beds with torn canopies. It had two windows looking out on the drive, and Fin guessed that this was the room where Mariula had spent the night. There was a third window at the end which looked out on the eaves of the kitchen wing. The peak of the roof concealed all view of the river. Below the window the roof was carried out over a porch which no doubt protected the kitchen door. Possible way to get out in a hurry, Fin's subconsciousness registered.

They looked into other bedrooms, some meagerly furnished, some completely bare, and returned downstairs again. The Slav woman was hanging about in the lower hall.

"What's your name, sister?" he asked, flippantly.

"Nastya," she muttered.

Fin winked at Daisy, as much as to say, Well named!

"Bet there's an elegant view from the back of the house," he suggested.

Daisy nodded indifferently.

"Let's take a look outside."

She fetched a coat to put around her shoulders, and they went through the front door.

After the ugly spell that rested on that house the blue sky was like a benediction. Fin breathed deep to clear his lungs of the poisoned air.

"Don't see how you can stand it," he said to Daisy.

She shrugged helplessly.

They strolled around the veranda. Fin's object was to discover if there was any opening into the cellar from the outside. They had not gone far before they ran into Mike on his knees, clipping the edge of the grass with a big pair of shears—a hollow pretense like his wife's dusting indoors.

"What's the gardener's name?" Fin asked Daisy, audibly.

"Mike," she murmured.

Fin walked up to him. "H'are ya, Mike!" he said in Bill's loud, hail-fellow style. "I'm Daisy's brother. Reckon we'll be seeing each other often now."

The man muttered unintelligibly and bent lower over his shears. Fin laughed and returned to Daisy. "Quite a crab, ain't he?" he said, loud enough to carry. "But at that I bluffed him," he added, *sotto voce.*

Daisy glanced at him, biting her lip, both terrified and admiring.

Having stopped to admire the view up and down the wide river—it bucked Fin up to see normal human fellows like himself paddling canoes and driving speed-boats—they stepped off the veranda and continued around the house. Fin saw that the lower floor was built almost flush with the ground, consequently there could be no cellar windows. He remembered this had been given as one of the reasons why the Slav nobleman had bought the house.

However, there was one opening which perhaps led into the cellar. It was a rectangular hole about one foot by two at the base of the main block of the house, near the point where the kitchen wing jutted out. The hole was filled with a stout galvanized wire mesh. Fin could not guess what its purpose might be, and he dared not ask for fear of arousing suspicion. Mike was close behind them.

Only a few steps farther along was the spot where Fin had found the two men excavating under the kitchen. The place was now so cunningly hidden under leaves and gravel no one could have guessed it was there. To the north of the kitchen wing was the old stable. The doors were open and Fin could see the black sedan that had once figured so prominently in the news. It bore an ordinary New York license now. The sound of their voices brought a man to the door, another Slav, younger and better-looking than Mike, but with an evil cast in his eye.

"That's the other one," murmured Daisy. "His name is Paul."

Having rounded the wing and passed the kitchen porch, Fin discovered another oblong opening in the base of the main house which presumably led into the cellar. Coal dust on the ground in front of it revealed the purpose to which this hole was put. It was closed with a heavy iron door which discouraged any chance of getting in that way. I've got to find the cellar stairs inside, Fin told himself.

Back in the dining-room with Daisy, he affected to shiver. "Gosh! it's cold in here!" He glanced at the fireplace. "Is there any wood to make a fire?"

"Please, no," murmured Daisy, imploringly. "Please go now."

Fin ignored her plea. "I'll fetch it," he said, moving toward the pantry door.

Daisy gasped at his temerity. "Let Mike . . . let Mike! . . ." she stammered in terror.

"Oh, I don't mind," said Fin, affecting a loud cheerfulness. Privately he winked at Daisy. "Just watch me," he whispered. "It's wonderful what a little gall will do."

Daisy was too terrified to follow him. She remained in the dining-room.

As he entered the pantry he was just in time to see the whisk of the Slav woman's skirt through the kitchen door. He followed. The kitchen was a squalid room with a heap of unwashed dishes in the sink, and old clothes flung over the chairs. There were two other doors in the same wall with the pantry, and one of them, Fin knew, must lead to the cellar stairs. Mike was in the room. He and his wife glowered at Fin, breathing hard, and it was clear they longed to leap on him like animals and bear him down; but Fin's very boldness confused them.

"It's cold in the dining-room," he said, with his loud vacant laugh. "Show me where the wood is and I'll make a fire."

The man and the woman hesitated and glanced at each other. Fin saw he had them guessing. Probably he was the first who had ever dared to storm Nipperg's castle, and they were uncertain how to act. They were thinking that if it was true he was Daisy's brother, Nipperg might order them to propitiate him.

Finally the man bestirred himself. "I'll fetch wood," he growled. Taking a heavy, old-fashioned key from his pocket, he moved toward the middle one of the three doors.

"I'll help you," said Fin, cheerfully.

"Stay here," growled Mike, with a black scowl over his shoulder.

Fin obeyed, not wishing to push the matter too far all at once. He moved toward the stove, thrusting his hands in his pockets and whistling between his teeth. "Nice and warm out here," he said offhand. The woman scowled at the floor.

Mike opened the door and clumped down the stairs beyond. Fin's eyes followed him desirously. How he wanted to have a look at that cellar! The key was in the door. How could one get possession of it long enough to have a duplicate made? With a duplicate key he could await his own opportunity for entering. Modeling-wax was what you needed to take an impression. An idea leaped into Fin's brain. Wax? Why not chewing-gum, then? His mouth was full of it!

His next acts were purely instinctive. He started violently, and turned a scared face towards the pantry door. "Who's that?" he murmured. It worked. The woman glided like a snake into the pantry and on into the dining room. With one hand Fin took the gum out of his mouth and flattened it against the door frame; he had the key ready in the other. After pressing it into the gum, he returned it softly to the door, and carefully peeled off the gum with its pre-cious imprint. All this was a matter of three or four seconds. As Fin turned his back on the door Mike started to mount the stairs.

There was a small box of matches on the table. It was not full. Fin slipped the gum in on top of the matches and dropped the box in his pocket. When Mike came through the door Fin was lighting a cigarette. The woman entered from the pantry at the same mo-ment, and gave Fin a furious glance of suspicion. But Fin's face was as bland as a baby's.

Nothing was said. Mike locked the cellar door and put the key back in his pocket. He carried the wood into the dining-room, Fin following, and dropping it on the hearth, retired. Fin knelt down to make a fire, thankful for the diversion that permitted his fast-beating heart to quiet down. It had been a breathless moment. Daisy was gazing at him in a kind of scared wonder. Clearly she thought he was a superman, and at the moment Fin was rather inclined to agree with her.

He wanted to leave then, since he had got all he could hope to get that day. But having ordered the fire, he felt obliged to stay on for a while and make believe to enjoy it. They pulled up two of the uncomfortable dining-chairs and sat down upon them. The pantry door had been left open a crack.

They might hear in the pantry, but they could not see because the door opened the wrong way; and it was clear from Daisy's self-conscious manner that she considered Fin might now evince a little ardor to make up for all he had made her suffer. He pretended to be oblivious, and began to tell her the imaginary adventures of Bill Zell since he had lost touch with his sister. Fin got more fun out of the story than his listener.

"... After that I enlisted in the navy. That's the life for a young feller. You don't have to worry about being laid off. A man can let down for a while in the navy and enjoy hisself without worrying about the future. It's a grand bunch in the navy, too. Them fellers ain't on the make, get me? and all being in the same boat and all, they're friendly, as you might say; they stand by each other. As for the girls, boy! There's nothing like it! It's always a case of sail away in a few days, so neither has any strings on the other. It's wonderful how a girl will let herself go with a sailor! . . ."

When he felt that he could do so without arousing suspicion in the pantry, Fin got up to go. Out in the hall there was a moment or two when they were free from observation, and Daisy partly broke down.

"Take me with you," she begged, clinging to Fin. "If Nipperg comes home tonight I haven't the nerve to face him!"

"Steady, kid!" said Fin. "I haven't made any arrangements yet. Just give me a day or two!"

"But Mike will tell him a story that will drive him wild! I can't face it!"

"Listen, kid. You're foolish to let Mike get away with anything like that. I'll give you something on Mike that will make him eat out of your hand!"

She looked her startled question.

"Listen," Fin went on. "As soon as I'm gone you have a talk with Mike. See? Start friendly. Tell him you lead a dog's life here, and if he said anything to Nipperg that would stop my coming any more it would be just too bad. See?"

"What does Mike care?" she muttered.

"Wait a minute! . . . When he turns ugly you just mention casually that if he makes any trouble for you, you'll have to tell Nipperg about the big fellow that comes to see *him* every night just after dark."

"What!" gasped Daisy.

"Tell Mike you don't want him to lie about me," Fin went on. "He'll have to tell Nipperg I was here, because Paul saw me. But let him tell it in such a way it won't make trouble. He can say that I looked like you. See?"

"But Nipperg will see for himself . . ."

"Bless your heart, kiddo, I'm not going to let Nipperg see me. I'll call afternoons. . . . Now get this straight: A great big man who came with a spade over his shoulder. You can say you were standing out on the veranda night before last and you saw him come up from the direction of the railway tracks. And last night you heard his voice behind the kitchen. A kind of a gobbling voice."

"But who is it?" faltered Daisy. "And what do you know about it?"

Fin reflected that Daisy was committed too far to let him down now. So he coolly refused to answer her questions. "Can't tell you now, kid. Just wait till I get you out of this dump. You try this on with Mike, and it will work like a charm. I'm not supposed to know anything about it. See?"

"But . . . but . . ." stammered Daisy.

Fin asked for the private telephone number. She gave it to him in a daze.

"I'll call you up at three tomorrow," said Fin. "Stick around where you can hear the bell. . . . So long, kid!"

CHAPTER TWENTY-ONE

AT THE APPOINTED HOUR NEXT DAY Fin called up Nipperg's house from a pay station in Riverdale. In his various pockets he had a false key for the cellar door; also a short-handled hammer, a couple of cold chisels, and a flashlight. He had no settled plan in his mind, but trusted to luck to provide him with an opportunity to use his tools.

Mr. Mappin had said that the mysterious hole into the cellar covered with a wire mesh was undoubtedly the air inlet to the furnace. All old-fashioned hot-air furnaces had one, he said, and they were always placed on the west or north side of the house where the cold winter winds came from. This one faced north. But when Fin suggested it might make a good way of entering the cellar, Mr. Mappin had shaken his head.

"You could easily cut out the wire mesh with a proper tool," he said, "but inside you'd find yourself in a big galvanized pipe leading to the base of the furnace. You couldn't cut or break out of that without raising a racket that would arouse the whole house."

So Fin had determined to concentrate on the cellar stairs.

Daisy's frightened voice came over the wire.

"Hello!" cried Fin. "How's every li'l' thing today?"

"All right," she faltered.

"Was Nipperg home last night?"

"Yes."

"Had you told Mike what I said to tell him?"

"Yes."

"Did it work all right?"

"Yes."

"Did Nipperg cut up rough over my call yesterday?"

"Not so much," she said, hesitatingly. Fin guessed that the Slav woman was within hearing of the phone.

"Well, did he leave this morning at the usual time?"

"Yes."

"He isn't there now?"

"No.

"All right. Then I'll fluff down to see you."

"Oh! . . ." breathed Daisy in a voice that expressed both terror and longing.

Fin had no intention of entering into an argument on the subject, so he hung up.

Five minutes later he was ringing the bell.

As soon as the door opened he perceived that there was a great change in the atmosphere today. Nastya was trying to smile at him in a friendly fashion. Her sullen features found a good deal of difficulty in accommodating themselves to it. "Good day," she said. "Come in."

"Hello, Nastya!" he cried, in Bill Zell's breezy style. "Howsa girl! Buttered side up to-day, eh? It suits you!" In the dining-room there was actually a good fire burning. "Hello, sis!" he cried. "Gee! that's a swell rig you got on! Ain't it nice to have a family to visit."

Daisy smiled bleakly.

Nastya passed through the dining-room into the pantry and closed the door behind her. This was just a little too good to be true, and Fin's instincts took alarm. He felt he ought to have a look at what these people were doing in the kitchen, and he coolly opened the door and followed Nastya. She was saying something to Mike in their own tongue. Both faces were convulsed with rage and fear. Mike made an attempt to smooth his features out and to grin. "Good day! Good day!" he said, nodding his head rapidly. But his little pig eyes were sharp with hatred.

"I just wanted to give you a cigar I brought," said Fin, producing it. "Here, smoke up!"

Mike accepted it, nodding and grinning.

On his way back through the pantry Fin thought: I've thrown a scare into them, all right. But there's nothing so dangerous as a thoroughly scared man. Watch out for a bullet in the back!

Daisy was less frightened than on the day before, but her brows were stormy, and Fin needed no perspicacity to see that he had a difficult interview before him. However, he was confident of his ability to handle Daisy. He closed the pantry door behind him and also the door into the hall on the pretext of keeping the heat in the room. Thus they were safe from spies for the moment.

"Nipperg seemed to take it all right?" he said.

"So-so," she, said sulkily. "Mike didn't make any trouble, but Nipperg was suspicious, anyhow. He would be. . . . He said if you came again today to ask you to stay to dinner," she added, with a sour smile. "So he could meet you."

"That was brotherly," said Fin, grinning, "It's too bad I got another engagement."

There was a silence, and then she burst out, bitterly: "What do you come here for, anyway? It isn't me you're after."

Fin took a look at her angry face and decided that frankness was his best line. "Well, that's right," he said coolly. "But at that, I didn't lie to you. Everything I said to you goes. See?"

She was disconcerted by this attitude. "What do you mean by that?" she demanded.

"I promised you I'd get you out of this dump," said Fin, "and I stand by that."

"I don't know that I want to go now," she retorted, stormily. "Anyhow, Nipperg is crazy about me in his own way. That's something."

"Sure," said Fin, "and he'll cut your throat in the end. That's his way!"

The angry woman turned pale.

Fin relentlessly pursued his advantage. "If he don't land you behind the bars first," he added, grimly.

"Behind the bars!" she faltered.

"Well, murder is his line, isn't it?" he said. "I reckon you know what an accessory is."

She stared at him in speechless terror.

"He has already forced you to kidnap a girl," Fin went on, "and it was only by the grace of God that he didn't kill her here in this room before your eyes."

Daisy began to shake. "You . . . you know that, too?" she gasped.

"Sure I know it," said Fin. "And a lot more besides."

"Who are you?" she whispered.

"I haven't got time to go into that now," said Fin. "You stick by me and I'll stick by you."

"What do you want here?"

"I want to get into the cellar," he said. "And you've got to help me."

Daisy looked more frightened than before. "O my God! What is down there?" she gasped, staring at the floor as if she expected the horror to rise through it. "What is the matter with this house? Nipperg has already dug the cellar from end to end!"

"Steady!" whispered Fin with an uneasy glance toward the pantry door. An ill-timed fit of hysteria would wreck everything. He took her hand. "Get a grip on yourself, kid," he said, sympathetically. "God knows it's natural you should feel that way! Come over here and sit in front of the fire. I'm your friend and I'm on the level. Look at me and you'll see."

Slowly she raised her tormented eyes to his. What she read there reassured her. She became calmer.

As on the day before, they sat down on two stiff chairs before the fire. The untidy remains of Daisy's lunch still lay on the table behind them. Outside, a boisterous east wind, the precursor of rain, was threshing among the branches and rattling the old window-panes.

"Oh, I wish it would stop blowing!" murmured Daisy, nervously. "Often I wish I was dead!"

"I was your friend before I ever saw you," said Fin, encouragingly. "Because you were kind to that girl. It was partly owing to you that she escaped."

"You know her, then?" said Daisy, surprised.

"Why, sure!" said Fin. "What did you think?"

"I don't know what's behind it all," she said, helplessly. The tears began to roll silently down her cheeks.

Fin was moved by a genuine pity for the weak, pretty woman who could resist no outside influence, either bad or good. Any man who might get hold of Daisy could make her do whatever he commanded, he reflected. Was that her fault?

"It's going to be all right," he said, soothingly. "Just as soon as I get what I'm after, I'll take you away from here. . . . 'Most any place else would be an improvement on this," he added, grinning and glancing around the dismal, dirty room. "But as a matter of fact, if you do the right thing you're going to find powerful friends. We'll put you where Nipperg can never find you, even if he's free to look. We'll find you a job if you want to work, and in any case you'll be . . ."

Fin in his efforts to soothe Daisy had his shoulder turned toward the pantry door. Daisy was facing it. He got his first warning from her face. A choked cry escaped her. Fin sprang up, and his hand instinctively closed on the back of his chair for a weapon. He had no time to draw his gun.

The pantry door had opened without a sound, and he saw Nipperg in the act of snaking his body around the frame, his stained fangs showing and his green eyes blazing with hate. He was more deadly than a black leopard crouched to spring. He had a gun in his hand.

Fin slung the chair and Nipperg fired. The chair saved Fin by a hair's-breadth. It collided with Nipperg as he pulled the trigger and his bullet ploughed into the floor. Nipperg sprawled, helplessly entangled with the chair. Fin could have shot him then, but he had not the instinct of a killer. His first thought was of escape, his second of Daisy. If he left her behind, Nipperg would certainly kill her.

Seizing her wrist, he yanked her toward the other door. As he banged it open Nipperg shot from the floor. They got out of range in the nick of time. The gross figure of Mike was crouching between them and the front door, his features fixed in an inhuman grin. He was not armed, but he had the strength of an ox. Fin saw that even if he shot him, Nipperg would be upon them before he could get the heavy door open. So he pulled Daisy to the stairs. They flew up on wings. As they rounded the landing Nipperg shot from the dining-room door. His bullet went through one of the green panes with a musical tinkle. They ran for Daisy's bedroom. Fin slammed the door shut, and thankfully turned the key.

"Oh!" gasped Daisy. "We're trapped in here!"

Fin pointed to the end window with a hardy grin. His blood was racing. "Open it quietly," he said. "Get a hat and coat." He remained listening at the door.

Presently Nipperg rattled it like a madman, and Fin stepped around the frame. "Bring up the ax!" Nipperg yelled down to Mike. "I have them safe."

"Oh, come on, come on!" whispered Daisy from the open window, sick with terror.

"Wait till we get Mike up on this floor," whispered Fin.

He presently heard him lumbering up the stairs. "Nipperg!" cried Fin. "Can you hear me? Watch that man! He's sold you out to General Diamond. The two of them are digging under the kitchen floor every night!"

He heard a snarl like an animal on the other side of the door, then Mike's voice roaring: "It's a lie! a lie! He's trying to trick you!"

Fin did not wait for the outcome of this argument, but ran for the window. Daisy had dressed herself in hat and coat. There was no time to take more. They slid down the steep part of the roof to the flatter roof of the porch. Fin could hear the dull blows of the ax on the bedroom door. Paul ran out of the garage, but Fin drew his gun, whereupon Paul ran back and was not seen again. It was an easy matter to slide down the porch posts to the ground. Inside the kitchen, Nastya set up a squall.

"There they go! There they go!"

The dull blows from inside the house ceased. Fin seized Daisy's wrist and ran with all his might for the tangled wall of green at its nearest point. Putting up an arm to shield his face, he plunged into it regardless, dragging Daisy after him. Scratches and tears were nothing to them at such a moment. Fin knew that the boundary of Nipperg's place was not far on this side, perhaps two hundred feet.

Soon they were scrambling over a low stone wall. On the other side was a well-kept property; a belt of trees, a sloping lawn.

In the middle of the lawn stood a handsome new house. No one was in sight about it. Fin debated whether he dared apply at the house for refuge, but decided against it. It would take too long to explain their predicament. He ran diagonally up the lawn toward the entrance gates, pulling Daisy. His heart sank when he got out in the street and looked up and down. Not a soul in sight; not a car.

Straight ahead of them a street ran on up the hill for two or three hundred yards and dipped down on the other side. Down at the bottom of that hill lay the busy principal street of Kingsbridge and safety. They ran on with pounding hearts.

"You're doing fine!" Fin said to Daisy, grinning. "It's no cinch to run uphill!"

As they rounded the top of the hill the black sedan turned into it at the bottom. Paul was driving it; Nipperg inside. Fin grunted with discouragement. All around were fine houses standing in their own grounds, but scarcely anybody in view. Where could they apply for shelter from a madman's bullets? There was a car parked across the street, but it was pointing the wrong way.

"We'll have to take cover and shoot it out," he muttered.

Just at that moment a taxicab turned in front of them and drew up at the curb. A man and woman were coming down the walk from one of the houses to take it. The two couples arrived at the cab simultaneously. Fin acting from blind instinct, violently shouldered the man out of the way, pitched Daisy through the open door, and climbed after her. He pressed the muzzle of his gun against the chauffeur's ribs.

"Step on it, kid," he said, hoarsely. "My finger is trembling!"

The chauffeur laughed. He was that type. "'S all right with me, boss," he said and the car leaped down hill.

"Hey! Hey!" cried the man on the sidewalk in an outraged voice. But nobody regarded him.

Fin could see the grin in the back of the chauffeur's cheek, and his heart warmed toward that hard guy. "You won't lose by this, fellow," he said. "I'll pay the meter, and a damn good bonus besides, if you can keep ahead of that black car behind us."

"Okay," said the chauffeur, coolly. "Don't let your heads show in the back window."

"He won't shoot if we can get where there are plenty of people," said Fin.

They catapulted down the steep hill. Daisy fell over against Fin in a faint. He callously propped her up in her own corner so he could have his arms free. As they neared the bottom of the hill he said:

"Turn downtown. The thicker the better."

The taxi turned the corner into Broadway, just escaping a capsize and no more. They made the first traffic light by a hair, and bowled over the Harlem River bridge. Evidently the driver knew exactly what his car would do. Fin congratulated himself. The Slav could hardly be so good a driver. Looking back through the window, Fin saw that the black car had taken a chance and run by the red light. They had gained nothing yet. Daisy returned to her senses and began to cry helplessly.

"Buck up! Buck up!" said Fin. "There are plenty of cars around us. Nipperg will never dare use a gun here."

Approaching the intersection of Dyckman Street, they saw that the light was about to turn against them. "Shall I run by it?" asked the chauffeur.

"No," said Fin. "This is as good a place as any to see what he'll do."

They stopped. Looking back, Fin saw that the black sedan was the third car behind them. As soon as it stopped Nipperg jumped out. Fin drew his gun, but Nipperg was ostentatiously showing empty hands. His ugly, convulsed face appeared at the window. With scarcely a glance at Fin's gun, he addressed himself to Daisy.

"Come out of that!" he snarled. "You're my wife. You can't get away from me."

Daisy's eyes were closed. She moaned in an extremity of terror.

"What do you say, kid?" Fin asked her, grimly. "It's up to you!"

There was a terrific silence in the taxi. People in the surrounding cars were staring curiously at the scene. Fin held his gun too low for them to see it. Finally the taxi driver said:

"Light's turning, boss."

"Quick!" said Fin. "Do you want to get out?"

"No," whispered Daisy.

"Drive on," said Fin.

It was the critical moment. Nipperg hesitated, and looked around at the press of cars. His face became inhuman with balked rage. They started to move. "I'll get you!" snarled Nipperg. When his own car moved up he swung himself on the running-board. Daisy was at the point of collapse.

They sped on downtown; Washington Heights, Manhattanville, Morningside, Central Park. Fin chose this crookeder route, hoping by some chance to shake off the following car. But luck refused to favor them. As they approached the center of the city the black sedan was still clinging like a dog at their heels. It was the most crowded hour of the afternoon.

Then Fin's thoughts took a new turn. Nipperg had chosen to follow Daisy instead of stopping to guard his place. When it came to the test there was something human in this madman. All right! It was all to Fin's advantage. He guessed that Mike and Nastya would never dare to face Nipperg's return with that incriminating hole under the kitchen. Hence the house would be unguarded at this moment. Gosh! if I could only get back ahead of Nipperg! thought Fin. If I could only get back!

As they ran out of the Park their chauffeur said, "I'll be able to shake them in the traffic all right."

"Don't try it," said Fin, brusquely. "I got a better idea now. Lead him into the side streets in the Grand Central district where traffic is all piled up now. This is his own trick I'm trying to turn against him. I want to slip out without his seeing me, and let him go on following you and the girl."

The chauffeur glanced around in his surprise. "Hell! Ain't you runnin' away with the girl?" he said. "I don't get this."

"Not exactly," said Fin, grinning. "I can't tell you the whole story now. You're all right, anyhow. I'm grateful to you."

"Oh, that's all right," said the chauffeur. "I liked your face better'n hisn."

"Listen," said Fin. "You want to keep this guy in the black car guessing as long as you can. I don't care how long you drive around.

I'm good for it. But if you happen to lose him, or if he finds out the trick and gives up the chase, then you drive the girl to the Vandermeer Hotel. She has the money to pay you."

"Okay, boss."

Fin gave Daisy half his roll.

"Oh, don't leave me!" she whimpered.

"Listen, Kid," he said patiently. "This is easy! You go to the Vandermeer and engage a room. You'll be as safe there as in a castle. Nipperg couldn't pull anything in a joint like that. There's a telephone switchboard and bellboys in every corridor. Register as Miss Daisy Zell. As soon as you get in your room call up my friend Mr. Mappin, and tell him everything that has happened. He'll tell you what to do. I'll call you up myself when I can get to a phone." He wrote down the telephone number.

They had to turn many a corner back and forth across town before Fin saw the opportunity he was looking for. It came in West Forty-third Street, which was filled with cars and trucks from curb to curb. They crawled through at a snail's pace, often stopped by a block ahead. The black sedan was four or five cars behind them. During one such stoppage Fin saw that the view behind was blocked by a big express truck delivering a load of goods at the curb. Opposite the taxi door was the rear entrance to a big department store.

He opened the door, and pressing Daisy's hand, made it in six jumps. Since he could not see Nipperg, he was pretty sure Nipperg could not see him. The procession of cars moved on again. He waited inside the store far enough back not to be seen. Presently the black sedan passed by, Nipperg sitting beside Paul now, writhing with impatience and squinting ahead. He had not discovered the trick.

After he had gone by, Fin ran in the other direction for Grand Central station. At this hour there were frequent suburban trains. If he had the luck to catch an express for Riverdale, he would get there half an hour before Nipperg, even supposing he started right back. Fin was a wild-looking figure, hatless and scratched from the thorns; but it was nothing to him how he was stared at so nobody tried to stop him. He still had key, hammer, cold chisels, and flashlight in his various pockets.

CHAPTER TWENTY-TWO

ACCORDING TO FIN'S THEORY, Mike and Nastya would have decamped the instant after Nipperg left. Not knowing how soon their master might be back, they had probably slid down the ravine and escaped by the railway tracks. He could not be sure of this; however, he boldly entered the place by the main gate. As soon as he was out of sight of the street he took out his gun.

Standing at the edge of the lawn, gun in hand, he surveyed the house window by window. It showed no sign of life. He hailed the silence. No face appeared anywhere. Keeping close to the trees, he moved first to the right, then to the left until he could see completely around the house. Nothing showed. The garage was open and empty.

Finally he ventured to try the kitchen door. Finding it unlocked, he went in. The moment he saw the kitchen he knew they had gone. There was a heap of their belongings—or Nipperg's—on the floor, and a trail of dropped articles through the dining-room. Obviously they had snatched up what they could, and had fled. A deathlike silence held the house in its spell.

Hesitating no longer, Fin unlocked the cellar door. He stood on the top step and locked it behind him, turning the key so that it could not be pushed out by another key. Switching on his light, he descended the stairs. That cellar was an obscene spot. The heavy air pressed on the lungs, suggesting imaginary horrors. It smelled of dead earth which had never known the sun. The floor had been dug up from end to end and the dirt heaped anywhere, making it look like a little rifled graveyard, or a battlefield wrecked by miniature shells.

It extended under the entire house excepting the kitchen. Once it had had a cement floor which had been taken up bit by bit and heaped down at the far end. With no power available but the human arm, Fin pictured the immense labor involved. And all for nothing.

The foundation walls were of rough field stone, evidently very thick. Once they had been kept whitewashed, but no fresh coat had been applied in many years, and most of it had flaked off. On his left as he stood at the foot of the stairs was a coal-bin partly filled; on his right the old-fashioned furnace with its immense cold-air pipe leading from the base up to the opening that Fin had marked outside, and a whole crop of smaller heating flues springing from its head like the tentacles of an octopus and leading in every direction to the different rooms.

The furnace was Fin's goal. It was built in a shallow pit so close to the foundation wall that amid the mess of pipes springing from it he found it difficult to worm his body behind it. So much the likelier hiding-place, he thought. The base actually touched the wall, consequently there was nothing "behind" it but the wall, and the hiding place must be there.

With his light he went over the stones inch by inch. After all these years there was nothing to indicate they had ever been disturbed. With his hammer he tapped them one after another, listening carefully. None gave off a hollow sound. Finally he attacked the mortar with his chisel. Reflecting that a man working there would likely choose a spot about the level of his eyes, he started at the top. Cement had been mixed with the mortar, he discovered, and it was almost as hard as the stone itself. His heart sunk. It would be a couple of hours' job to loosen even one stone.

However, he kept on trying the mortar one place after another. Finally at a tap of the hammer his chisel sank in half an inch and the loose sand trickled down. Fin's heart set up a thick beating that made his throat tight. Exploring with his chisel, he found that the mortar surrounding one big stone in the center of the space behind the furnace was of a softer sort, everywhere else hard.

Fin fell to sweating and trembling. He had been through so much! But the hammer and the chisel never stopped, and a continuous cascade of loosened mortar rattled down on the hollow base of the cold air pipe on which he was standing. Soon at a tap of the hammer the chisel sank in up to its head. There was a hollow space behind the stone. He had to stop for a moment to wipe his face and get a grip on himself.

In a short while he had the stone loosened in its place, but could not yet get a purchase on it to draw it out. Suddenly his arm was arrested by a sound from above. The front door banged open and two pairs of footsteps strode into the house, reverberating loudly on the floor overhead. He heard Nipperg's voice speaking angrily in his own tongue. Fin had become so absorbed in what he was doing, he had completely forgotten the danger from this source. His first feeling was one of grinding anger. Five minutes more would have been enough! It seemed as if chance were deliberately sporting with him. Silently and helplessly he cursed his luck.

Overhead, Nipperg was shouting for Mike and Nastya. He came out into the kitchen; he returned and went upstairs. Paul was waiting in the hall. Fin could no doubt have escaped from the cellar at that moment; but with success all but in his grasp he simply could not leave the place. Any risk was preferable to that. There was no reason why Nipperg should come down cellar at that moment, he told himself, and he could keep tab on him by the sound of his footsteps. If he watched his chance he could escape later. It was dark by this time. It was always easier to get out of a house than to get in.

Nipperg, cursing his treacherous servants, came out into the kitchen again, followed by Paul, and left the house. The back door slammed. Taking off his coat, Fin spread it under his feet to deaden the sound of the falling mortar, and softly set to work once more.

In a few minutes he found he was able to work the loosened stone out of its place. Dropping hammer and chisel in his pocket, he laid the stone on the ground to one side. He cast his light into the hole with a trembling hand. Suppose, after all, there was nothing there. But it revealed a little iron box of antique design neatly fitted into its place, and quiet descended on him. There lay treasure.

Taking it out and laying it on the ground in front of the furnace, he knelt down to examine it. A little iron chest about nine inches square, deeply rusted but solid still. He did not need to be told that it was of immense age. It was cunningly wrought of thin strips of iron woven together basket fashion, the corners heavily reinforced. A mediaval treasure chest in miniature. It locked with a key, but the key was not in the hole. Fin did not trouble about that. His cold chisel would do the trick. While he was turning it over, he was startled to hear Nipperg's furious voice apparently issuing from the furnace. An instant later he realized that it was coming down the cold-air pipe. Nipperg was outside. He had discovered the excavation under the kitchen and he was mad with rage. Fin put on his coat, not knowing when he might have to make a dash for it.

Nipperg stormed into the kitchen, cursing alternately in English and in his own tongue. Paul was trying to soothe him. Suddenly he rattled the cellar door with the greatest violence. "Damn him! he's taken the key!" he yelled.

And then Fin heard the words that caused his heart to stand still. "By God! the key's inside! There's somebody down there!"

There was a silence, then Paul's scared voice saying: "It's not Mike. Mike has gone and taken his things."

Fin's backbone stiffened. After, all, he thought, they can only come down the stairs one at a time and the light will he behind them. I have six bullets in my gun. He waited at the foot of the stairs, gun in hand, and the little chest pressed against his ribs.

One of the panels of the door was split with a crash. Nipperg had evidently driven his heel through it. A stream of savage vituperation poured down.

"Look out!" yelled Paul. "He'll shoot . . . You don't know how many there are!"

Nipperg quieted down. "I'll fix them!" he said, with a maniac laugh. "Watch that door and shoot the man who opens it!"

He ran through the house. Fin heard him enter the locked room at the foot of the stairs. In a few seconds he was back, laughing.

A frightful cry escaped from Paul. "My God! What are you going to do!"

"Quiet, you fool!" snarled Nipperg. "I'm not going to blow the house up. It's only gas."

At the same moment a small hard object was pushed through the hole and came bumping down the steps.

"Stop up the hole with paper," said Nipperg.

Fin heard the thing hissing on the ground. All his blood seemed to turn to water. To be suffocated like a rat in its hole! His head whirled around. He dropped his gun and struggled to get the flashlight out to find the thing. But it caught in his pocket. He retreated to the farthest side of the cellar, sobbing for breath. Already he felt himself choking.

The thing did not explode. It only fizzed out, rolling this way and that on the earth. Fin leaned against the wall with the sweat running down his face, looking at death in the dark. But when he caught, or imagined that he caught the first deadly whiff in his nostrils, the blind instinct of self-preservation leaped into play. Air was his need. Dropping the iron box, he flung his arms around the big galvanized pipe and yanked at it madly. As he felt it give, he yelled to drown other sounds:

"Let me out! Let me out!"

No doubt Nipperg laughed heartily.

The pipe parted at a joint and the middle section came away in Fin's arms. He laid it on the ground. The upper part was firmly fastened and braced. He dived into it and scrambled through, working knees and elbows until his face pressed against the wire mesh at the top. Ah! how sweet the air of Heaven tasted in his lungs!

His panic passed away. He managed to get out hammer and chisel, and spreading his knees to keep from slipping back, cut the wire with light swift strokes. It yielded easily to the chisel. He cut around three sides and pressed it up out of his way. As he was about to drag himself through the hole he remembered the iron box.

It took nerve to return to that deathly hole. He hesitated, trying to work himself up to it. Finally he filled his lungs and let himself slide. Holding his breath, he searched frantically around the floor with his hands. They touched cold iron. He thrust the box inside his buttoned coat. He had to let the gun go. Not until head and shoulders were thrust far up the pipe did he dare to breathe again. A minute later he was lying on the ground outside in an ecstasy of relief and thankfulness. Life! Life! Life! Until that moment he had never known how precious it was.

It was quite dark by this time. When he got up he saw a light in the kitchen window, and could not forbear taking a glance inside before he turned away. The hideous Nipperg was watching the cellar door like a cat at a mouse hole. The smashed panel was stuffed with newspaper, and Paul on his knees was pressing strips of paper into the crack all round with the blade of a knife.

Fin gave them his blessing so to speak, and ran down the old garden path with a thankful heart. As he slid down the side of the ravine he realized that he was shaking in every limb and actually babbling to himself in the reaction that had overtaken him. "A damn close shave! A damn close shave, old fellow!" Laughing weakly, he sat down for a moment to pull himself together.

Climbing to the railway tracks, he turned toward the Riverdale station, a furlong distant. A fluttering newspaper in the ditch gave him a wrapping for his precious iron box. As he came within radius of the station lights he realized that he was covered with dirt and blood. What did it matter so long as he had his prize? People are quick to stare at anything that departs from the normal; fortunately, they are less quick to interfere.

A train came in. It was bound in the wrong direction, but he got on. Anything to put distance between him and that place. He got out at Yonkers and learned on the other side of the tracks that there would be an express for Grand Central in five minutes. He called up Mr. Mappin while he waited.

"Well, I've got it," he said, in a voice that tried to be offhand, but was choking with excitement.

"Got what?" came the startled question back.

"I don't know what it is because it's locked up in an iron box."

"Where are you?"

"Yonkers. . . . Listen, Chief, if you were to give the police a quick tip now they might nab Nipperg in his own house. He's trying to asphyxiate me in the cellar."

"What?"

"Oh, I squeezed out on him," said Fin, chuckling.

"I'll do that," said Mr. Mappin.

"But listen," Fin went on. "If he slips through their fingers, Mariula ought not to be allowed to appear tonight. The man will be maddened by disappointment. He might . . ."

"Quite," said Mr. Mappin. "That occurred to me as soon as Daisy told me her story. So I went over to Hoboken and got Mariula. She is here with me in the apartment."

"Thank God!" said Fin. "Where's Daisy now?"

"I put her on a train for Chicago at her own desire," said Mr. Mappin. "Friends of mine there will take care of her for the present."

"Here comes my train," said Fin. "Home in half an hour."

That was a dramatic homecoming. When Fin's key turned in the latch, Mariula, Mr. Mappin, even Jermyn came running to the door. Mariula's face of joy turned to dismay when she looked at him.

"Oh, Fishy!" she cried, clasping her hands. "What have you been through?"

"Just a pipe," he said, airily. "I dusted it out for the first time in fifty years or so!"

"Don't joke! Are you hurt?"

"Hurt!" he cried. "I'm the livest man in New York! I'm born anew. I'm just an hour old!"

"What do you mean?"

"Never mind now. Look what I've got!" He held out his uncouth package in its newspaper.

"Bring it in here!" cried Mr. Mappin, leading the way into the dining-room with shining spectacles. "Put it on the table where we can all see it."

Fin put it down and the newspaper fell away, revealing the rusty little treasure chest, ancient and secret-looking. It brought the dim past into that elegant room; it belonged to a ruder and more exciting world than ours. A cry of astonishment went around the table, and Fin was repaid for all he had been through.

"Oh!" said Mariula. "How quaint! It looks a thousand years old!"

"About half that," said Mr. Mappin, with a collector's enthusiasm. "Fifteenth-century work. A perfect miniature! It's a museum piece!"

Fin produced his hammer and chisel. "Sure," he said, dryly, "but let's see what's inside it."

"The lock is probably unique," protested Mr. Mappin. "What a pity to smash it!"

"Where would we get a modern locksmith to open it?" said Fin.

"You're right," said Mr. Mappin. "Go ahead."

Fin sat down and took the little chest between his knees, while the others looked on in strained suspense. His little hammer was obviously inadequate, and Jermyn fetched him a heavier one from the kitchen. It was only a sort of toy chest, and a dozen strokes loosened the cover. Fin put it back on the table.

"Open it," he said to Mariula. "It's yours!"

She put her hand out, almost afraid to look, and slowly lifted the cover. Inside they saw a bag made of antique crimson velvet much stained by mold. Upon it lay a white envelope, likewise warped and stained by the damp. It bore no superscription. Mariula hesitated.

"Open it! Open it!" urged Mr. Mappin. "It is certainly for you."

Mariula's slim fingers trembled. The envelope contained a double sheet of notepaper folded once. Owing to its outer protection, it was in a better state of preservation. She read it, starry-eyed with excitement. "It is from my father," she murmured. Lifted quite out of herself, she pressed the paper to her lips. "I do not quite understand it," she said, passing it to Mr. Mappin.

"This is your father's testament," he said, gravely, after reading. "Don't you see, it establishes your identity beyond all question." He passed it to Fin.

There were some curious marks at the top, followed by several lines of writing in a distinguished hand, and signatures. Fin read:

> Above are the fingerprints of my infant daughter Mariula. She is my only child and heir.
>
> Constantine Constantinovich.

Witnessed by:
Olga Maria
Lina Maximova

Meanwhile Mariula was fumbling with the cord that drew the neck of the velvet bag. When it refused to yield she lifted the bag clear of the little chest. In so doing the ancient fabric parted and a golden crown rang on the dining-table.

They fell back with cries almost of fear, and stared at it in silence. So much is symbolized for men by the crown—sovereignty, war, treason and assassination—that their senses reeled. Moreover, this crown had a character of its own. A wide band of soft yellow gold decorated with innumerable leaves of thin gold, laurel leaves folded upon each other all around the circle, it bore no resemblance to the conventional crown with its points and jewels. It was older and simpler than other crowns.

Mr. Mappin was the first to break the silence. "I expected something of the sort," he said, huskily.

"I don't want it!" cried Mariula, rebelliously.

As for Fin, he said nothing. His heart was heavy.

Finally Mr. Mappin ventured to pick it up. "This is older than the casket," he said. "I should say that it dated from the ninth century. Notice how strong the Byzantine influence is. . . . How beautiful! How beautiful!" he murmured. "Wherever it belongs, it is one of the great treasures of earth!"

"But where did it come from?" cried Fin. "If any such crown has been lost you ought to have heard of it?"

Mr. Mappin shrugged. "Who could keep track of all the changes and upheavals during the past sixteen years," he said. "More than one crown has been lost."

"Then we have not yet discovered the secret!" cried Fin.

"Oh, the rest is easy," said Mr. Mappin. "All we have to do now is to advertise our find."

"Advertise it?"

"Surely. Let us call in the reporters and show it to them. Allow them to photograph it. A golden crown a thousand years old! That ought to be news!"

"But if the whole story comes out it will make complications," said Fin, scowling. "It will give the murderer a chance to escape."

"The whole world will not be big enough to hide him now," said Mr. Mappin, gravely. "However, let us not tell the whole story. It is our secret. We have a right to withhold a part of it for the moment. Let us show them the crown and refuse to tell where we found it. Mystery will increase its news value. The story will be flashed over all six continents, and within twenty-four hours we are bound to learn the history of this crown and the circumstances of its disappearance." He addressed Mariula with a smile. "What do you say, Princess?"

She started, and glanced at him with immense scared eyes. Then a deep flush overspread her delicate face. "You decide," she murmured.

"Very well. If I call up the newspaper offices at once, we can get it in the morning editions."

CHAPTER TWENTY-THREE

THE STORY OF THE ANCIENT CROWN duly appeared in the morning news-papers with photographs. At the breakfast table Mr. Mappin, Mariula, and Fin passed the different versions from hand to hand. Mariula's name was not mentioned in connection with the affair. Mr. Mappin said:

"I expect the police will interest themselves in this. We cannot refuse to answer their questions. I had better go call on the Com-missioner before he sends for me."

Fin was left to keep the reporters at bay. No further informa-tion was to be given out for the present, and Mariula was not to be exhibited.

Two hours later Mr. Mappin returned, bringing word that Nipperg had slipped through the hands of the police the night be-fore. However, they promised an arrest within twenty-four hours. Mr. Mappin and Fin exchanged a smile. They had become accus-tomed to this formula during the early days of the Nick Peters case.

"How about General Diamond?" asked Fin.

"Oh, he's still at the Madagascar," said Mr. Mappin, dryly. "His conscience is clear. He is in a rage, I am told, over the loss of his trunks. I have agreed to reimburse the hotel for any damages he may be able to collect."

The three friends were in the living-room, talking things over, when Jermyn entered, looking rather queer.

"What is it?" asked Mr. Mappin.

"General Diamond is calling, sir."

"Well, of all the nerve!" cried Fin.

"But how characteristic!" murmured Mr. Mappin. "Ask him to come up, Jermyn."

Mariula retired to her own room. "The best way to get information out of the General," suggested Mr. Mappin, "is not to appear to require any."

"I'll let you do the fishing," said Fin.

A moment later the hearty slap of the General's feet was heard in the hall. He charged in, gobbling: "Good morning, gentlemen! Good morning! Good morning!" But on this occasion he did not shove out the fat hand. The excessively dry expression of Mr. Mappin's face may have warned him. "So your labors have been crowned with success!" he went on. "Heartiest congratulations!"

"Thanks," said Mr. Mappin; and, "Thanks," said Fin, grinning.

"We have really all been working toward the same end," said the General, affably. "Unfortunately, the strictest secrecy had been enjoined upon me, and so I was under the necessity of deceiving you."

"Oh, don't speak of that now," said Mr. Mappin, with a wave of the hand.

There was a polite silence. Each gentleman was waiting for the other to give him a lead. Mr. Mappin had the advantage because he was on his own ground. He had the air of waiting for the General to explain the object of his call.

"Of course you know a great deal more than you gave out to the press," said the General, jocosely.

"Of course," said Mr. Mappin, matching his roguish smile.

"Why were you so guarded with the press?"

"I don't get you, sir."

"I mean, why did you say nothing about Mariula?"

"Queen Mariula," suggested Mr. Mappin, with delicate emphasis.

The General swallowed hard. "Queen, of course," he said, bowing. "I was not aware that she had assumed the title."

"She has not done so," said Mr. Mappin, equally polite. "But of course it is hers when she wants it."

"You and I know that, sir," said the General, "but the world will require legal proof. The other governments of Europe will have to be satisfied before extending recognition, and . . . er. . . the present incumbent . . ."

"Your employer?" ventured Mr. Mappin, slyly.

"Yes, my employer will certainly demand proofs of her identity."

"We have them, sir," said Mr. Mappin, blandly.

"But the girl's father and mother are dead," said the General, spreading out his hands; "her nurse is dead; the nurse's husband is dead. How can you produce legal proof of her identity?"

"The late King Constantine with admirable foresight inclosed it in the chest with the crown."

"Proof of what nature?" asked the General, eagerly.

"I will produce it at the proper moment," said Mr. Mappin, dryly.

The General's eyes bolted. He was beginning to grow angry. "But surely as King Alexander's representative I have a right to know what it is!"

King Alexander! thought Fin. There's the first lead. Who the hell is Alexander? He ran over in his mind all the crowned heads he knew, but no Alexander was forthcoming.

"Certainly," said Mr. Mappin, with dry politeness, "whenever it suits you to show your credentials."

The General bit his lip. "A birthmark I presume, or something like that," he said, sarcastically.

"Oh dear, no!" said Mr. Mappin, with an amused smile. "Birthmarks are entirely out of date as a means of identification."

The General was losing his usual aplomb, and he knew it. With an effort he recovered a semblance of good-humor. "But why don't you bring the Queen forward, sir?" he asked.

"No reason in particular," said Mr. Mappin. "I don't want to proceed too fast, that's all. . . . Why should I bring her forward?"

"When the news of the finding of the crown reaches Kuban there will be a revolution," said the General, impressively.

Kuban! thought Fin; there was the cat out of the bag! From his school days he remembered the little triangular country based on the Black Sea. Tinted green it always was on the old maps.

Mr. Mappin never changed a hair. "Of course Alexander's re-gime is at an end," he said, carelessly, "but why should there be a revolution?"

The General turned evasive. "Well, it's not for me to say, sir. The event must speak for itself."

"Quite!" said Mr. Mappin. He refused to be drawn.

"Have you any objection to showing me the crown?" asked the General, presently. "A man is naturally curious to see the thing he has been searching for so long."

"No objection whatever," said Mr. Mappin. He left the room.

As soon as he was gone the natural man peeped out. "Where did you find it, Corveth, hey?" the General asked, with an eager-ness he could not conceal. "There's no harm in telling me, is there?"

"I guess not," said Fin, grinning. He was not averse to enjoying a little triumph at the fat man's expense. "I found it in Nipperg's cellar."

The General's face fell. "But my agents reported to me that the cellar had been dug up from end to end!"

"So it had. The crown was not buried under the floor, but in the wall."

"How did you stumble on the spot?"

"I was led to it," said Fin. "The clue was in the seemingly blank piece of paper we showed you. After you left we discovered that when you touched a spark to the pencil dot, the message wrote itself in fire. Mariula's father must have dabbled in chemistry."

The big man looked pretty sick. In spite of iron self-control his eyes rolled painfully. How he would enjoy strangling me! thought Fin. "Yaas, I have heard so," said the General.

Mr. Mappin returned, bearing the crown. The General looked at it in bitter chagrin. He did not offer to take it in his hands. "So that's what it's like!" he said.

"Irrespective of its historical significance!" remarked Mr. Mappin, "the mere workmanship is marvelous!"

"Well, it's supposed to have had a heavenly origin," said the General.

"Yes?"

"Don't you know its history?"

"No," said Mr. Mappin, coolly. "Only that it is the crown of Kuban." (And you just told me that, he might have added.)

"It's called the crown of St. Karel. St. Karel was the gazebo who christianized Kuban a thousand years ago and became their patron saint. They say he went up to the top of a mountain to pray and when he opened his eyes the crown was lying on the ground before him. To this day the peasants will show you the print of his knees up there. That crown is the holiest thing in Kuban. The people believe that the fate of their country is bound up in it."

"'Is' bound up in it?" said Mr. Mappin, quickly. "Then they don't know it's ever been lost?"

"No," said the General. "Though there have been rumors flying."

"How could Alexander reign without it?"

The General merely shrugged.

"I suppose he's been putting off his coronation on one pretext or another until he could recover the crown?"

The General said nothing. His failure to answer was answer enough.

Mr. Mappin retired to put the crown away again.

"What's the old fox's next move?" the General muttered to Fin.

"I don't know," answered Fin, grinning. "He keeps his own counsel."

When Mr. Mappin came back the General said, somewhat surlily: "Just the same, you ought to let the world know that Mariula has been found, too."

"Why?" said Mr. Mappin.

"If Alexander is overthrown and there's no other royal claimant on deck, the Reds will take the opportunity to set up a republic. That's what happened before."

"There is something in that," said Mr. Mappin, thoughtfully. "Well . . . in an hour or two all necessity for secrecy will be over and we'll give the whole story to the press."

Fin thought: He means he'll give out the story as soon as he fishes it out of you, old fruit!

"In an hour or two?" echoed the General, anxiously.

"Nipperg," murmured Mr. Mappin, meaningly.

"Ah, you want to nab him first, I see."

The old game of fence between these two, thought Fin, with the advantage, for the moment, on the chief's side.

"If Alexander is eliminated you'll be out of a job, General," said Mr. Mappin.

The General affected to laugh heartily, but his expression was far from a merry one. "Sure! Sure!" he said. "It's the fortune of war. Johnny must seek a new master!"

Mr. Mappin neither accepted nor rejected the implied suggestion. "I don't understand why King Constantine was obliged to fly from Kuban in 1914," he said. "There were no popular upheavals as early as that. I suppose I read about it at the time, but I've forgotten."

The General was anxious to propitiate him now. "There was so much happening in the world then that the affairs of little Kuban passed unnoticed," he said. "No news got out of the country at all. Kuban came in on the side of the Allies. King Constantine had just married a Russian princess. Unfortunately, his country lies adjacent to Turkey, and at the outbreak of war the Turks simply overran it. It was the Turks, not the Reds, who forced Constantine to fly. Constantine was a popular monarch. His dynasty had ruled Kuban for two hundred years."

"What happened in Kuban after he left?" asked Mr. Mappin.

"As the war went on," the General continued, "the Turks had all they could do nearer home, and they were gradually forced to withdraw their armies from Kuban. That provided the Reds with an opportunity to seize the government and proclaim a republic. They never had any real hold, because the people were monarchist at heart and devoted to the ruling family. But in the absence of the king and his only brother the royalists had no leader. The republic only lasted eight or ten months."

"Who overthrew it?"

"The king's brother, Alexander."

"Mariula's uncle," murmured Mr. Mappin.

"By this time the Bolshevist revolution had taken place in Russia," the General went on, "and the Tsar and his family were no more. However, South Russia, as you may remember, was strongly White in its sympathies. Several powerful White armies were operating there, and Alexander applied to the leaders for aid. The Whites wanted Kuban for a base, so they marched in and put Alexander on the throne as regent-dictator. The Reds, who were cut off from their northern comrades, fell with scarcely a struggle."

"And then followed the White terror," put in Mr. Mappin.

"How did you know that?" asked the General, staring. "The censorship . . ."

"I didn't know it," said Mr. Mappin. "But it always did follow."

"I'm afraid your sympathies incline toward the Reds, sir," remarked the General.

"Not at all, sir," returned Mr. Mappin, blandly. "Neither Red nor White. Pink. Please go on."

"Alexander then sent word to his brother in America that the way was clear for his return," resumed the General, "and Constantine started for Kuban, accompanied by the young Queen Olga Maria, who refused to be separated from her husband. Unfortunately, as they crossed the border into Kuban they were set upon by a party of Red sympathizers and foully murdered. The actual details have never been established."

"That is not exactly the popular version of what happened, is it?" suggested Mr. Mappin, mildly.

"Oh, I see," said the General, without turning a hair, "you have heard the monstrous story that it was Alexander himself who lured his brother and sister-in-law back to Kuban and had them murdered."

"No, I never heard it until now," said Mr. Mappin.

The General looked a little foolish. "Well, that story was set in circulation by the Reds to divert attention from themselves," he said, hastily. "I can assure you there is not a word of truth in it, sir."

"Still, Alexander did become king as a result of his brother's death," Mr. Mappin pointed out.

"He could not avoid it, sir. The country required a strong hand at the helm!"

"That's what they all say," murmured Mr. Mappin.

"Alexander is a hard man," said the General, enthusiastically. "I may even say ruthless. The times demand it. But he is the soul of honor! I would stake my own honor on his!"

Mr. Mappin's spectacles twinkled. "Constantine must have had some suspicion of what awaited him," he suggested, "because he left his two most precious possessions in America—his baby and his crown."

"You should have seen Alexander as I have seen him," said the General, earnestly. "Crushed with grief, sir! Crushed with grief! The anniversary of Constantine's death has been appointed a national day of mourning in Kuban. The whole court goes into black. Special services are held in the cathedral, which the king attends in person, though not otherwise a religious man. . . ."

"Now come, General," said Mr. Mappin, persuasively; "it is agreed that Alexander's goose is cooked. Why bother to stick up for him any longer. You and I are practical men."

The General executed a rapid right-about-face. "You're right, sir," he said laughing, heartily. "After all, I'm only a plain soldier of fortune. I worked for Alexander and I got my pay. I owe him nothing further. Thank God, I'm an American citizen! I don't have to lose any sleep over Kuban!"

"Bravo!" cried Mr. Mappin, very dryly indeed. . . . "Some time after Constantine's murder Nipperg appeared in America," he prompted.

"Yes. Nipperg is an agent of the Reds' central committee," said the General. "It was rumored in Kuban that Constantine had carried the crown of St. Karel out of the country, and had not brought it back. It was also rumored that Olga Maria had borne him a child in America. Nipperg was sent over here to find out what there was in it. The Reds considered that a child of Constantine's and the holy crown were greater obstacles to their success than Alexander."

"And Nipperg was to destroy both if found."

"Certainly. In the beginning he was well supplied with funds and he was able to buy Constantine's residence when it came into the market. Latterly the Reds have lost interest in Kuban. A simple, pastoral people devoted to the monarchical idea, they are not considered worth bothering about. So Nipperg has been kept pretty short. But he is a perfect fanatic, as you have seen. He is determined to set up a republic in Kuban if he has to do it single-handed. No doubt he sees himself as President. But he never succeeded in finding either the crown or the child."

"And Alexander sent you over?" suggested Mr. Mappin.

"Oh, that was quite recently," said the General. "King Alexander had had many agents before me. They spent his money and did nothing. But I produced results. I succeeded in locating the supposed daughter of Constantine, and in learning that the secret of the crown's hiding-place was said to be contained in an emerald pendant that Nick Peters had hidden. Nipperg found Nick Peters through following me, and in his savage fury killed the man and ruined all my work."

"Have you any proof of that?" asked Mr. Mappin.

"No proof I could take into court," said the General. "But the fact is self-evident, isn't it?"

Mr. Mappin nodded non-committally. "How did you learn that the emerald contained the secret?" he asked.

"Oh, by a little sleuthing," said the General, vaguely.

"I suggest that you received a hint before you left Kuban," said Mr. Mappin.

"No, sir!" protested the General, virtuously.

"I suggest that Constantine and Alexander had had a meeting," persisted Mr. Mappin, "and that Constantine, trusting in his brother, had partly revealed the secret—or possibly one of his servants betrayed him to Alexander. Who can ever know now?"

"Impossible!" cried the General.

"Then how did you know that the blank paper would yield its secret to the touch of a spark?"

"I didn't know it until Corveth told me just now."

"Then how came you to start digging under Nipperg's kitchen?"

The General puffed out his cheeks and blew helplessly. His eyes roiled. That voluble man was silenced for the nonce. Fin took a grim satisfaction in the sight.

But the fat blackguard was not yet licked. All his life his effrontery had served him, and he called upon it now. He spread out his hands and hung his head in a touching gesture of surrender. "You have me, sir," he said. "You have me! . . . I am obliged to confess that I did receive a hint in Kuban. Fact is, I couldn't bring myself to give Alexander away. The habit of loyalty is too strong in an old soldier like me."

"Hum!" said Mr. Mappin.

Suddenly the General started as in horror of a thought that had just come to him. He dramatically struck the back of his hand against his brow. "My God!" he cried. "You are right! Alexander must have been privy to the death of Constantine. I see it all now! I took the King's story at face value. I never paused to think the matter out. I am a man of action!"

Mr. Mappin's expression was a treat as he listened to this. "In case you found the child and the crown," he asked, quietly, "what were your instructions?"

"To bring them back safely," protested the General, piously. "I swear it!"

Mr. Mappin said nothing, but only rose and helped himself to a fresh cigarette. There was an air of finality about the simple action which suggested to Fin that having got all he wanted out of the General, the chief was now ready to show his hand. The atmosphere of the pleasant room was tense. The General was anxiously studying Mr. Mappin out of the corner of his eye.

"The damned bloody villain!" he cried. "You have opened my eyes, sir. I won't work for him another hour! I'll cable him instantly saying that our relations are at an end!" His voice broke touchingly. "As I told you, sir, my instructions were to guard the child and keep her safe if I was able to prove her identity. I took it at face value, and that is why, as soon as I read the story in the papers this morning, I came to offer the little queen my homage and my services."

Mr. Mappin still said nothing, and the General's eyes bolted like those of an animal at bay. As his morale weakened he made the common mistake of laying it on too thick. "Such a little queen!" he gobbled, unctuously. "The situation appeals to a man's tenderest instincts! Use me in whatever capacity you see fit, sir. With my knowledge of Kuban and the Kubanians I can be of very real assistance to you. . . ."

A hot anger flared up in Fin. The damned hypocritical scoundrel! he thought. I can't stand much more of this!

At last Mr. Mappin began speaking. "Well, I think the hardest part is over, General," he said, with a sort of steely affability. "Mariula has the crown, and, as you said yourself, the crown of St. Karel is all-powerful in Kuban. I am really very much obliged to you for all the information you have furnished." He paused to let this sink in. "It is good of you to offer to accompany us to Kuban," he resumed, with deadly quietness; "but I fear you will be detained in New York by your own affairs."

Fin's heart suddenly began to thump.

The General was panting a little, too. "New York . . . my own affairs!" he echoed. "I don't get you, sir."

Mr. Mappin pressed a bell beside the window-frame. When Jermyn answered it he asked, "Have the two gentlemen come?"

"They're waiting in the dining-room, sir."

"Show them in."

The General, with a surprising celerity in one so fat, heaved himself out of the settee, and, turning, anxiously watched the door. The instant the two entered, he recognized them for plainclothesmen and his face turned livid. As they came around one side of the settee to greet Mr. Mappin, he edged away on the other. Seeing a clear space before him, he made a dash for the door. One of the detectives took two steps to the rear, shot out a foot, and the General came down with a shock that made all Mr. Mappin's ornaments rattle. It was like the collapse of a rhinoceros. In a twinkling the two had him handcuffed. Jerking him to his feet, they thrust him in a chair.

"What does this mean!" he gobbled, puffing and blowing. "Outrage! . . . Outrage!"

Mr. Mappin said to the detectives: "I promised the Commissioner to deliver the murderer of Nick Peters to you. There he is."

"It's a lie!" bellowed the General.

One of the detectives moved closer to him with a hard smile, and he shut up like the closing of a door. In an adventurous life it was obviously not his first encounter with the police.

The suddenness of the denouement caused Fin's head to spin. He had believed Nipperg guilty of the murder. He wanted to send up a cheer. Up to the last moment he had feared that this slippery scoundrel might escape them. Fin was not generally vindictive, but he regretted now that electrocution provided such a merciful end.

"You've got no proof," muttered the General.

"General," said Mr. Mappin mildly, "they say that every murderer makes one mistake. How could you hope to escape doing so? You are a remarkably vigorous man in most respects, but your eyes are beginning to fail, as is customary at our age. You cannot read print without glasses. You are careless with your glasses and you possess several pairs. When you flung Nick Peters on his bed and bent over him, you had a pair of glasses in the breast pocket of the rough workman's coat you were wearing.

"In the struggle that took place on the bed one of the lenses was broken, and a small piece of glass dropped down inside of Peters' clothes. I found it there. You made your mistake in not throwing away the broken glasses. I found them in the old coat when I opened your little leather trunk. When I put the piece I had together with the remaining pieces they made a perfect whole. . . . I have other evidence, but that will do for the moment. You may take him away, gentlemen."

The General had nothing to say. So complete had been his confidence in his own cleverness he had no reserve with which to meet the blow. He broke up before their eyes, and Fin in very shame looked out of the window. The detectives led him out, sagging and stumbling as if his legs were no longer capable of supporting that triumphant paunch.

AN HOUR LATER word came from the police that an unknown man, presumably the much-wanted Nipperg, had committed suicide by leaping from an upper floor of the Vandermeer Hotel. This was the last place in town where the police had expected to find him.

In his pocket there was a newspaper clipping telling of the discovery of the ancient crown, also the photograph of a woman on which was written "Daisy."

The man had approached a telephone operator in an upper corridor, asking for the room of Miss Daisy Zell. When informed that Miss Zell had checked out, he refused to leave, but went from room to room, trying the doors. The operator sent for a house detective, and upon his approach the stranger had run through a room that was being cleaned and had leaped through the window, taking the glass with him. Mr. Mappin was asked to come to the police station to identify the body.

THAT EVENING THE THREE FRIENDS were sitting in the big living-room, discussing their future plans, when Mr. Mappin was called to the telephone. Left alone together, Fin and Mariula became miserably self-conscious. The crown of golden laurel leaves lying on the table seemed to have destroyed at one stroke the happy, candid, thoughtless relation that had existed between them from the first. She glanced at him timidly.

"Why do you look so queer?" she murmured.

"Reason enough," muttered Fin.

"What are you thinking about?"

"I was thinking," he said, with a stiff smile, "that five days ago I fell asleep with my head on a queen's shoulder!"

"What of it?" said Mariula, stoutly.

"Well . . . it makes a fellow feel queer!"

"I won't be a queen," said Mariula, stormily, "if it's going to change my friends!"

"I reckon we've started something we can't stop now," said Fin, gloomily.

"But even if I was a queen I'd still be me inside, wouldn't I?"

"Sure! But you wouldn't belong to yourself any more. You would always have to think first before letting yourself go."

"Oh, this is terrible!" cried Mariula.

He laughed briefly at the sight of her dismayed face. "That's a funny way to take the queen business."

"If I have to be a queen," said Mariula more firmly, "you shall be a nobleman. You shall be the greatest nobleman in my country. The one who sets the king or the queen on the throne is supposed to be greatly rewarded. It was always so in history."

Fin shook his head. "I can't see it. There is something comic in the idea of a ready-made nobleman nowadays. I haven't got the crust for it."

"You just have notions about noblemen," said Mariula. "I expect they're exactly like anybody else. Look at me. I'm no different. It's just your notions."

"Well, I feel as if I belonged in this low-life country," said Fin, stubbornly.

"Maybe I won't be a queen for long," she said, hopefully. "The last remaining thrones are insecure, they say."

But Fin wouldn't have this, either. "Nothing doing!" he said. "We'll organize this kingdom and start it right!"

The corners of Mariula's lips turned up. "You do it, Fishy," she said.

Fin picked up the crown gingerly. "Gosh!" he murmured. "You read about crowns, and sometimes you see them in glass cases, but a fellow never expects to handle one. Certainly makes you feel queer. Think of the dozens of royal pates this has rested on! . . . Excuse me! I didn't mean any disrespect to your forefathers."

"That's all right," said Mariula. "They were no better than anybody else's."

He looked at her somberly. He was thinking that if crowns were still being worn, he knew of one head beautiful enough to bear one. "Say," he said, diffidently, "let me try it on you once."

"Oh no," said Mariula, startled. "Not until I am sure I have the right."

"Just while we are alone here together," coaxed Fin. "Let me be the first one to see it. No one will know."

"It's too big," said Mariula, weakening.

"I'll soon fix that."

She was wearing a silk scarf knotted on one shoulder. He untied it and, twisting it, bound it around her forehead like a fillet.

He then placed a big renaissance chair against the drawn curtains of old brocade, and seated her there. Standing before her, holding the crown high in his two hands, he lowered it upon her bright hair.

"I'm the blooming archbishop," he chuckled.

But when he stood back to observe the effect, the jokes died on his lips. He was startled by the fitness of the crown. That little head was made to bear it. The sight of the pale, fine maiden, her hands on the arms of the chair, her head up, and the consciousness of a proud destiny in her eyes, suddenly swept him off his base. All at once he understood the inner meaning of the old stories of our race. He dropped clumsily on one knee.

"What is it you ought to say?" he mumbled, with a sheepish grin. Then the words came: "Hail, Majesty!"

Mariula looked at him with a kind of horror. "Oh, Fishy darling, get up!" she murmured, tremulously. "You really frighten me!"

He rose, and she cast herself in his arms most unqueenlike. "Fishy, promise me you'll see me through this dreadful time!" she begged. "Promise me! Promise me!"

"Sure, I'll see you through," he said, scowling. "Who said I wasn't going to see you through? Who the deuce has got a better right to see you through than me?"

Her head dropped on his shoulder, and the golden laurel leaves scratched his neck. He plucked off the crown and laid it on the table behind them. "Buck up, old kid!" he said, patting her shoulder. "We're going to get some sport out of this. Think of the fun we'll have razzing the royal show after business hours."

COACHWHIP PUBLICATIONS

COACHWHIPBOOKS.COM

ISBN 978-1-61646-256-6

THE MURDER
THAT HAD
EVERYTHING!
HULBURT
FOOTNER

ISBN 978-1-61646-258-2

COACHWHIP PUBLICATIONS

COACHWHIPBOOKS.COM

THE MUMMY
CASE MYSTERY

DERMOT
MORRAH

ISBN 978-1-61646-250-7

VULTURES
IN THE SKY
A HUGH RENNERT MYSTERY

TODD DOWNING

ISBN 978-1-61646-149-2

COACHWHIP PUBLICATIONS

COACHWHIPBOOKS.COM

ISBN 978-1-61646-232-1

MURDER

À LA RICHELIEU

THE ADELAIDE ADAMS MYSTERIES

ANITA BLACKMON

ISBN 978-1-61646-222-2

www.ingramcontent.com/pod-product-compliance
Lightning Source LLC
Chambersburg PA
CBHW031319280626
47169CB00019B/2214